FATHER AND DAUGHTER

Romayne was by her father's side, and her strong young arms about his neck, lifting, lifting with all her might. And now the thing she lifted was like lead. She could not get a hold with her trembling hands. She could scarcely breathe as she forced his head from the floor and into her lap. She lifted wild angry eyes to the face of the young man she loved, Evan Sherwood, who came forward now and tried to help her loosen the collar of the fallen man.

"Don't touch him!" she cried in a terrible suffering young voice. "You have killed him!"

Bantam Books by Grace Livingston Hill
Ask your bookseller for books you have missed

Grace
Livingston
Hill

Coming Through the Rye

BANTAM BOOKS
TORONTO · NEW YORK · LONDON

*This low-priced Bantam Book
has been completely reset in a type face
designed for easy reading, and was printed
from new plates. It contains the complete
text of the original hard-cover edition.*
NOT ONE WORD HAS BEEN OMITTED.

COMING THROUGH THE RYE

*A Bantam Book / published by arrangement with
J. B. Lippincott Co.*

PRINTING HISTORY
Lippincott edition published 1926
Bantam edition / March 1972

2nd printing	.... June 1972	5th printing	.... August 1974
3rd printing	...... October 1972	6th printing	.. December 1975
4th printing	.... April 1973	7th printing	...... August 1979

ISBN 0-553-12228-2

Published simultaneously in the United States and Canada

PRINTED IN THE UNITED STATES OF AMERICA

Coming Through the Rye

CHAPTER I

ROMAYNE RANSOM walked through the station and out to the street door looking for a taxi. There were usually three or four in sight. What had become of them all?

She set down her shiny suit-case and tapped the little new suede slipper toe impatiently while she waited, thinking how vexatious the whole day had been. Not a thing the way she had planned it, the whole day spoiled.

She had started off bright and early that morning in her pretty spring costume with the dearest new wardrobe any girl had ever owned, expecting a wonderful week. Her first house party! And nothing short of a miracle that Father's new business had materialized just in time for him to give her a substantial check wherewith to provide the wardrobe and the suit-case. She had thought when the invitation first came that of course she must decline it. She hadn't a garment fit to wear at a great beautiful house party by the sea.

But the look in her father's face had been wonderful when he handed her that check and asked her if it was enough. Enough! She had never dreamed of having half that much money for her own. And it had come so suddenly! Right out of the blue as it were!

What fun she had had spending it!

She couldn't remember the time when she hadn't been poverty-stricken, never enough to get the bare necessities of life! Poor Mother, even up in heaven she must be glad to see them having it easier now. To know that her dear ones were actually going to be able to have luxuries as well as necessities. Father was talking about a car for her own driving! Wouldn't that be wonderful! If only Mother had lived to see it all. Of course, heaven was better than anything down here, but Mother had so wanted to have things nice, and Father not so down-hearted and discouraged all the time. If only she might have stayed with them just one year during their prosperity, so they could have enjoyed it together!

It had been wonderful to start off in a taxi, an expense she never dared afford before. Father had been so pleased and proud when he carried her suit-case into the parlor car for her and kissed her good-bye. The stoop in his shoulders was almost gone and his eyes were bright as if he were happy. Poor Father, he would be so disappointed to see her coming back this way, without even a glimpse of her house party after he had gone to all the trouble and expense. But, then, she had the pretty things, and there would be other house parties.

And, of course, Isabel had been awfully nice about it, offering to send her home in the limousine, and so distressed that the note she had dispatched to her the night before, calling off the invitation until fall, had not reached her. Of course, the mistake was all on account of her having moved recently, and Isabel not noticing the new address when she had accepted, but one couldn't expect a girl to stay home from a sudden invitation to spend three months abroad just for a house party. Isabel had tried to reach her by 'phone, and failing had sent a special-delivery letter. It would probably be forwarded from the old address and reach the house tomorrow, and, anyhow, Romayne was glad that she had had the trip even if she didn't stay. It was a glimpse into another lovely world and a bit of experience for her.

She made a pretty picture standing there, slim and graceful in her dainty spring costume of soft green. Her eyes were brown, and her hair had just a hint of copper in its glowing waves that peeped out from under the trim little hat. She couldn't help being conscious that she looked well. It was such a new experience not to be trying to hide the faded place on her dress, and the worn spot on the tip of her slipper, and the darn in her glove. Everything new and lovely, and all for nothing! Oh, well, Isabel would have a wonderful summer in Europe with her father, and there would be a party in the fall. She could be getting ready for it all summer. And Father and she would have wonderful times together, especially if they got that car.

But where were all the taxis? Perhaps she would have to walk two blocks and get the trolley after all. It would be hard in the hot sun, for the suit-case was heavy.

She turned her glance toward the side street where a group of children were playing noisily on the curb in front of a row of two-story red brick houses. Such a contrast of life to the great cool mansion at the seashore where she had lunched before coming back to the city. A wave of pity came over her for the poor little ones who lived in that hot street and never got a sight of ocean except for a sticky, noisy, crowded picnic, perhaps once a year. She, standing on a small pinnacle of recent prosperity, half way between the fortunate wealthy friends and the unfortunate little strangers, could pity them.

Then suddenly she remembered that it was down that very street that a little Sunday-school scholar of hers lived, and the minister had asked her not long ago if she wouldn't call on the child and try to brighten her up a bit. She had been run over by a truck and broken her hip and there was danger that the spine was involved, and she might never walk again.

In the joy of her new fortunes Romayne had completely forgotten the request. Now it suddenly came back to her. That was awkward. She might meet Doctor Stephens almost any day and he would be likely to ask her about the child. Why couldn't she just run back in the station and check her suit-case and make the call now? Of course, she was rather too much dressed up for that sort of thing, but it would be so good to get that duty done and off her conscience. Poor little thing! She was a sweet little girl with gold curls and blue eyes! What a pity! She would get some oranges at the fruit-stand and take them to her. There was no reason in the world why she shouldn't do it. Father wasn't likely to be home from the Corporation meeting before six, and he didn't even know she was coming. She would just get it done at once!

So she checked her suit-case, bought some oranges and a child's lovely magazine full of pictures, and started on her errand of mercy with a heart full of loving kindness.

She asked the group of children if they knew where Wilanna Judson lived, and they pointed out a house half-way down the next block. But when she rang the bell it was a long time before anybody came to the door, so that Romayne almost concluded that nobody was at home until she remembered that Wilanna was not able to get up. Then she debated whether she should attempt to open the door and walk in, for perhaps the child was all alone.

But a faint step was finally heard, the door was opened a

crack and a tear-stained face peeked out and looked her over half belligerently from a dainty shoe to tip of hat.

"Could I see Wilanna Judson a few minutes?" she asked, half wishing she had not come. "I'm her Sunday-school teacher."

"Oh, come in," said the girl, opening the door grudgingly. "I didn't know it was you at first. Yes, she'll be glad to see you. Nobody's paid much attention to her to-day."

Romayne stepped in and saw that the girl was one of those tawdrily dressed little flappers that sat in the girls' Bible class next to her own, and sang a high clear soprano. The girl looked anything but a flapper now. Her stringy hair was out of curl and her nose was swollen with crying. Even now the tears were brimming over again.

"It's awful good of you to come—" said the girl, "I 'spose you've heard?"

"Heard?" asked Romayne. "Are you in trouble, dear?" It wasn't like shy Romayne to speak to a stranger that way, but there was something in the girl's woebegone countenance that made her sorry.

"Oh!" said the girl, bursting into tears again, "I can't never hold up my head again!"

"What is the matter?" asked Romayne in a soothing tone. "Can't you sit down here and tell me about it? You look awfully tired. Is Wilanna worse?"

"No!" wailed the girl. "She's doing all right. It's papa. He's in jail! I thought you'd seen it in the papers."

"Why, no," said Romayne, "I've been away—that is, I didn't see the paper yet. Who are you? Wilanna's sister?"

"Yes; I'm Frances."

"Can you tell me about it? Is there anything I could do for you?"

"I don't know," sobbed the girl. "I don't guess there is! Mamma's gone out to see a lawyer, but it all depends if the woman dies. You see he'd been drinking again, and he ran over a woman and just missed killing her baby, too. They took the woman to the hospital, but they think mebbe she won't live——"

"You poor child!" soothed Romayne, trying to think what to say to one in a predicament like this. "You say he had been drinking? Why, where in the world could he get anything to drink?"

"Plenty of places!" shrugged Frances. "It's all over. There's a new one almost every week somewhere, and there's devils around here always coaxing him to drink. You don't know ——"

"You poor little girl," said Romayne, laying a gentle hand on the girl's shoulder. "Tell me all about it. I'll tell my father and brother, and we'll see if we can't do something to get those places closed up. Did your father always drink?"

"No," sighed the girl, "he don't drink when they let him alone, but it's always going around. He wouldn't go get it hisself, but everybody he goes with has it or treats him."

It was half-past five when Romayne came away from the Judson house, her mind filled with the sorrows of little Wilanna and her sister Frances, and turning it over how she would ask her father to get his new friend Judge Freeman to do something about the places where they were selling liquor. Of course, Frances had probably exaggerated it. There couldn't be as many places as she said there were, or people would hear more about it. Of course, there was bootlegging, but that was mainly people who stole automobiles and ran away across the border of Canada, or made moonshine whiskey down in the South somewhere. It was all very vague to her. She had never taken much interest in such things. Her life had been so safe and guarded all these years, the companion of her mother during her lifetime, and now the companion of her father. But Father would be interested in this. After they had had dinner together she would tell him the whole story, and then perhaps he would take her out to call on Judge Freeman and she would tell him. She had always wanted to go with her father when he went to the Freeman's house, but there had always been some reason why it wasn't convenient when he had to go on business.

Thinking these thoughts she reached the station, claimed her baggage and signalled the taxi that had finally appeared on the scene.

"I thought there were always taxis here by the station?" she said to the man. "I waited for fifteen minutes a little while ago."

"Well, there usually is," said the man apologetically, "but you see we all ben down to the Commissioner's office trying to get our rights."

"Your rights?" said Romayne faintly, wishing she had said nothing to the man, and reproaching herself for giving him opportunity to talk with her. Isabel Worrell would never have done that. It was because she was not accustomed to riding in taxis.

"Yes, Miss," said the man, as if he had just been looking for someone to whom he could tell his troubles. "You see us fellers has to pay fifteen dollars a week to the Commissioner to get our licenses, and we ben hearin' there's a guy in the city ben makin' it hot fer everybody what's in this here graft game, so we jest kinda got together and decided we'd tell the Commissioner we was going to give evidence 'gainst him ef he didn't do somepin about it. So we went together, a gang of us, an' we give him a line of talk, and waddaya think? He give us our money back! Yes, sir! Every last man of us, we got our money back! Sorry to keep ya waitin', Miss, but you see how 'twas. I jest had to have that money. I got a sick kid and she has to go to the hospital fer a noperation, an' I needed that money."

Romayne was all sympathy now. She asked questions about the child and promised to send her a doll and a picture-book. How much trouble there was in the world, and she had been fretting for years just because she had to make over her dresses and they couldn't ride in taxis. And now money had come to the Ransoms, but here were the Judsons, and the taxi-drivers, and a lot of other poor people who were still in trouble. It really spoiled much of her own pleasure in her good fortune to know that there were so many people in such deep trouble. And it all seemed to be the fault of a few rich politicians who were trying to get richer than anybody else without doing anything. At least that was the way it looked. Or, perhaps, it was the fault of the people who voted to put men who would do such things into these offices of trust. Fancy a Commissioner trying to live off a poor taxi-driver whose little girl was having to wait for a much-needed operation until her father could scrape the money together to pay the doctor and the hospital! Something ought to be done about it. She meant to ask Lawrence and Father to start at once organizing some kind of a society to look into these things. They could do it. Now that they were going to have a little money they would have a real chance to do good in the world.

She gave the driver a generous tip, took down his address, and promised not to forget the doll. Then the car drew up in front of the old respectable brown stone house into which they had moved but the month before.

She glanced up at the house with a thrill of pride and pleasure. To think that was their home after all these years in a little tucked-up apartment! And she was presently to have a good sum of money put into her hands wherewith to furnish it with fine old furniture such as belonged in a respectable old family mansion. Of course, it wasn't one of the newer houses. But it had an air of ancient grandeur about it that pleased her. She liked the high ceilings and the big rooms.

As she looked toward the front windows where now her father had his office she saw the curtain stir and a hand draw back. It must be her father had come home and he would be coming to the door to meet her!

She paid the taxi fare and hurried up the steps, wondering what Father would say when he heard her story, and wouldn't he be glad after all that she had come back? She knew he had been going to be lonesome without her in spite of all his joy in her holiday.

Inside that stately old front parlor thick rough silk curtained the windows, in a deep amber shade. A great walnut roll-top desk occupied the centre of the room. In the wall opposite the hall archway was set an old mantel with cupboards on each side and two tall graceful urns of alabaster stood upon the mantel-shelf. A large old Kerminshah rug, worn but still beautiful, in rose and amber covered the floor. A few walnut chairs and a desk chair completed the furnishings. On the desk were several specimens of ore and some tubes of oil in various stages of refinement.

"Oh, gee!" said a thick-set youth in knickerbockers and golf stockings, peering from between the curtains. "That girl's come back! I thought you said she was safe in Jersey for a week! *Now* what are we going to do? She'll be in here in a minute."

"We're going to do just what we planned to do, Chris," said a quiet grave young man in a plain business suit, with a face that had a rugged look of determined strength about it.

"But—why say—Sherwood,—she's a peach of a girl! I went to school with her."

"Sorry for the girl, Chris, but it can't be helped! This is the only time this could be done, and the stage is set. We can't afford to let the opportunity slip. We may never get it again. We're not fighting for one person's feelings, kid! This is righteousness! You get into your corner, Chris, and let me manage this thing."

"But, Sherrey, you can't——"

There was the sound of a key turning in the lock, and a lifted hand of caution silenced the youth at the window.

The other three men, two of them in policeman's garb, and one a plain-clothes man, showed no interest in the incident save by quick alert gleams of the eye. They maintained a grave aloof bearing and seemed to study to obliterate themselves as far as possible from the scene. Their time of action was not yet come.

The man they called Sherwood was seated just inside the arch from the hallway.

Romayne flung open the door and stepped inside, closing it after her before she saw him. Then she took a step forward and all the others were visible to her view, not excepting her old school mate, who had turned his back to the room and was earnestly peering through a crack between the curtains in the hope of not being recognized.

The girl stood still for a moment, eyeing each of the five men questioningly, then turned toward the young man who obviously dominated the scene.

"Where is my father?" she asked coldly, as if she felt he were somehow to blame for the presence of these uniformed men.

"That is what we hoped you might be able to tell us, Miss Ransom," said Sherwood courteously. He had risen as she entered the doorway.

She looked around at them keenly once more.

"Then if my father has not been here," she asked crisply, "how did you get in here?"

For just an instant she stood facing the five men, then she stepped quickly over to the desk and laid her hand on the telephone.

Just as quickly another hand, firm and strong and determined, was laid upon hers, and the man called Sherwood looked sternly down at her.

"I'm sorry, Miss Ransom, but we can't let you do that—not now."

CHAPTER II

ROMAYNE cast a frightened glance from one stern face to the other, her eyes lingering with sudden recognition on the broad shoulders of the boy.

"Chris Hollister!" she said sharply, "what are you doing here? Why don't you tell these men that they have no right to come in here and tell me what I can do and what I cannot do?"

The boy turned shamefacedly.

"I'm sorry, Romayne, I didn't know you would be here—I understood you were to be away——".

"Oh!" said Romayne haughtily. "So you knew what my movements were, did you? And you were in some plot against my father in his absence, it seems. Well, I thought better of you than that. I've always supposed you were a very nice boy—that is, in the days when we used to go to school together."

Her tone was as if she had finished with him forever. Then she turned toward Sherwood.

"I don't know who you are, but I'm sure you look as if you might have been a gentleman once. Will you please let go of my hand?"

"Not until you give me your word of honor that you will go over and sit down in that chair and not go near this telephone again," said Sherwood gently but firmly. "I'm in command here, and I can't run the risk of your messing things."

"You're not in command of me!" said Romayne, giving her lithe hand a quick twist and jerking it from his hold. It hurt her cruelly, but she did not wince. With a quick motion she turned toward the front door, but to her dismay she was suddenly confronted by the two men in uniform, standing like an impassable wall before her.

With a dazed look she stopped, gave each a frightened

glance, and turning back to Sherwood she drew herself up proudly.

"What does this mean?" she asked indignantly. "Do I understand that I am a prisoner in my father's house?"

"I'm afraid you are, Miss Ransom" answered Sherwood gravely. "I hope it will not be for long. You need not be troubled. No harm will come to you. If you will sit down I will see that no harm comes to you."

"Thank you. I prefer to stand," she said frigidly.

"Just as you please," answered her captor, "only I advise you to stand right where you are if you do not wish to be interfered with again."

Romayne caught her underlip between her white teeth to steady its trembling. She could feel the tears smarting in her eyes. Slim and straight she stood in her pretty spring costume looking like a frightened child. Chris Hollister could not stand it and turned his back, pretending to be looking out from between the curtains again.

The girl had wonderful self-control. She was trying to think what she should do. It was unthinkable that she should submit to such a situation.

"What is the meaning of all this anyway? What right have you to order me about in this way in my own house?" she said, trying to hold her temper and see if she could find out what it was all about. "There certainly must be some explanation. You don't look like a bandit!"

There was just the least tang of contempt in her voice.

"Aw, gee!" breathed the boy, Chris, under his breath.

"I can explain," said the young man gravely, "but I would rather not. I hoped perhaps that you might be spared the pain——"

"Oh!" interrupted Romayne. "Don't trouble yourself about that. You haven't seemed to care how much pain you inflicted. I beg you will inform me at once what all this means! It isn't necessary to use any oratory or false friendliness. I want the facts. I'll bear the pain!"

Her face was haughtiness itself. Her tone stung the young man and brought a flush of indignation to his cheek, but he kept his quiet voice.

"Very well, then. I will tell you. This house is under suspicion and we have been ordered to investigate. I am sorry our duty brought us here while you were at home, but if you will consent to be seated quietly in that chair where the guard can watch every movement I give you my word you shall not be personally disturbed."

Romayne stared wide-eyed.

"This house! Under suspicion? But for what?" she demanded angrily.

"For illicit dealing in intoxicating liquor."

"Oh!" unexpectedly laughed out the girl with a relieved hysterical giggle, "is that all? Isn't that funny!"

She dropped into a chair still laughing, her eyes dancing merrily.

"But," she said, looking into the young man's face, "you surely didn't mean that seriously?"

"I surely do," said the young man sadly. "I'm sorry, but we have all evidence———"

Romayne turned toward the boy.

"Chris, why in the world don't you tell him we're not that kind of people? What do you get out of this farce that you can let it go on? You surely know how absurd this charge is!"

Chris turned earnestly toward the girl.

"I did, Romayne; I told them all about you. I said you were a peach of a girl! I wanted to put this off when I found you were home———"

"Put it off!" said Romayne, scornfully turning back to Sherwood. "If you would allow me to call up my father's friend, Judge Freeman," she said with an edge of haughtiness in her voice again, "he will be able to explain how impossible this all is," she said loftily.

A quick meaningful look passed from one man to another around the group.

"I have no doubt he would," said Sherwood meaningfully, "but we will not call the Judge at present."

"Or if you will call my brother," she went on more soberly, trying to realize that it was not going to be as easy to convince these determined men as she had expected. "He is probably still in the office—I can give you his number. He never gets out till a quarter past six."

Another lightning glance went round the circle. She could not tell what it was about, that quick motionless look. It seemed to be more of a light coming out of the eye, like a signal flash in the night, than anything tangible; but it gave her a chill of foreboding.

She suddenly turned to Sherwood quite gravely, as one

would speak to a naughty child in a tantrum who needed quieting, speaking slowly and distinctly as if to bring him to reason.

"I should think it would be easy enough to prove that your suspicions are absurd," she said. "Why don't you look around and see that this is nothing but a plain everyday home?"

"Are you willing to take me over the house, Miss Ransom?"

"Certainly, if you insist on being so absurd," she said freezingly.

"Very well. We will begin in this room."

"In this room?" She lifted her eyebrows amusedly. "I should say everything was perfectly obvious here."

"What is behind those doors, for instance? Can you open them for me?"

Romayne laughed.

"Some old dusty papers. Files of sales of Father's business. It's nothing but a shallow cupboard. Father had to have a carpenter come here and make it deeper to get his papers in. Did you think it was a wine closet?"

Another of those quick lightning glances went round the circle of men, though when she looked again no one seemed to have paid the least attention to her words. Their eyes were thoughtfully on space.

The steady eyes of Sherwood did not waver nor show special interest. His voice was just as quiet as he said:

"Yes? Well, can you open them for me?"

"Why, certainly!" said Romayne, walking briskly over to the fireplace and touching the little spring knob.

But the door did not open as she expected.

She looked at it puzzled.

"Oh, I remember! Father had a lock put on. He said there were valuable papers here and he did not want them disturbed. Perhaps I can find the key. Of course Father wouldn't object to my opening it for you to see."

She searched in the drawers of the desk, the men meanwhile noting every movement, and taking in at a glance the contents of every drawer, without seeming at all to be looking.

Romayne came upon a bunch of keys and tried several but without success. She lifted somewhat mortified eyes to the young man at last.

"Well, we'll have to wait till Father comes, I suppose. But there really is nothing in there but papers."

"I see," said Sherwood gravely, as if the matter were dismissed. "Now, this house, it's a double house, is it not? Do you happen to know what is on the other side of this mantel? Have you ever been in the other house?"

"I have not," said Romayne haughtily. "The house is vacant, of course, you know."

"Yes?" Sherwood lifted his eyebrows in that maddening way he had done before, as if he doubted her word. "Is the house for rent?"

"I believe it is," said Romayne, vexed. She felt somehow that he was making game of her, yet his tone and manner were entirely respectful. There was about him an air of knowing more than she did about the things she told him. If he knew things why did he ask? Was he trying to get her tangled up? Oh, if Father or Lawrence would only come home. It was outrageous! But perhaps she ought to play the game and keep them here till one of them did walk in, so that these intruders might be brought to justice.

"Do many people come to look at the house?"

"I really don't know," haughtily again. "I've noticed an agent once or twice. It may be rented now for aught I know."

"Yes?" and then quite irrelevantly it seemed to her, "And your father's business is?"

"He is Manager of a Corporation. It has to do with ore and oil products." She waved her hand toward the bits of rock and oil tubes on the desk. She had the air of endeavoring to graciously satisfy an insatiable curiosity on his part, endeavoring to show him how contemptible he was. But his quiet grave manner did not alter.

"Miss Ransom, have you ever been down cellar in your own house?"

"Really!" she shrugged. "How absurd! Of course."

"Can you tell me what it contains?"

"Why certainly. A furnace, and a coal-bin, and a wood-pile."

"Where is the furnace located?"

What possible interest could that be to these strangers? "Why, almost directly under this room, I think."

"Yes? And the coal-bin? Is it located on the right wall or the left?"

Romayne stopped to think. This was rather interesting, like a game. What could the man possibly be driving at? Or was he merely trying to kill time and asking any question that came into his head?

"It is on the right wall, just in front of the fireplace, I believe. Yes, I know it is. They fill it from the basement window on the sidewalk, just under that window over there, I think. We haven't been here long, and haven't needed to get coal yet."

"Did you ever examine the coal-bin?"

"Well, no. I couldn't possibly take any interest in a coal-bin. Father always looks after those things."

"Then you have no knowledge of a door or passageway leading from that coal-bin into the cellar of the next house?"

Romayne gave a startled glance from one intent face to the other. For the first time it seemed to her the men were off their guard and openly watching her.

"Of course not," she said, trying to keep her voice calm. Oh, if Father or Lawrence would only come. "You must have been reading dime novels or mystery stories."

The young man controlled a desire to smile. She could see it in the quiver of his lip. He had a nice mouth. But how outrageously impertinent.

"Did you ever notice anything else in the cellar?" went on the steady voice. "Nothing but some boxes and barrels that came from the mine and have to do with the business," she said wearily. Would this inquisition never end?

"I'm hungry," she said suddenly. "I don't suppose you'll mind if I go and get something to eat, will you? In my own house?"

"I'm sorry, Miss Ransom, but you'll have to remain right here in this room for the present." She had a queer sensation as she swept him a glance of disdain that his eyes were asking her pardon. "Hollister here will go where you direct him," he added, "and get something for you. You can trust him to find what you want I'm sure."

"No!" said Romayne contemptuously. "I certainly cannot trust a person who has done what he is doing to an old friend. Thank you! I will remain hungry!"

The color swept in a crimson wave up to the roots of Chris's hair and he turned switfly toward the window once more.

"I'm sorry," said Sherwood with genuine concern in his

voice. "It was no part of my plan to drag you into this mess, Miss Ransom!"

"Oh, yes, you're very sorry!" retorted Romayne angrily, and suddenly sat down in the chair he had offered her several times, with a defeated look on her face, and stormy eyes. Oh, if her father and brother would only come. It was ten minutes after six! Surely they must come soon!

And then there was a sound of a key in the latch, a tense silence in the room, the front door opened, and Mr. Ransom, followed by his son, entered and looked around with white startled faces.

CHAPTER III

In AFTER years when Romayne looked back on that silence that followed her father's entrance into the room, it seemed to her to have lasted for years, and to have encompassed three distinct eras of emotion.

There was the first instant of relief that her father had come and that now all would be set right. During that instant her own firm little chin was lifted just the slightest, haughtily, with an assurance, the perfect assurance which she had always felt in her father to dominate any situation; an almost pity for the cocksure young man who had been so condescending and so dictatorial to her in her own house, and she swept him a brief glance of contempt that included the whole room. The boy, Chris, seemed suddenly to have been submerged in the amber-colored curtains. She had forgotten that he existed.

Her eyes went back to her father's face, expecting to find a certain look, the expression of an aristocrat who had arrived in time to discomfort interlopers. She knew the look, he had worn it often through the years in protecting herself and her mother from impudence or presumption on the part of servants or officials. It became him well, that look of righteous indignation, tempered with severity. She was always a little sorry for anybody who had incurred his displeasure, when her father was really roused. He had a command of fine terse sarcasm that was really withering to listen to. That he would use it now she did not doubt. She waited to hear him speak, and realized that the silence had been long, with something vitally terrible in it that she did not understand. Of course, her father would be much disturbed that she had been here alone in the house with a company of men of this sort. He would be fairly overwhelmed.

She turned her attention fully to his face again. Was it something in the expression of the uniformed man who stood at his elbow that made her look more closely? Why, her father's face was ashen! His eyes! There was nothing haughty in them. They looked—why, almost *frightened!* Perhaps he was sick. The doctor had said there was a little weakness of the heart—nothing organic. It was not good for him to be excited. She flashed a glance of condemnation toward the leader of the men, who stood just ahead of her to the right. Then her eyes went again to her father's face.

Mr. Ransom was a handsome man as the world counts beauty in a man. He had regular features and a fine old-fashioned bearing, which his silver hair and well-clipped pointed beard accentuated. He habitually bore himself as one who respected himself, and dealt gently, almost reverently, with himself. He was the embodiment of lofty sentiments, and his well-groomed person was always an object of observation and admiration, as he walked the streets and went about his daily business. One thought of him as a man who wore his glasses attached to a fine gold chain over his ear, and carried a gold-headed cane. He was the kind of man who was always well dressed, carried his papers in a fine cloth bag and wore silk hats whenever there was the slightest excuse for them. He might have been an elder in a church, or even a minister, so dignified, so conventional, so altogether fitting was everything about his appearance. People had always looked upon him as a good man, well-born, well-bred, and upright to the core. This was the general essence of the character which his daughter had always revered, and of which more than anything else in her life she had been most proud. And now she turned eyes that were accustomed to watching him proudly, tenderly, to his face once more, and all those things which she had been accustomed to see in his beloved face had vanished. Instead the lips had grown more ashen, the eyes wild, like a hunted animal, as they glanced from one intruder to another, the skin of his face white like death as he stood perfectly still looking slowly around that room, only his eyes moving in their ghastly setting. He did not seem to be aware of her presence—or—was he?

She sprang to her feet.

"Father!" and instinctively reached out her hands toward him.

It was just at that instant he crumpled and went down.

You have seen a balloon that was pricked suddenly lose its inflation, or a tent, let loose from its holdings, sink slowly to the earth. It was like that. The thing that had made the man what he had always been seemed suddenly to have gone out of him. He lay on the marble floor of his entrance hall, a limp heap of cloth. A white face, from which the inhabitant seemed to have departed, and the white skin, withered and lying in loose folds as though that which had held it buoyant and plastic had been suddenly withdrawn from beneath. There was something drawn about the features as if they had been misplaced, and had nothing to give them form or continuity. The thought flashed through the girl's consciousness as she flew toward him that that could not possibly be her father, lying there, collapsed, inanimate. She must reach him quickly. She must lift him up, as if the life and buoyancy would return to him once more if she could but lift him quickly enough.

She was by his side, and her strong young arms about his neck, lifting, lifting with all her might. And now the thing she lifted was like lead. She could not get a hold with her trembling hands. She could scarcely breathe as she forced his head from the floor and into her lap. She lifted wild angry eyes to the face of the young man, Sherwood, who came forward now and tried to help her loosen the collar of the fallen man.

"Don't touch him!" she said in a terrible suffering young voice. "You have killed him! Oh! *Father!*"

That one anguished cry stabbed the young man's heart as if it had been a bayonet. He stepped back sharply.

"Go for a doctor!" he said to Chris in a low tone. But the girl's senses seemed to be abnormally alert.

"No," she said sharply. "Don't one of you stir from this room! You are all going to stay right where you are and answer for this. My brother will go! Lawrence! Where are you?"

She turned her head sharply to look up and back where her brother had stood, but Lawrence had vanished. His white face had disappeared from the doorway almost as soon as it had appeared.

Romayne lifted a proud head.

"He is gone for the doctor!" she said in a clear, high voice, calm with a terrible excitement. "He will be here in a moment."

Sherwood motioned to Chris to go, and the boy stepped out from the curtains with a low murmured expression of horror. In order to get out he had to step over her feet as she sat huddled with what was left of her father in her arms. He went stumbling out into the darkened street with tears rolling down his nice boyish face. He had always liked Romayne. He had always looked up to her. She had been the head of his class, and he the foot. He had looked upon her as a sort of an angel. And now this! And he having to go against her. But he knew what to do in an emergency. He darted across a hedge and two back fences, and was soon ringing the bell of the nearest physician.

Inside the house Sherwood had quietly organized his forces. Water was brought, and someone produced aromatic ammonia. Stern faces stooped gravely, but the girl's slender hand took the water from them and held it to the still ashen lips that somehow seemed like lips no longer.

Frantically the girl applied the remedies that were brought, and held in her aching, eager young arms the form that was so dear.

"Father!" she called, "Father!" as if she were crying to him to return from a great distance. "It is all right, Father, you needn't worry! They did me no harm. It was only a ridiculous mistake. They intended to go somewhere else, of course. You needn't mind, Father! Of course, when they know they will be very much ashamed!"

But there was no sign or stir from the limp form in her arms.

Finally she lifted great eyes of appeal to Sherwood's face.

"If you ever have been a gentleman, I beg that you will go to the telephone and call my father's friend, Judge Freeman. He will explain it all to you, and then perhaps you will have the grace to apologize and withdraw. When my father becomes conscious, if I tell him it was a mistake and that you have apologized and withdrawn, he will be calmer and perhaps he may get over this. You must get Judge Freeman quickly! There is no time to waste! Tell him I beg that he will come to us at once. We are in great trouble!"

The young man's voice was very gentle.

"I'm so sorry," he said, "but Judge Freeman cannot help you now. He——"

"Oh—you needn't be *afraid* to call him!" she said contemptuously. "I'll see that you do not get into any trouble through it. We are not the kind who prosecute people even if they are—*murderers!*" she ended bitterly, with tears dropping upon the white face in her lap.

There was a little stir behind her. Almost as if a throng were entering. A strange doctor stooped beside her and slipped a practised finger on the patrician wrist of her father. Just behind came Chris panting. The men in uniform seemed to have multiplied. They were on all sides of the room— silently. Had there been only two of them before? How confused her mind was! Perhaps she was only dreaming. Where had she been going to a house party a little while before? Was this all real?

Stern-faced men were lifting her father now at the doctor's command, men in uniform, who walked with measured tread as if they were used to doing gruesome tasks, as if they were ordained of God for such terrible offices. They carried him upstairs. They did not ask her where to go. They swept her aside as if she were a child.

They opened a door at the head of the stairs. She stood dazed, watching them. How had they known which was his room? She seemed to know without seeing that they were laying him upon his bed, and now they were shutting the door!

She cast a look of rebuke about upon the men who stood there silently, the man Sherwood notably at their head, the boy Chris drooping, just behind him, and fled up the stairs.

But they put her out—silently, gently, but firmly, and shut the door. She stood a moment staring horror in the face and then went swiftly down the stairs as she had come up and stopped in front of Sherwood.

"Where is my brother?" she demanded breathlessly. Her face was stained with tears and her gold hair was ruffled about her sweet face. There was something fine and glorious in her eyes such as one sees in the eyes of a child who is in search of its mother.

A look passed between Sherwood and Chris, and back again. It said: "Did they get him?" Its answer: "They did. He is in custody." The miserable truth sat upon Chris's nice boy face written large. There was yearning tenderness in Sherwood's eyes as he looked back at the slender girl in her little bright spring costume, all rumpled now and a stain of water down the front where she had spilled it trying to make her father drink.

"He is not here just now," he temporized. "He had to go away. Will you not try to forget what part I had to play in all this and let me help you for the present?"

"*Had* to?" repeated the girl sharply, ignoring his offer. "Do you mean they took him away?" Her perceptions seemed suddenly sharply awake.

Sherwood looked at her compassionately. A flash passed between him and the boy again. She saw it.

"Have they?" she appealed to Chris.

He nodded miserably.

"Do you mean they have *arrested* my brother?" she turned back to Sherwood, her voice suddenly grown older, more mature.

Sherwood could only bow gravely.

"But—what for?"

"For complicity—with your father. They have acted together in this business—"

"Stop!" said Romayne, trying to speak calmly. "It is terrible for you to say such things with him lying up there!"

She caught her breath in a sob, and hurried on:

"But I want you to try to be sensible, and tell me what made you ever get an idea like this? You know you will have to *prove* a statement such as you have just made."

The young man bowed again.

"I'm very sorry, Miss Ransom, but it has *been proved*."

"Where is your proof?" she demanded, her eyes flashing with the restrained look of one who feels strong and sure of her position, and can afford to hold her anger in abeyance until facts come to her rescue.

The young man looked at her sadly for a moment, and then spoke.

"Miss Ransom, I would have spared you if I could, but I suppose you will have to know the truth sooner or later, although I would rather it were not my task to tell you. Can't you be persuaded to take my word for it, and spare yourself the unpleasant details? No one has any wish to bring trouble upon you."

"I thought you could not prove your charges," flashed the girl, with bitter contempt in her tone. "You are a coward and afraid to face the truth!"

For answer Sherwood turned to her, his face hardening.

"Come then," he said half bitterly, "I have warned you. It is your own fault if you have to suffer."

He stepped to the panel beside the beautiful carved mantel and touched a spring. The panel swung open and disclosed a set of shelves inside, shallow shelves, as she had told him a little while before, filled with papers fastened in neat bundles with rubber bands about them, official-looking documents, and each shelf labelled with letters of the alphabet. A gleam of triumph came in her eyes.

But even as it dawned, the young man silently touched what looked like a nail head, and the whole set of shelves, papers and all, began to move, slowly, smoothly, swinging around out of sight into a recess somewhere behind the mantel, leaving a dark opening into a cavern-like space beyond. It could not exactly be called a doorway, yet it was wide enough for a person to pass through.

Romayne stood staring in amazement and said nothing.

The young man reached his hand through the opening, touched a button, and a shaded light sprang up in the space beyond.

"Come!" he said, and with strange premonition Romayne followed him, stepping through the opening with a strange sensation of fright, yet unable to refuse to follow.

It was a room that she arrived in through the narrow door, a room with not a little attempt at beauty and luxury. There were tables and chairs, and pictures on the wall. Several of the chairs were pushed back as if their occupants had left them in a hurry. There was a lady's glove upon the floor, and a rose with a broken stem beside it. There were glasses on the tables and an odor of liquor faintly tanging the air. She looked toward the windows, doubting her exact locality and saw that they were closely and heavily curtained, and that the lamps were shrouded in dim draperies. Sherwood reached out and removed one shade, and the glare of electric light fell garishly over the place. A cupboard door

half open he swung wide, and disclosed rows and rows of
bottles, with many labels. She did not try to read them all.
Her eye caught one with terror-stricken gaze—"PURE RYE
WHISKEY" it read. There were other names which meant
nothing to her, vaguely associated in her mind with a world
of which she knew little. She turned bewildered, half questioning what he meant by it all, and why this should have
anything to do with her father.

"Come!" said Sherwood again, setting his firm lips to the
task he did not relish. Yet this girl must be convinced.

He led her through other rooms, and showed her other
closets filled with more bottles, and showed her cases half
open, from which the bottles had not been removed, and
more cases still in their wrappings. He let her read the labels,
"Utopian Refining Company"—her father's company!

And then he led her down a dark stairway into a dim
cellar where the lights were far apart, and where she wandered after him through a maze of more packing cases,
stopping now and then to make her read the painted lettering
on their sides, and now and again to lift a lid and let her look
within. They came at length to a large iron door that swung
back mysteriously in the dim light, at a touch, and they
stepped into what seemed a coal-bin.

Stumbling after him and groping, her hand touched his,
and she caught at it for support, as she slipped over the loose
coal.

"I must go back!" she gasped.

He caught her gently, and held her firmly until she was on
the smooth cement floor of the cellar again, and then he took
a flashlight from his pocket and lighted the way around a
strangely familiar furnace to another great packing case,
whose half-open top disclosed great lumps of mineral that
gleamed weirdly in the glow of the flashlight, and all at once
she began to realize where she was. This was the packing
case that had stood by the furnace for several weeks past.
The young man lifted what seemed like the top of the case,
and lo, below were rows of bottles packed in straw. He lifted
and flashed the light full into the lower compartment, then
put it down again, and led the way to the cellar stairs.

They mounted in silence, the girl ahead, her knees shaking
weakly beneath her. The young man tried to steady her, but
she drew away from him, and went on by herself. So going

they came once more into the wide hall, and walked toward the front to the room from which they had started.

Romayne stood still for a moment staring at the opening in the chimney panel, with the light still burning beyond and a glimpse of those awful bottles on their shelves, and then she sank into the big chair close by with a groan and covered her face with her hands.

CHAPTER IV

ABOUT that same time Frances Judson was dressing to go out for the evening. She called the function "I-gotta-date." They occurred almost nightly. But this one was a special date.

She was seated before a small pine dressing table in the room which she shared with her invalid sister. A cheap warped mirror was propped up against a pile of books, and Frances was working away with her crude implements, trying to attain a make-up for the evening. There were still traces of tears on her cheeks and her eyes had a puffy look. Now and then she caught her breath in a quiver like a sob.

"Oh, dear!" she sighed miserably, "I don't see why Papa had to go and act this way again, just when I was beginning to get in with real classy people! I don't think it's fair! When folks have children they oughtta think a little about them!"

Wilanna was to her elder sister something like a waste-basket, into whose little open mind she threw all her annoyances and disappointments. The little girl listened always patiently, with troubled countenance and sympathetic mien, and tried to suggest some alleviation or remedy for the trouble. Wilanna had troubles of her own, but she usually kept them to herself. Now she turned sympathetic eyes to her sister and watched her for a minute in silence as Frances dabbed a lump of cold cream on her sallow countenance and began rubbing vigorously.

There were traces of tears on the little girl's thin cheeks, too, and a burdened look much too old for her years in the eyes that searched her sister.

"You're not going *out—to-night*—Frannie—are you? Not *to-night!*"

"Sure!" said Frances apathetically. "I *gotta*. Larry'll give me the go-by if I stand him up. I can't afford to let the first real classy fella I ever had slip by. There's plenty a girls ready to ride with him in his automobeel if I don't go. Whadda ya think I went without lunches all last week t'save money fer that new dress for ef I was going to stay at home?"

"But Frannie! When Papa's in trouble?"

"Trouble!" sneered Frances, mopping off the cream vigorously with a soft rag. "Well, it's his own trouble, ain't it? *I* didn't do it, did I? *You* didn't do it, did ya? Well, I should say not! Then why should I give up my pleasure just because he's gone and got hisself in jail? I guess anyhow not, Wilanna! If Papa don't think about his children and his home why should we worry! We gotta think about ourselves, ain't we?"

"Oh, don't, Frannie!" the little girl began to cry. "Don't talk like that, Frannie! He's our own papa, Sister. He's always been good to us."

"Yes. When he didn't *drink!*" said Frances fiercely. "Whaddoes he wanta drink for? I ask you? Does he *havta*? You know he doesn't. You know he can come straight home with his pay envelope when he likes and give it to Mamma. It's just because he *doesn't care!* Larry says people don't *havta* drink unless they like. He says everybody has free rights ta drink or not ta drink if they like. He says this is a free country. Papa don't *havta* drink unless he likes."

"Oh, Frannie, don't you *love* our father?"

"No!" said Frances fiercely, with tears in her eyes. "Not when he makes a beast out of hisself. That's what they call it, Willie, when a man gets drunk, they say he makes a beast outta hisself. It ain't so bad to drink a little in a refined way. All the fellas I go with do that, of course. But they know when to stop. You can't ever think Larry would ever come home *drunk*, would ya? Nor *I*. I drink a little evenings when I go out. They all do, but they don't drink enough to run over a woman and half kill a baby."

"Oh, Frannie!" wailed Wilanna, "you oughtn't ta drink. You know you oughtn't. You know what we learned in school. You know what it does to the—the—the—*nerves*, and the—the—the—*brain!*"

"Aw, that's all rot! Larry says that's an exploded theory. He says young people to-day know a lot more'n their fathers and mothers did when they was our age, and they know how to control theirselves."

"But, Frannie! Suppose you *couldn't!* Suppose you got drunk yourself! Some folks can't. Papa *can't* stop!"

"Aw! Cut that out, Willie! I hope you don't think I'm like Papa! Papa could stop if he liked. He don't *like!* He *wantsta* get drunk! He does it on *purpose!*"

There were two great tears in Wilanna's big blue eyes and her underlip was trembling.

"But, Frannie, don't you think there's something about drinking that *makes* people wantta?"

"Aw, shut up, Willie! You're only a baby. You don't know anything about such things. I'm grown up. I gotta do as the rest of the young folks do. How'd I look saying 'No thank ya!' when everybody else was drinking? They'd all think I was afraid. They'd all know my father couldn't control hisself."

Frances was pencilling in a supercilious eyebrow now, and it required all her attention. The room was very still for a minute or two while the slow sorrowful tears flowed silently down the younger sister's cheeks. Then Wilanna roused to the attack once more.

"Frannie, I wish you wouldn't go out tonight. I *wish* you wouldn't! Mamma may not come home till a long time yet, and I'm afraid here alone tonight. I keep thinking maybe that woman might die and her spirit come here. I keep thinking it all the time. She would know our father had killed her—and her little baby—and—I wish you wouldn't go, Frannie!"

"Aw, shut up!" cried out Frances impatiently, rubbing away at one very rosy cheek. "Now you made me put too much rouge on! You make me tired! As if a woman that was dead could come back. You wouldn't see her if she did. Think about your nice Sunday-school teacher and the book she brought you. Didn't she have a swell dress on though! Her hat was some class, too, only I'd have liked a little more color on it. She's a real pretty girl."

"Frannie, why do you put that old rouge on your cheeks? I think you look a lot better without it. She didn't have any on. She just had her skin. It looked more real. I don't like to look at you when you get your mouth all red and kind of pointed like that and so white around your nose. You look like one of those false faces you see at Hallowe'en. I don't feel like kissing you when you look like that."

"Well, there's others that do," preened Frances self-consciously, with a little unholy laugh her sister did not understand. "Oh, if you aren't a *scream*, Wilanna! Wait another year till you grow up, if I won't have piles of fun telling you how silly you were! Why, baby, I wouldn't be considered *dressed* if I didn't have on powder and rouge. Your teacher probably does it too when she really goes out to parties and things. She didn't bother to waste it on us, that's all. You can see by her clothes there's some class to her. But I don't think she has very good taste, myself. If I could dress like her I'd go to a real Beauty Parlor every day of my life and get my face done, and a wave. Her hair looked almost like natural curls. I don't think it looks neat all irregular like that. If I had hair like that I'd get a boy-bob, that's what I'd do."

"Oh, Frannie, I thought her hair was *lovely!*" There were signs of tears once more.

"There, Baby! I guess it was all right, only she probably gets it fixed up when she goes to dances and things."

Frances was arraying herself in a flimsy apricot-colored crepe de chine with an apron of sleazy yellow lace and a scarf going around her throat and over one shoulder, surmounted by a bright red silk rose where it crossed. She was very busy smoothing down her draperies and plastering a half-moon of dark slick hair out over each cheek as far as the cheek bones.

The little girl surveyed her half in admiration, half in trouble.

"My but you look pretty, Frannie! But I can't think you oughtta go t'night, with Papa in jail. It don't seem right!"

Frances wheeled about upon her.

"Well, I gotta, Willie! What I gonta tell Larry when he comes? Say I can't go to the dance and the movies and take a auto ride because my papa's in jail fer murdering a woman getting drunk? Would you like to tell a young man that? And such a classy young fella as Larry? Why, Willie, he ain't like the other fellas. He's polite and handsome and he has just rolls of money. He's free with it, too. I'm going to get him to get a whole box of chocolates for me to-night, and I'll bring them home to you, all except one or two pieces I have to eat for politeness, you know. Say, Wilanna, can you shift yerself a little farther over on the other side of the bed? I wantta get out my hat and these springs sag so in the middle the box won't budge. That's it. Now I have it. I hope it ain't mashed!"

Frances pulled out a tiny hat of silver, faced with a dash of flame color. It did not hurt the hat for her that it was a bargain on account of a slight spot of tarnish on one side. It was what she called a "classy" hat. She fitted it carefully on before the unflattering mirror and then sat down at the front window to watch for signs of her escort.

"He's coming in a car," she told her sister over her shoulder. "It's a car he's thinking of buying. Just think of me going out with a young man to try a car! Wilanna, wouldn't it be great if we'd have a car some day?"

"I'd rather have Papa out of jail!" wailed Wilanna, and buried her face in her limp little pillow.

"Well, nat'ally, Baby, we all would. Disgrace isn't the pleasantest thing in the world, but I'm going to forget it for one night. I'm going to have the time of my life to-night. But I hope it won't be the last time either. Larry seems to be real fond of me."

"Where do you go when you go out, Frances? What do you do all the time?"

"Go? Oh, lotsa places. Ride in the Park, and then away off on the hills. There's a drive they call Lovers' Lane, with the trees overhead and it's real dark, and there's a little brook across the road, and sometimes we park the car—oh, you wouldn't understand, Baby! Wait till you grow up. Then we go to a road house and dance and have a supper. That's the kind of a fella Larry is. He never skimps things. We're going to the whole show to-night, he says, and then some. There's a place where they have dancing and a dandy orchestra, and they have suppers—they say the suppers are great, and only real refined people go there. Society people, you know, that is, kind of *select* people. It has a private entrance. You wouldn't know there was such a place when you go in. It just seems like it was some sort of rooming house. It's way down Vinegar Lane, just small houses there, but you go to this man's room—he's an awful rich fella and he just does this fer fun—I forget what his name is—and when you get into the room it's just a common room with a bureau and chairs and things and you open a door into a closet or something and that opens into another hall you didn't know was there, and it leads to a secret room in between buildings! They say it's a wonderful place, with carpets and pictures and soft chairs and lots of lights and flowers, and they have a big dining room too. I've been dying to go there for weeks, ever since Gladys and Vivian told me about it. Heaps of the girls have been. I think we're going there to-night. You see, Larry has a pull with the man that owns it, and he's given Larry a ticket to get in. Only fellas with tickets can get in—and girls, of course. Every fella takes a girl."

"Oh, Frannie," broke in the little girl. "They don't have wine there, do they? I don't want you to drink wine, Frannie. Please, Frannie!"

"Oh, now stop being a goose, Wilanna! They just have refined kinds of wine there, not the kind Papa drinks. Why everybody drinks refined kinds of wine now—not whiskey, of course—!"

"It's against the law," wailed Wilanna. "The teacher in school said you got arrested if you bought it or sold it, and my Sunday-school teacher, too, she said it was *wicked* to be a bootlegger."

"Oh, Baby! You silly thing! These people are not bootleggers, they are just classy society people. Why, Willie, they are real high-up people, these people. Some of the Government folks, you know, that *make* the laws. Nothing couldn't arrest *them*, you know, and, anyhow, of course they know what the law is, and they wouldn't break their own laws, would they?"

"I s'pose not," admitted the little girl hesitatingly, "but, Sister, I'm *afraid*——"

"Oh, now stop that nonsense! Listen, Wilanna, I want you to be a real good girl and not cry if I havta go before Mamma comes. You see I have a special reason for wanting to go to-night. It's about Papa. It's to help Papa. Now, will you be good?"

Wilanna beamed.

"What is it, Frannie. Tell me quick. I'm afraid you'll have to go before you tell me. Will it get him out of jail?"

"Will you promise not to cry? Not to let anybody *know* you're alone in the house when Larry comes?"

"I promise," said Wilanna eagerly.

"Well, you see, if I can get Larry to go to that place to-night, I might meet a high-up officer-in-the-Government man, and if I do I've got a real good story made up about

Papa and I'm going to beg him to help Papa. That's why I put on this dress and hat, Baby, so he would like me and I could get to sit out a dance with him and talk about it."

"Oh, Frannie, how wonderful!" The little girl's face was bright through her tears. "And you'll tell him our father wouldn't drink if they would just close up those saloons, like the law says they must, won't you? You'll tell him how down at Booker's corner they go in the back door and pretend like it's closed in front, and how Jimsey's is running all the time in the back. You will, won't you, Frannie?"

"Oh, I guess so," said Frances impatiently, her face against the window pane. "I don't see why Larry doesn't come! It's half past eight now. I wish he would hurry. Mamma oughtta be here any minute now. Don't say anything to Mamma about where I was going. You tell her I've gone out to see if I can't get a friend of mine to speak a word for Papa."

"I will," promised Wilanna willingly, "but why don't you want her to know all about that man and his secret room and everything? I think it's a lovely idea."

"Well, I wantta surprise her, Baby. Now, you lie still. I'm going downstairs. I think I hear someone at the door. Maybe it's Larry. He don't like to be kept waiting. You won't mind my going before Mamma comes, will you?"

"No, I'll just lie still and hold God's hand like Miss Ransom said to-day to do. She said when I felt pain in my back to do that, it would help, and I tried it once, and I think it did. Oh, I wish you liked her! I think she's so sweet!"

"Oh, sure, I liked her. She's kind of high and mighty, but she's all right. Now, I'm going, good-night."

Frances slipped down the stairs breezily and opened the front door, but it was not the young man she expected who stood on the front steps. Instead it was three very much excited girls. They crowded into the room without noticing the lack of cordiality on Frances' part and all began talking in loud tones at once.

"Oh, Fran! Have you heard?"

"Say, Juddie, when did you hear from Larry?"

"We're up against it, old girl! Larry's pinched!"

"Whaddya mean, pinched?" shouted Frances excitedly. "What for? Who gave you a line like that?"

"It's true, Frannie. Larry's pinched. It's all over our crowd. I'm not giving you any line. It's the straight truth. They *got* him."

"I always knew that Lawrence Ransom was too soft for our crowd! He didn't know the ropes," said a bold girl with black eyes and hair that looked as if it were cut with a bowl. She was chewing gum vigorously.

"*Ransom!*" said Francis suddenly. "Was that his name? I always thought you called him Rawson."

"No, it was Ransom. Lawrence Ransom. He lives up on Clinton Avenue with the swells. Don't you know who he is? His father's thick with Judge Freeman, and our 'Towney' who gives us the suppers. What's eating you, Fran? You look as if you'd seen a ghost."

"Oh, nothing. I was just thinking. Wilanna has a Sunday-school teacher by that name. She was here this afternoon to see her. But it can't be any relation of his, of course."

"He's got a sister," put in the girl they called Vivian. "I saw her once. She's real stuck up. Doesn't run with our crowd. She's in with the Worrells and Freemans. Thinks nothing is good enough for her but the millionaires. I guess she don't know how speedy her brother is? That's the trouble with him, he's soft. But I guess he'll get his now."

Frances' face blanched. Two arrests in a day was almost too much for her small nerves.

"Why'ncha explain, Viv? I don't think that's smart. How'd he get arrested?"

"Oh, that Sherwood bunch is around again, hot trail fer trouble. They rounded up Merty and she had to run all the girls off in taxis quick. They say there's nothing doing whatever to-night. Even the road house is quiet. Got pink candles on the tables and advertising a family dinner, with wholesome movies afterward."

"But, Larry," faltered Frances, "why should they get Larry?"

"I'm sure I don't know," said Sybil crossly. "What difference does it make? We lose our fun anyhow and that's enough. I'm sick a this town. I'm going to N'York, where you c'n have a real time! These folks here are run by a bunch of old maids and Sunday-school teachers. You girls all better come with me. We'll hire a house fer ourselves and do the town. Say, Fran, your father and mother ain't here? D'ya mind if I smoke? I'm near dead fer a smoke. It's ridiculous they let the boys smoke in the streets and won't let us."

"Oh, I wouldn't, Syb," said Frances in a panic. "Mamma

might come in any minute and besides, Wilanna's upstairs. She'll smell it and tell."

"I should worry," said Sybil, taking a box of cigarettes out of her pocket, lighting one, and throwing the match down on the carpet carelessly.

Frances stooped and picked it up nervously.

"I wish you wouldn't, Syb. Mamma don't like it. She'll can my going out nights if she sees you smoking. She don't know I smoke. You haven't any right to spoil all my good times. Go outside if you wantta smoke."

"Rats!" said Sybil inelegantly. "If you've got a back number like that fer a mother you better clear out. That's what I'm going to do. I'll take you along if you won't be a sissy. But you've got to get some money together first. It'll be fifty-fifty if you go with me. I mean to *live!*"

"Hush!" said Frances suddenly, "Mamma's coming!" She threw up the window quickly, and snatching Sybil's cigarette flung it out on the sidewalk, as Mrs. Judson opened the front door and came in.

She was a heavy woman, with a strong tread, and creases of habitual anxiety on her broad sagging face. She had a dreary sorrow in her eyes as she looked around on the girls with their gaudy little frocks, her own daughter in their midst. Her sad, keen eyes searched her daughter's face.

Frances had snatched off the little silver hat with its nasturtium facing, and was swinging it nervously in her hand.

"I was just coming out to hunt you, Mamma," she explained, looking apologetically down at her bright dress.

"H'm! I don't know as you had any call to go out in a rig like that to hunt fer me!" said her mother witheringly.

She sat down heavily in the nearest chair, however, as though she was too weary to pursue the subject further. She drew out two long black-headed hatpins and removed her rusty black toque, smoothing her graying hair with a work-roughened hand. Frances hoped the girls had not noticed how old-fashioned her mother was. She cast a furtive glance at Sybil chewing away at her gum indifferently. She half expected Sybil to be angry about the cigarette. Sybil was considered a sort of leader in their set. She dared more and talked more than the rest. She wondered tremulously what her mother would do in case Sybil broke forth into one of her tirades.

But Mrs. Judson did not seem to have noticed any of the

girls, or to realize which girls they were. She looked about on them drearily, or rather over them, and continued to talk to her daughter.

"Well, I've been to see the lawyer," she said in that same sort of hopeless voice. "He says there ain't much hope 'ithout yer father is willing t'turn state's evidence an' help the Sherwood bunch. He says they've got things in their own hands fer a while now, till the whiskey folks can get organized. He says they've got to lay low, and the Sherwood gang has some men who are helping them that'll do a good turn fer your father if he'll just say where he got the liquor."

She paused and looked impersonally around on the gum-chewing group.

"I ben to see your father, too," she went on, "an' he says he'll do it. He ain't got no compunctions about tellin' where he got it—they weren't no friends of his'n. He seems real sorry—yer Father!"

She sat stolidly a moment gazing off at nothing, her loose sorrowful cheeks sagging more than usual, the little pouch of flesh under her chin quivering. Then two large slow tears most unexpectedly rolled out and down her face. They looked as out of place as a steam-roller going down a church aisle. She was not the kind of woman who cried. One didn't know that she had tears. She seemed unaware that she was weeping. She sat a moment longer, looking into space across the little tawdry room with its golden oak furniture and its crayon portraits, and then she rose heavily, gathered her two old-fashioned hatpins and her rusty toque and trod wearily out of the room and up the stairs.

The four girls sat still for a moment, even their jaws arrested in their regular rhythm, in a strange new embarrassment. Was it possible there had been a kind of dignity in that fat, homely, stolid woman? Had she ever been a pretty girl with bright frocks, going out with the boys? And it had come to this!

Would it ever end in something like this with any of them?

There was a stillness in the room for a moment while they turned this new idea over in what they had left of a mind. Then suddenly they all four started into alert guarded attitudes, as a loud knock sounded on the door!

CHAPTER V

THE startled silence lasted until Mrs. Judson came heavily to the top of the stairs and called.

"Frances! Why don't you open that door?"

The stentorian voice seemed at once to lay bare the four shamed girls sitting in breathless silence, seemed to reveal to the one outside the door that they had been afraid to open it. Just what they were afraid of they did not quite know, only that there had been so many unforeseen happenings, so many startling events during that day that they hardly knew what was coming next. Then, too, there was in their countenances a confession of the many things in their lives that they would not care to have revealed. An admission, to themselves at least, that they were open to unpleasant investigation as well as the ones who had been that day arrested.

Not that there was any such open admission. Oh, no. Each girl straightened her frills and ruffled her bob, and went on chewing indifferently as though that knock were nothing to her.

Frances hurried into the hall with a belated and breathless "Oh, yes'm. Did somebody knock? I didn't notice!"

She made a time wrestling with the latch, although her mother had not locked the door. Then she opened it a crack with her foot behind it and looked out, chewing her gum nervously, with an assumed indifference.

A man stood outside with some papers in his hand, which he seemed to have been trying to read by the fitful light of the street. He looked up at Frances and asked sharply:

"Is Mr. Lawrence Ransom here?"

Francis was past master in delaying an attack.

"Mr. Who?" she asked stupidly.

"Mr. Ransom—Mr. Lawrence Ransom. I was told I would find him here."

"This is Judsons'," stated Frances with finality. "I don't know any Mr. Ransom."

"You're Frances Judson, aren't you?"

Frances was frightened, but she put on a bold face.

"Well, what's that got to do with the man you was talking about?"

"You're the girl that was with him the other night when I stopped him on the road, up by the road house. You remember. You were trying to make a get-away."

Frances cast a frightened glance up toward the stairs and stepping out the door hurriedly drew it to, lowering her voice.

"Oh, you mean Larry!" she whispered. "He's just a kid I met that night. I didn't know his name. He was taking me to ride. I don't know him, honest I don't. A friend of mine introduced us——"

"You can't pull that off with me!" said the man gruffly. "I want to see Lawrence Ransom and I mean to do it! You had both been drinking that night, and you had a whole case of liquor in your car——"

"Don't talk so loud!" pleaded Frances in a whisper. "I've got a little sick sister and they don't know if she's going to live or not. They had a consultation t'day—they said she must be kep' quiet——"

"Very well," said the man, lowering his voice a trifle. "I'll be quiet if you'll step aside and let me in. But you can't put anything over on me."

"You needn't bother to keep still," said a calm, stern voice over their heads. "He isn't here, but I'll come down and show you through the house. Frances, you come in the house and go to bed."

Frances cringed at her mother's voice from the window above, and ducked into the house as her mother withdrew her head from the window and came heavily down the stairs. The girl hastily reviewed the interview and wondered how long her mother had been listening. There had been an ominous sound to her voice. She slid into the parlor with a defiant fright in her eyes and tried to look nonchalant before the girls, hoping they had not heard. But Sybil left no rag of doubt about that.

"I wouldn't stand fer that, Fran! Now's the time ta get out!"

But with strange suddenness Mrs. Judson stood beside her.

"Yes, now's the time ta get out!" she repeated. "You girls better run right home ta yer mothers! Frances! There's the stairs!"

Then she turned her attention to the man who had entered in Frances' wake.

"Will you have a chair?" Her tone was sad and formal. Then to the girls:

"You girls run along!"

With defiant malice in their eyes the three visitors, chins up, sidled along the wall toward the hall, under the grilling gaze of the stranger. Suddenly the man pointed his pencil at Sybil.

"Wait! You're another!"

His words were like sharp scissors snipping off the words.

Sybil lifted her chin and her eyes grew hard and wicked. The sad eyes of Mrs. Judson looked at her for an instant startled, and then glanced toward her own child with sudden understanding. She had thought these creatures were little children, and here—suddenly—! What would come next? Her eyes went sternly to the frightened Frances standing huddled in her corner like a draggled nasturtium in her bright cheap draperies, and Frances quivered and slunk toward the door. But the bold black eyes of Sybil jeered at her, and Frances was forced to put up a feeble fight.

"I ain'ta going upstairs now, Ma. I got company!" she said, trying to make her voice both conciliatory and defiant, although she could see from her mother's face that her stand would be short-lived. When her mother was really roused there was no gainsaying her.

"Let her stay, will you, Mrs. Judson? I want to ask her some questions. And you three, you stay too. There's another one I want to see!"

He was pointing at Sybil. Gladys and Vivian huddled behind her with furtive glances toward the door.

Mrs. Judson sat down heavily, her stolid face blank with burden and despair. She was looking straight at Sybil as if a revelation was slowly dawning upon her.

Sybil leaned back nonchalantly against the door frame, took out her cigarette and lighted a match with an air of supreme contempt of the whole scene. She eyed the officer with an assumed amusement.

Then with surprising agility for one who seemed so massive Mrs. Judson was upon her feet and standing close to the bold-eyed girl, speaking in a calm low tone of command.

"Stop that!" she said. "You can't do that in my house! I may be old-fashioned and ugly, but I still know what's right, and there ain't no little huzzy like you goin' to over-step me. You c'n blow out that match and put that box in your pocket, but you can't stand there and smoke in my house. I've always been respectable, if my husband is in jail, and I intend to keep so!"

And, strange to say, Sybil obeyed her. She did it with an air of contempt, but she did it. Frances was amazed. She drooped in her corner and wondered what awful thing would come next.

Then spoke the officer.

"You kids had better look out," he warned. "If you keep up the speedy gait you're going you'll all be landed in jail in another week. I know what I'm talking about, and you're headed straight down hill!"

The girls were frightened. Frances' face grew white, and she watched her mother with a sideways glance, but Sybil stood her ground contemptuously.

"It's none of your business what we do," she said to the man boldly. "And you've got no right to make us stay here. I don't know anything about your Mister Ransom, if that's what you call him, and I'm going where there's some fun."

"You're not going until you've answered me a few questions," said the man firmly, and he flashed a badge from under his coat. "You're the girl that was in that seven-passenger Cadillac that was stolen from Seventh and Broad the other night. You got away then by lying, but you don't get away now. I've got this house watched back and front, and it won't do any good for you to try to slip out. If you answer my questions straight you can go where you like, but if you try to put something over on me I'll have you taken to Headquarters. Now, what's your full name?"

"Sybil Mary Johnston," answered the girl sullenly.

"Where do you live?"

"Thirty-two Maple Street."

"Is that your parents' home?"

"No. I live with my grandmother."

"I see. And where do you go to school?"

"Oh, I quit school ages ago. I work in the silk fac'try."

There was a swagger to Sybil Mary's voice now. She felt that she was going to "get by" after all.

"I see. And do you go out every evening in the week? Does your grandmother approve?"

"Oh, sure! Nobody can't keep me in. Let 'em try. I never ast her could I go. I just go."

"I see. And how early do you leave home?"

"It seems to me you're mighty nosey. I'm sure I don't know. I go when I like!"

"And where you like, I suppose. Well, do you happen to remember just what time you started out last Thursday night and where you went?"

"I don't recall," said the girl insolently.

"Well, *recall!*" said the officer in a compelling tone. "You left your home somewhere about seven-thirty and went to the drug store at the corner of Third and Pine Streets. You had several sodas and a sundae, and then walked down the street toward Fourth in company with the two girls who stand behind you, where you met this other girl—" he looked toward the shrinking Frances— "and all of you stood on the corner until four boys came along. Now, from there, Miss Johnston, will you continue?"

Sybil Mary's eyes had been getting less and less bold as he told crisply the tale of her doings, and the other three girls were plainly shaking with fright and looking at one another aghast. Frances put her face down on her arm and began to cry. She did not dare look at her mother. Sybil looked from one to the other of her partners in crime, helplessly, like a wild thing suddenly cornered. Then her eyes glinted hardly and she tossed up her chin.

"Why, one of the fellas said his uncle left his machine round the corner a little piece and said he might use it for the evening, and he ast us if we didn't all wantta go fer a ride. Ain't that so, girls?"

The girls hurriedly chorused, "Oh, yes. Yes, indeed! That was so."

"Which of the boys was it said that?" asked the officer, his keen eyes taking in each girl with surprising understanding.

"Oh, I couldn't say," said Sybil Mary airily. "I really don't remember. Do you, Fran? Was it Bob or Timmy? I didn't pay attention. I just heard the word ride, and that was all I cared." She laughed jauntily.

"It wasn't Lawrence Ransom, was it?" quizzed the officer.

"Lawrence Ransom?" repeated Sybil thoughtfully. "I don't think I know him. Mebbe he was one of the strange fellas that was along with Bob and Timmy. I really didn't pay attention to their names. I never do when I'm introduced. It's too much trouble. We always give them nicknames anyway."

"I see," said the officer, writing something down. "And now, could you just tell me where you went after you got into the car?"

"Why——" Sybil Mary paused thoughtfully and bit her vivid lips as if she were trying to recall. "Why, I don't really just remember. We go on so many rides. It mightta ben to the Park, and it mightta ben out Fielding Road. It was real dark that night and I don't recall."

"Could it by any possibility have been toward Pine Woods Inn?"

"I—don't—think—so." She drew her brows thoughtfully. "I've never been there much."

Suddenly the interrogator turned to Frances.

"Which one of the men waited on you at your table that night, Miss Frances? Did they call him Jim or Joe?"

Sybil was raising her eyebows at Frances and signalling all sorts of warnings, but the miserable Frances was beyond using subterfuges.

"Joe, I think," she answered with quivering lips, and then saw what she had done, and putting her head down sobbed bitterly to hide the angry glances of her mates.

"That will be about all, thank you," he said to Mrs. Judson as he closed his little note-book and put it in his pocket. "I'll leave your daughter in your hands, Mrs. Judson. I'm sure you know what is best to be done *for the present*, and if all goes well I hope we sha'n't have to trouble you again. I shall have to ask these other three girls to take a little ride with me. There is an automobile waiting outside, and it isn't a dark night to-night."

The three girls looked at each other with frightened glances, and Frances stopped sobbing and held her breath.

"Oh—I—gotta date——" began Sybil Mary.

"That's all right," said the officer. "This date comes first. Just step right outside."

"But my grandmother will worry," persisted Sybil Mary.

"You should have thought of that sooner," said the officer, taking firm hold of the shrinking girl's arm. "If it becomes necessary we'll see that your grandmother is informed where you are."

"I'll tell you where Lawrence Ransom is if you leggo of my arm!" she ventured at last as the man opened the door.

The officer led her on grimly silent.

"He's pinched," affirmed Sybil Mary anxiously. "You don't need me. They got him half an hour ago."

But the officer herded the girls out and closed the door behind them.

It was not until the sound of the automobile outside had died away among the city noises that Mrs. Judson turned to her cringing daughter.

"So it seems we have *two* fools in the family," she said dryly. "It ain't just the time I should ha chose to find it out, but I s'pose it don't matter. It's well to know just what one is up against."

There followed a pause, during which Frances' slender young shoulders shook pitifully under their flimsy silk covering.

"So that's what you ben doin' all these evenin's when I thought you was staying overnight with Mary Johnston studying stenography so's you could help pay for Wilanna's operation!"

The shoulders shook still harder.

"I never thought my girl would disgrace me!"

The mother's voice was dry and empty.

"One woulda thought you'd had enough of drinkin' with your Pa takin' them spells. But I s'pose it's in the blood somehow and just came natural. I tried to do my duty by you, but it seems I ain't. Well—it ain't too late to begin. Frances May Judson, I ain't never spanked you enough. I know that. You was such a kinda pretty little thing. I never thought you'd grow up to be *bad!* I done wrong. I can see it now. But I'm gonna give you one good spankin' yet that you'll remember all your days. After that ef you wantta leave home as that bold-eyed huzzy told you, I s'pose you can go, but you'll have that spankin' to remember wherever you go, and mebbe p'raps it'll remind you what you oughtta ben. But anyhow you ain't gonta have no more such carryin's on while you stay in your home! You can just make up your mind to that. Now you can go upstairs to my room and take off that silly rag you've got on and get ready, and when I come up I'll tend to you."

"But, Mamma,"—Frances lifted a woebegone face—"I

ain't never done anything dreadful. I didn't steal any car, nor have anything to do with any folks that did—Larry was tryin' a car to buy——"

"Ain't it bad enough to go with a young man that drinks and carries whiskey round in his car? I ask you, Frances May Judson, was you brought up to do things like that? You, a baby, that oughtta be goin' to school yet, runnin' round in the night to hotels in the woods, dancin' with men you don't know their names! I ain't got words to tell you what I feel about it. It's no use."

"But, Mamma, he's a real classy young man, and his car was something swell. We didn't have whiskey either. It was a real refined kind of wine!"

"Fiddlesticks end! Don't talk like a fool! As if liquor wasn't liquor! You can't refine the drunk out of it, can you? Ain't it breakin' the law just the same if it's refined or not refined? Whadda they have a law for ef it ain't the best thing to keep it, d'ya s'pose, Frances May? And whaddaya think a classy young man wants with a girl like you outta tha ten-cent store, an' her papa runnin' a truck? You don't s'pose he was meanin' to make *real* friends with you, did you? Them kind don't. They wouldn't wipe their feet on you before their own home folks. They just run with you to act crazy and then they throw you away and don't care what becomes of you. Talk about classy young men, Frances Judson! There'd be some class to you ef you kep up that sortta thing. You wouldn't be even in the workin' class. You'd be outside where folks don't count you at all. There ain't never any of our family been like that, child. We've always ben respectable, an' that's a sight cleaner an' better than bein' classy. Some time you'll find that out. Now, go upstairs and I'll do my duty by you."

Sobbing bitterly, Frances went slowly upstairs, the tears making long streaks on the bright flimsy silk, the gay little streamer that was meant to go around her neck straggling down her back at half-mast and dragging on the stairs unheeded.

Into her mother's bare room she crept in the dark, still sobbing, and on the other side of the thin wall her little invalid sister Wilanna lay in her bed and prayed.

"Dear God, don't let my sister get drunk and get in jail. Please don't let her! 'For Jesus' sake,' like my Sunday-school teacher said. And please, dear God, if you've got any more time you can spare, won't you see what's the matter with our home? It's got something the matter all through. Amen, and I thank you."

Then Wilanna closed her eyes and tried to think of her prayer going out the window and up through the skies on wings like a bird to heaven. Wondered if it would have trouble finding the way in and how it would ever get to God with all the singing of the angels, and how He would know it was hers.

But her sad little heart was comforted with the thought that she had done all she knew how to do, and her teacher with the pretty dress had said God would hear.

Mrs. Judson came heavily up the stairs after locking up the house, and grimly performed her duty by her eldest child. With set face and dry eyes, she chastised the shrinking Frances, utterly subdued now and thoroughly frightened. Mamma seemed suddenly a new strange person whom she did not know, whom she had vastly sinned against without knowing.

And when the sad rite was over—which might as well have been performed upon Wilanna's poor little suffering body so fully did she bear the pain for her sister—Frances slunk away to the next room and shrunk sorrowing into the other side of her sister's bed, still quivering with sobs. By and by a little skinny hand, hot and nervous, slid softly over and lay upon the heaving shoulders with a little patting motion on the coarse nightgown.

Its comfort reached to the repentant young sinner, and gradually she turned to the little sister till their arms were about one another, and their tears mingling together. And so they slept.

But in the bare front room at the window the sad-eyed mother sat, staring out across the roofs of the opposite houses, past towers and steeples and tall buildings, to where in the distance like a battlement against the sky the grim walls of the jail arose.

So she sat the long night through and thought her sorrowful thoughts, visualizing the man who sat alone and awake in his dark little cell, sober and repentant now. She thought of him as he was years ago when she gave up a good home and parents who loved her to try the world with him. His hair had a glint of gold then where it turned into curls about his brow, and his eye was Irish blue with a twinkle. The world had looked good to her when she left her world for his. She was not so bad-looking herself in those days, with a pink dress and her black hair braided smooth and bound about her head. And when the little baby Frances came how proud they had been to see her father's twisted smile in miniature and her cute little ways! And now here! *He in jail!* And *Frances—what?*

She held her hands together hard where they smarted from the pain she had administered, and her heart ached with the horror of it all! She thought bitterly of the rich man who had financed the saloons where her husband got the drink, and kept them protected and going in spite of the law, and wondered again dully, as she had wondered many a time before, why God didn't kill the devil, and why such rich men had to be in a world with poor people who couldn't help themselves?

And, then, weary to exhaustion with her vigil and her sorrow, just as the first streak of dawn crimsoned the battlement in the horizon, she dropped her head down on her arms, and the tears flooded her face. The morrow was here, and what would it bring to them all?

CHAPTER VI

IT WAS very still in the room. Only the soft tread of the doctors overhead and the subdued voices intermittently broke the utter quiet. It was almost as if there were no one in the room.

Evan Sherwood was not easily embarrassed nor upset, but he felt as if he had just completed the murder of an innocent.

Romayne, after that first long shudder as she sank into the chair, had not moved. She did not sob, nor even quiver, yet the whole attitude of the little despairing figure expressed utter anguish. Suddenly he felt that he had done a terrible thing in thus revealing to this gently reared girl the folly and sin of her beloved father. He should have saved her this terrible knowledge at all costs. He should have gone all his days in the light of her contempt rather than shatter her faith and joy in her father. He should have let her walk upon his very soul, and trample him under her poor little feet, rather than to have brought this awful shame upon her!

How was it, he questioned his own heart in the silence, that he had so far forgotten his first resolve to keep the daughter out of the affair at all costs? Was it that she had hurt his pride by her imperious ways and her scorn of him?

The quick blood crept into his face. He felt that he had dishonored his purpose in thus yielding to a personal feeling. What did it matter if she despised him? He would probably never see her again, and far, far rather that she should hold him lightly than that her idolized father should be torn from his pedestal and she crushed under the shame of it. Still, could she have been kept in ignorance of the truth and kept her faith in her father even if he had not revealed the truth to her? Somebody would have made her know, and perhaps even more sharply than he had done. Well—let somebody else have done it then! Anything rather than that he should bear this deed on his soul the rest of his life! He felt that he could not forgive himself.

The stillness of the little crouched figure became intolerable to him. He felt as if he could not stand it. His soul swelled with sorrow for her. Such a frail little thing, so beautiful, so tenderly reared, and so utterly cast down. A frenzy seized him to do something for her if only to show his sympathy.

He stepped forward and touched her ever so lightly on the shoulder.

"I'm so sorry," he pleaded in a gentle voice.

She shrank from him as if his touch had been upon raw flesh.

"I did not want to hurt you——" he began again, trying to search his mind for something that might be said under terrible circumstances like this. What could be said? He had only shown her the truth and there was no way of taking it back even if that were a right thing to do. It was too cruel that men had to sin and their children must suffer for it.

She shrank still further from his touch and lifted her face dry of tears, with a terrible look of despair and horror in her eyes.

"Don't!" she said sharply. "You do not need to offer me sympathy—*now!*"

Her lips were white and trembling, but she was very quiet otherwise. There was a look in her face as if she had

suddenly grown old, very old, with the sharpness that sudden
great sorrow and revelation of sin brings.

"I know," he said simply, with miserable humility in his
voice. "I must seem terrible to you. But I wish you would
believe me that it was not my *pleasure* that brought me here.
It was to save others from awful suffering! I did not know
about *you*. I did not realize that there would have been you
or anyone except the wrongdoer to suffer——"

"*Don't!*" she said so sharply this time that he started as if
she had struck him.

"Of course!" said he. "I am a fool! I should have kept my
mouth shut. I am only making things worse. But at least you
will let me do something for you. I could send for anyone
you want."

She swept him with a silencing glance.

"It is too late!" she said significantly, and then with a little
despairing gasp like a suppressed moan—"and it would not
have mattered anyway, of course. But oh, won't you *go* now?
Haven't you done all the awful things you had to do?
Couldn't I be alone?"

He took one determined step toward the door, and then
paused hesitating, and looking up the stairs.

"I see," she said with a tired voice, "you have to remain on
guard. Never mind. If you will just let me alone till you are
allowed to go, and if you will try and manage it so that I will
never have to see you again if possible, I shall be very much
obliged. You are anxious to help me. Do that if you please."

He stood looking straight at her sorrowfully for a moment.
She had risen now and was looking straight and coldly at
him. She seemed like a little sinking thing that was begging
him to let her sink, and he stood trying to see a way out of
it. Some strong emotion swept over his fine young face and
passed.

"Very well," he said quietly, and looked at her again,
thinking rapidly. "Very well, I will—on one condition, that
you will let me know if there is any way in which I could help
you."

"There would never be any way!" She held her head
sorrowfully high. "I have friends."

He was still again for a moment, then said slowly, as if
realizing a new phase of her situation:

"Of course—yet—if there *should* come a time when there
was no one else who could help—I will do anything in my
power for you—or your father—or brother!"

"There is always God," said Romayne briefly, and turning left him without a look, holding her head high and walking up the stairs with brave steps.

He watched her go, a gallant little figure with the look of wreck upon her, yet a spirit that would not surrender.

She took up her position outside her father's bedroom door as if she intended to stand right there for hours if it were necessary; standing by, till time passed and she was needed. She did not glance downstairs where the tall young officer stood guard. If she must bear her anguish thus in the eyes of a stranger she would at least ignore his presence. She wanted him to know that henceforth for her he no longer existed. It was the only possible way in which she could go on and live. And live she must for her father's sake. He might have done wrong, but he was her father still and needed her all the more if he had done wrong. She could not make it seem real that he had knowingly broken the law or put himself under its power. There must be some explanation by which others were to blame, and her father had been deceived about the business somehow, and thought he was carrying on a legitimate affair. That didn't seem reasonable either after all that she had seen. Her father was not one easily deceived. Well, this was not the time to reason terrible possibilities out to a logical end, not while her father lay between life and death, or perhaps had even already gone over the borderland out of a world that *must* have misjudged him! Her work now was to watch by that door and pray.

As she stood there trembling through what seemed hours although in reality it was but minutes, her mind was fixed on the memory of the white drawn face of her father. She seemed to see like a panorama the scene upon which he had entered, the chalky face of Lawrence appearing an instant and then gone! *Lawrence!* What part had he in it all? Had it anything to do with his staying out late nights, and his surly air at the table of late? And those lines that had been etching about her father's eyes and lips, that she suddenly realized now were deeper and more anxious than they had ever been? Had they been wholly on account of Lawrence?

But her shocked senses could not reason. She swept such thoughts away, and stood there praying.

"Oh, God!—Oh—God!"

But she could think of no words further, than merely to cry out that she was in dire need. As she had just told the young man there was always God, and now all at once she knew there was *only* God. If all this was true that they were charging on her father and brother, there would not be other friends. Of course, there might be some who would be willing to share ignominy, but none that she would wish to drag down to so low a level. No, she would have to face this thing alone, and bear what the world gave her. There would be God, and she must just keep on crying till she knew He heard, and let Him do His will. She had no power in her even to suggest what He should do. She did not know what to ask for. She dared not ask that it might all be a dream, and morning bring sweetness and sanity and a fair future once more. She had too much good common sense to deceive herself into any such hope or possibility. She must just cry till she felt God heard and then wait till He helped. If they might only all have died before this happened!

In the course of time the door opened silently, and a doctor came out, almost falling over her as she stood crouched close. Her eyes asked leave to go to her father, and he half waved assent, eyeing her curiously, sadly, as she slid like a wraith over to the bed, and down upon her knees, taking the cold resistless hand in her warm one and laying her lips against it.

One look at his face told her he was no better. The features were even more drawn than she remembered them, yet she knew he was not dead. She could see by the faces of the nurse and the other doctor that they were still doing things for him, and when she lifted her eyes to the doctor who came near the bed and asked if she might speak to her father he shook his head.

"He can't hear you," he said. "He's unconscious. Later he may rally. They do sometimes."

The tone was kind but merciless. Romayne sensed that everything after this was to be merciless. She must just understand that.

There was a long period when she knelt there trying to think, wondering if she had prayed as hard as she ought to have done, seeking vainly for a way out of this terrible situation, a friend upon whom she might really rely.

Downstairs the telephone rang several times and a man's voice answered in low tones. Twice she heard the front door open and close and voices in the hall, but it seemed to be no concern of hers. Others were in charge. She must remain here until something came, she knew not what.

Now and again the thought of her brother wrenched

through the blank of her mind and gave her pain, her bright
handsome brother of whom she and her father had been so
proud! Surely, surely they must be mistaken about Lawrence.
He was always so gay, and so ready for a good time. Only
that morning they had been talking about the car they were
going to get and the long trip they were going to take when
his vacation came. He had told her how he was staying out
late to earn more money. She had pictured him working hard
over the books of the tailor who pressed his suits for him,
and spending hours at the invoices in a little grocery store
where the proprietor didn't understand bookkeeping very
well and had taken a fancy to Lawrence. Several times in the
past months Lawrence had told about "helping out" these
humble men and receiving a few extra dollars in return.
Surely, surely they were mistaken about Lawrence's having
anything to do with this terrible business. Surely, if it were
true at all it was only Father, and he had done it for love of
them. Poor Father! He wanted to give them beautiful things!

She thought of her pretty suit crushed now beneath her
weight on the floor, rumpled beyond restoration to freshness
perhaps! Poor, poor Father! How could he have fallen? No!
She would not believe yet that he had! There would be some
explanation when he came to himself!

"Oh, God, please let him come to himself and explain!" she
cried in her anguished young soul. And then came another
thought! "But if he were guilty! If he could not explain!"

And then she went back to her first prayer, just "Oh, God!
Oh, God, don't *You* know what to do?"

Presently the nurse stooped and lifted her away from the
bed.

"It's no use your staying there," she said in a low professional voice. "He'll be like this for hours—days perhaps—
before there's any change. You better save your strength.
You'll need it. Did you have your dinner? You better go
down and get it. I'll sit right by him and call you the first sign
of any change; but there won't be any. The doctor was sure."

Romayne looked about and saw that they had all gone but
the nurse and a man who seemed to be on guard outside the
door. She shuddered as she realized that her father, in what
might be his last illness, was having to be watched by an
officer of the law. *Her father!*

She was glad the officer was not any of those who were in
the house when she first entered. She slid past him as if he
had been something to fear and sped down the stairs. It had

been slowly coming to her that she ought to do something to
set Lawrence free at once. They ought to be consulting
together about their father. If that terrible young man with
the iron hand and the square jaw were downstairs would he
let her telephone to Judge Freeman? For, of course, if Judge
Freeman was her father's partner he was responsible for
things and he ought to be able to do something about setting
Lawrence free.

It was humiliating to her to think of opening a conversation once more with her obnoxious young jailer, but she
would have to do something at once. Perhaps it was not true
after all. Perhaps Lawrence was not arrested. Perhaps he had
only gone for friends and would soon be back.

These thoughts all went through her mind as she glanced
furtively in every corner for sight of the young man, Evan
Sherwood.

But he was not there. Not anywhere apparently.

The little doors by the fireplace had been closed, and the
chairs set straight and everything looked normal again in her
father's office. Not until she searched twice in the dim light
of the single shaded lamp that was lit, did she discover the
square shoulders of the boy Chris, standing half within the
amber-colored curtains as if he shrank from being found.

Very well. She would not find him. She would just go
ahead and do her telephoning as if no one were there.

So she turned her back on the shrinking Chris and sat
down at the desk, drawing the telephone toward her.

She called Judge Freeman's home, but after waiting some
time was told that he had suddenly been called out of town,
and they did not know when he would return. It might be a
week or more.

She hung up the receiver with a feeling that the props had
been knocked from under her and she was slowly sinking.

She grasped for the receiver once more and called another
number, the home of another of her father's associates, with
the same result. A third time she tried for another friend of
the family with a like failure, and it dawned upon her that
this might not be a mere coincidence. Could it possibly be
that these men who had been the promoters of her father's
business had found it convenient to get away while her father
bore the penalty of the law for them in their absence?

After sitting for some minutes, silently turning over in her
mind her list of friends who would be helpful now she called
one of her brother's gay friends who had been much at the

house during the past few weeks of their prosperity, and whose family were influential people.

Carefully she explained the situation as she saw it. Lawrence was gone. They had told her he was arrested! Of course it was some mistake. The whole thing was—but never mind! Her father was terribly ill, suddenly, a stroke of paralysis the doctor said. Would George kindly hunt up Lawrence and do whatever was necessary to get him out and get him home at once? He was needed——"

But a lofty ruthless voice at the other end of the wire answered her.

"Awfully sorry, Romayne, but I don't see how I can possibly do anything. I've got an awfully important engagement for this evening. I'm late now, and you know you can't stand up a lady. S'pose you call up Cholly. He's a good friend of Larry's. I guess he'll do something. He has more time than I. And I hope your father'll be better in the morning, Kid, I really do!"

Romayne spent a precious ten minutes chasing over the wires from club to club after "Cholly" and finally found him. Cholly professed to have great concern for his old friend Larry, but suggested that Albert Huston had more influence at court than he had and gave her Albert's 'phone number.

Romayne tried Albert and received a flat refusal.

"Can't do it, little girl. Sorry, but I'm in bad with the authorities now, 'count of a little affair last week, and it simply wouldn't do for me to come out in the open yet. Hope you find somebody to help, I surely do! And say, Girlie, when you see Larry give him my best and say if there's anything he wants brought to him I'll see't he gets it. He'll understand. Good luck, Girlie. He'll get out all right. Don't you worry. Larry's got lots of good friends."

Romayne rattled the receiver tremblingly into place and let her head sink down on her arms on the desk, utterly forgetting the ambushed Chris.

"Oh!" she moaned softly in despair. "Oh-h-h! Is there no one to help?"

Chris wheeled from his window and marched over to her suddenly.

"I'll help, Romayne. I'll do anything you want. But you can't get your brother out now. I've been off trying for the last hour. They've refused him bail and nothing anybody says will do any good. Evan Sherwood has gone off to try himself. He says he knows where he can find somebody that'll go bail if he says so, but they won't let him do it, I know. I heard 'em talk. They're mad and they think he's the key to the whole situation. They say he's slippery. I came back and told Sherwood, and he's just gone. If anybody can do anything that guy can, Romayne!"

Romayne's face was white and set.

"I wish you would telephone him and tell him to do nothing," she said with a hard edge to her voice. "He is insufferable! I am sure my brother would rather remain where he is than have that man do anything about it. He is presuming. I told him I did not wish his help. A man who did what he has done is beyond the pale of helper."

"You don't understand, Romayne; he didn't want to do all that, no more did I."

"Then why did he do it? Why did you?" asked Romayne fiercely.

"Because we belong to the League, and we were following out our orders. We didn't know it was going to lead us in on friends, or give trouble to women. Evan Sherwood is all for helping people. You don't know that guy. You'd like him, I know. When it's all over I want you to meet him and be friends.

"Chris Hollister! This will never again be over! And we shall never be friends! He is a terrible man, and I hate him!" She cried out the last words as if they were a pain. It was not like Romayne Ransom to say she hated people. Chris looked at her startled, and realized he wasn't being much of a help. He looked down awkwardly and then looked up.

"I say, Romayne, if there's anything I can do I'd be all kinds of glad. I always liked you best of any of the girls——"

"Have the mercy then to keep still!" cried the girl desperately. "There is nothing you nor anybody else can ever do! You have done it all and more. Get over there to your window and watch the house as long as it's your duty, but don't try to talk to me again."

Chris retreated crestfallen, but was suddenly called into action again at the sound of the doorbell pealing through the house. It was a part of his duty to open that door.

A telegram was handed in addressed to Romayne.

He passed it on to her silently and went back to his window curtain again. The girl's trembling fingers opened it nervously and she read:

"For the love of mercy, Kid, get into action and send some of my friends down after me if Dad can't come. I've got to

get out of here before seven to-morrow morning to look
after something or the mischief will be to pay!

(Signed) "Lawrence."

CHAPTER VII

ROMAYNE stood with the paper trembling in her hand and
looking helplessly from the telephone to the back of the hurt
boy, who stood just within the curtain awaiting her call. How
inadequate he looked. As inadequate as when he had been
required to translate a paragraph in Latin, or solve an Alge-
bra problem. He had never been a good scholar, but he had
always been a kindly soul, ready to do a good turn for
anyone, and she used to like him. Now she looked away from
him bitterly as she would look from any traitor. Where
should she turn? What should she do?

Her heart sank as she read the note over again. What was
it that Lawrence was so afraid of? Why must be get out
before morning especially? Was it then true that he had had
a part in this dreadful business which it seemed her father
had been carrying on? Or could it be possible he had just
suspected all was not right and that he hoped to get home
and to put out of sight some incriminating goods or papers?
Well, whatever it was, he was her brother, and she must
answer his call.

She racked her brain for someone else who might be a
help at this time, but she could not think of anyone she dared
ask, and she was not well versed in the politics of the town.
It ought to be somebody who had influence with the powers
that were doing all this, of course.

She walked over to the desk and dropped into a chair by
the telephone again, and as she did so a card attracted her
attention. She reached over and grasped it, hoping in some
way it might help her in this trying moment.

"EVAN SHERWOOD, ATTORNEY AT LAW," the card read, and
down in the corner, "772 Park Building."

She flung it from her as if it had been hot, and catching up the telephone called Judge Freeman's number again, asking, when the response came, for Mrs. Freeman, only to be told that Mrs. Freeman was away on a motor trip with friends and would not return for a week at least.

In her desperation she asked if the servant could give her Judge Freeman's present whereabouts, as she needed to telephone him on important business at once; something she was sure he would want to know. After some parley with the servant to establish her right to such an address, he finally gave her the name of a New York club, and Romayne started on an hour's long-distance search. She had made up her mind to fight this thing to a finish if it took all night. She felt positive that a telegram from Judge Freeman could set her brother free, and she determined if there was anything she could do to get hold of him this night she would do it.

In the long and patience-trying intervals between calls she sat back and wrought out other plans in case the present chance failed. She was so busy at this that she did not notice that the motionless boy in the shadow of the curtain was still standing, and that his shoulders had taken on an exceeding droop of discouragement. She was thankful only for this, that he let her alone and let her forget him.

At the end of an hour and ten minutes the club she was calling informed her that Judge Freeman had started on a week's yachting trip with friends at eleven o'clock that morning, and he had left no address where he might be reached by wireless. No, they did not know the name of the yacht nor its owner.

Sitting back almost in tears at last, she considered the brief list of possibilities she had written out on a bit of paper from one of her father's desk drawers.

The last name on the list was that of her friend, Isabel Worrell. Isabel's father was a rich man, a business man. He had some vague connection, too, with her father's business. But, anyway, business men had great influence. She had always heard that. Surely he could do something if she could only reach him. Had they left yet? She tried to remember whether they were leaving that night or not till the next morning. Isabel had been locking her trunk when she arrived there, and had said something about getting it off beforehand. Well, it was worth trying.

So she tried.

After a long wait and a parley with the toll operator, she succeeded in getting the house at which she had so blithely arrived that morning. The butler who answered was very explicit.

"Yes, Miss, she has left, Miss. She left on the next train after you went. Their boat left the dock at six o'clock, Miss."

Romayne's lips trembled. Then her friend Isabel was even now sailing out over a moonlit sea, while she was tossed about alone on a sea of trouble! And where—to whom—should she turn next? Would they let her telephone to her brother? She was all untaught in the ways of prisons. She would try.

So she tried that, only to be refused. And while she was parleying that matter someone came to the door and her young warden opened it and let in the newcomer, who stood silently by and listened until Romayne hung up the receiver again with a long drawn sigh of worry. Then the man came out of the shadow by the front door and spoke.

"I am sorry to intrude, Miss Ransom, but my duty makes it necessary——"

"Oh, but all means do your duty!" she said scornfully.

He looked a little as if she had slapped him, but he went on with his sentence in an even tone of voice.

"I have just come from the place where your brother is," he said. "I have done my best to get him released for the night, but find it impossible."

"You would, of course," she said loftily. In spite of her anxiety she felt angered beyond measure at this young man's cocksureness. "I have friends who could do anything," she added with equal assurance, "if I only knew where to reach them."

"I'm afraid even your friends could do nothing this time," he said sadly. "But I am come to ask if I can carry a message, or do your bidding in any way? I know you do not wish to trust me, but if you have no one else——"

"I do not need your help," she said wearily. "I am going myself. That is permitted, I suppose, isn't it?"

"I think it can be managed. Do you wish to go at once? I will call a taxi and take you to him."

"Why do you have to go too? Couldn't I go by myself? Am I a prisoner?"

"No, but I could not take the responsibility of letting you go unescorted."

"Well, let Mr. Hollister go then and you stay here. I at east know who he is."

Sherwood looked toward the shrinking Chris meditatively.

"I think I had better go," he said. "They don't know Chris, and he might have some trouble in getting the thing through smoothly. You see—well, there's been some other trouble about an automobile—and—well—a man was killed in a mix-up and your brother was in the party—which explains why they are taking unusual precautions."

Romayne heard his words as in a dream. They meant little to her save that it was necessary for some vague reason that she go with this officious young man. It seemed all a part of the horror that had suddenly fallen down upon her. She could not explain it and she did not try to, but back in her mind she had a conviction that a large part of the difficulty lay in his imagination. However she was in the clutches of the law and must humble herself and get to Lawrence as best she could.

She swept him with a glance that was almost annihilating and turned toward the staircase.

"Very well," she said, "if there is no other way I suppose I can't help myself; but I can't see that you are keeping your promise very well."

"I will go away if you say so," said Sherwood quietly, "but I think you will have to go with me if you go at all."

"He's all right, Romayne," put in Chris. "Everybody knows him——"

"Then take me quickly!" said Romayne. "I must get back to my father. He might rouse and want me."

He was certainly expeditious, and the taxi was at the door almost immediately.

Sherwood did not intrude upon her during the ride. He put her inside and sat with the driver, and she found herself trembling as they whirled through the lighted streets. They came at last to a grim, looming building where the taxi drew up sharply. Here she was going to jail to find her brother! How terrible! What if the dear little mother had lived to see this awful happening!

For the first time since her mother had been taken away she was glad that she was gone. At least she was saved this horror and shame.

Lawrence was white and nervous when they came to him. He seemed almost angry with his sister for not coming sooner, and for not having brought immediate release for him. There was something about his attitude that made her almost afraid to tell him how she had failed in trying to get hold of any of their friends to help him. He seemed to take it as a personal failure of her own instead of the accident of circumstance. He raved at her as much as he dared. Her drooping lashes hid bright tears that she would not let fall. She shrank from having her escort see how her brother treated her. Her brother seemed strange, almost beside himself. She scarcely knew him. All the courtesy of his lifetime seemed swept away. And, yet, he was her dear brother who had shared everything with her for years. She was bound to overlook his actions, to do all in her power for him.

He seemed aghast that his father was still unconscious, and, yet, he did not seem to feel it as much for his father's sake as because of his own captivity. It merely served to make his own strait the more difficult, since there was no father to lean upon. That, too, he took as a personal affront. Was it possible that Lawrence was the least bit spoiled? Romayne could not help noticing that he had not once said a word about her predicament, nor seemed deeply concerned about his father. But she quickly laid that to his excitement. Of course, he was not normal. It was enough to make one crazy to suddenly find one's self in jail!

Romayne found her mind running on aimlessly, excusing him while she tried to tell him what she had done, and listen to his excited sentences. Sherwood stood aloof from them, not seeming to notice them, yet nothing escaped his observation. He felt sorrier for that game little girl than for anybody he ever saw before. He wished he could just pick her up and carry her away from it all. Take her to his Aunt Patty up in the mountains and let her run with the wind and laugh with the sunshine—he felt sure she could laugh like a brook—such absurd thoughts to be racing through his head while he waited here in a grim jail for a girl he never saw before, whose father was a bootlegger! Was ever any situation more unpleasant! He would give all he had to be well out of it, yet he did not want to leave her, little, delicate, scornful, lovely thing!

There he was at it again! This business must be getting his nerve. He had never before fallen for a girl that snubbed him. But this one was so bravely pitiful in her terrible situation! No girl he ever knew had had to face a thing like this!

And then he jerked himself back to realities. The young man was telling his sister he wanted her to destroy certain papers that were in his bureau drawer, also certain letters which she would find in the pocket of his coat. And then he was giving her a note which he wanted her to personally give to a girl who lived in a street down near the railroad station—not a neighborhood to which Sherwood would have cared to send his sister hunting a strange girl at that time of night.

Sherwood stood with his back turned toward them, and patiently waited without a sign that he had heard anything. There were other men in the room. No one was especially noticing the brother and sister. The girl's white ethereal face stood out strangely incongruous in the grim surroundings. She shrank back as the door opened and a reeling, ribald man singing a snatch of a song out of the past peered gustily in.

"If a body meet a body,
Comin' through the rye," he sang mirthlessly, and bowed toward Romayne with mock ceremony.

Romayne looked up with a shudder, and grew whiter round her lips. She had her brother's keys and had written down his directions.

Sherwood hurried her away as soon as possible. It seemed now to him that he had done a terrible thing in bringing this sweet young girl here among drunken roughs. He ought to have prevented the visit somehow. Yet how could he?

Romayne did not cry on the way back to her home. She seemed to have grown old, so old, and to have things they called cares hanging all over her. She did not know which was the more terrible. To have her beloved father locked in a sleep like death, or to have her only brother spending the night in jail with all too apparently good reason.

"Did you wish to go anywhere else?" Sherwood asked her abruptly as they were about to turn into her street. "You had a message to take?"

"Oh!" she roused herself with a start, and told off the address; but when the taxi drew up in front of the number she had given she looked out to find it was the very house where she had spent an hour that afternoon before coming home, and with new horror she remembered that the little note had been addressed to "Frances" somebody. What could this mean? Surely Lawrence could have nothing to do with a girl like Frances Judson, common little painted thing that she was! What possible communication could Lawrence have to make to her?

She straightened up in her seat after glancing out.

"I think there is some mistake," she said to her silent

escort. "I will not take the message to-night. I would like to go home now, please."

There was a note of humility in her voice that had not been there before, and Sherwood felt his own heart go out to her in her despair. If only he were her friend now, and could help a little—really help!

They went swiftly back to the house, and Romayne looked up at the light in the upper window and remembered how she had glanced up that afternoon with such satisfaction. How soon and how swiftly her satisfaction had been swept away! How gladly now would she welcome back the hard sweet days when she and her father lived in a little old house in an uninteresting street, and were happy companions together! How happy poverty could be if she had it again, along with her utter trust in her father and brother!

There were men in the house again when she entered. They had opened the little door by the fireplace once more, and there was a light inside. Strange! Now she suddenly remembered that the house next door had been dark as they drew up to the curb! It must have been lit up other nights too and shaded somehow by those heavy curtains so that no ray of light penetrated to the street.

As she passed through the hall she threw just one glance toward the narrow open door, but she caught the gleam of the row of bottles with their labels "Pure Rye Whiskey." How indelibly that was stamped on her brain! And to think that she had been living in a house with all that hidden peril and had not known it; had, in fact, been hiding its presence and protecting it by her own presence there. Could it be that her dear father had realized that and had been willing to put her in such a position? She felt as if she were entering a charnel house.

She fled up the stairs that the men who were visible beyond the narrow door might not see her. She felt that she could not bear their eyes upon her. When she reached the top of the stairs she found her knees were all but sinking under her. Where was her fine vigorous strength of the morning? Oh, how had life fled away and left nothing but death. Death in life!

She went once more and stood by the bed, listening to her father's hoarse unnatural breathing, taking his twisted hand in hers and wondering how a single moment like that could have changed and distorted his form and features. Her heart was bursting with its heavy burden.

The nurse had shaded the light, and motioned her to go and rest, and Romayne slipped away to her own room. She took off her hat, and then remembered that she had yet a mission to perform. Perhaps even now men were on their way to her brother's room.

She slipped down the hall again, and was about to open her brother's door when she noticed there was a light streaming from the crack below. She drew back as the door swung open and saw two men, one with a flashlight, going through her brother's pockets. It was too late! The papers he had wanted destroyed were already in their hands! So she had failed to do even so much to help him! She made a little sound like a moan and turned to go, but her foot slipped on the polished floor, and she would have fallen if someone had not caught her. She looked up and found that Sherwood was steadying her with his arm. A sudden feeling of fury came upon her that he should be present everywhere as if he was at the bottom of all her trouble. Her overstrained nerves recoiled and she stiffened away from him.

"So that was why you were so anxious to go with me to see my brother!" she said with scorn. "You went to spy!"

He looked down at her sadly.

"You poor little girl!" he said. "What I heard made no difference. This would have all been done anyway." He swept the room with his gesture. "This has all been arranged since yesterday. I had nothing to do with it except as I have been obeying orders."

"Oh!" she moaned. "I wish I might never see you again!" and the tears flowed down in a deluge.

The young man recoiled at her words as if he had been stung again, but his voice was steady.

"If you will go into your room and stay an hour I will do my best to make your wish come true," he said, and walked away back to Lawrence's room once more.

Romayne hurried into her own room, locked the door, and fell upon her trembling knees in a deluge of tears.

Presently in a blinding search for her handkerchief a bit of paper fell from her pocket, and she remembered the note she had been trusted with. She stooped and picked it up.

It had fallen open, and her eye caught the words:

"Go tell Krupper I'll get him a whole truck load of the kind he wants—the real thing—if he gets me out of here. Do what I say and I'll see you get all the rides you want. Don't open your lips about last Thursday, and if anybody asks you about the road house say you went with Timmy."

The signature was a disguised "L."

CHAPTER VIII

ROMAYNE dropped down upon her bed weakly with the paper in her hand. She felt as if all the strength of her body were slowly ebbing from her through hands and feet. Her fingers seemed lifeless. The effort to keep her hold upon the flimsy paper seemed almost too great to be accomplished, yet she grasped it as if by so doing she were in some way withholding the words it contained from a ruthless and unsympathetic world. Her thoughts were in a tumult. All that had happened before seemed climaxed in that note of her brother's.

It was not that she had not already appreciated the shame and humiliation of the discovery of the evening to the full, but somehow this note to this common little painted girl so far below her brother socially, so much beneath him in education and breeding, so low in the moral scale, seemed suddenly to reveal to her the depths to which they all had fallen, and to sweep away in one stroke any illusions she might have entertained concerning her brother's innocence in these other matters.

Then Lawrence *did* know about it all.

Then he not only *knew*, but he was deep into the business himself.

Then that was where all his money had come from! It had seemed so wonderful that he should have stepped right into a great salary just because Grandfather used to know the grandfather of the man who was at the head of the business. Probably Lawrence's salary at the office was after all but a mere pittance. Probably he kept the position the better to hide his real business! These last suggestions only hovered in the back of her mind. She had not yet got adjusted to the idea of Lawrence as a deceiver. Never had she thought of anything like dishonor in connection with this brother who had always seemed to her just about perfect.

It is true that Lawrence had been away at school for years and she had seen but little of him except at vacation times. But he had written her the most charming letters, gay and breezy, telling her of all he did and of all his friends. Ever there had been an atmosphere of refinement and righteousness about him. How could it be possible that he could have descended to this?

She read the note over again, trying to torture its phrases into a mere business communication, or possibly a message he was transmitting to Frances from some friend of hers; but the truth stared her in the face. Lawrence must have had some kind of friendship with this low-born little ignorant child, whose limitations would necessarily have taken him among people with whom he did not naturally belong. Dimly she understood that a relationship like that must be one of temptation, must carry him to places where his own ideals would be cheapened by the contact.

Something rose up in righteous anger within her soul toward the pert little flapper who had presumed to be intimate with her brother. *Her brother!*

And then her pride winced at the thought that she could no longer hold her head up at thought of her family. Not that she had ever boasted or been unduly vainglorious about herself, but always she had been glad that she had been born into a family who were God-fearing, law-abiding, educated, refined people, above doing anything low or mean or beyond the pale of culture.

Now! Now where was she! *The daughter of a bootlegger!*

Down went her head into the pillow once more and the tears welled forth strangling her for the moment.

Back came the vision of her father's white face, and hunted look, just before he fell.

Like a rock upon her heart fell the conviction that her father had known what those men had come for, and that there had been guilt in his look!

Then there surged from her heart a reaction. She would not believe that of her father! He had *not knowingly* sinned! It might be that he had come to suspect something. There might have been things in the business to make him uneasy. But surely, surely he had not known all! They had been using him as a blind to the world to hide their illicit operations.

As she recalled it now, her father hardly ever went down

cellar—not in the daytime, and he could not have gone at night without awaking her. Why, she could remember but three times when her father had gone down cellar. Twice to arrange about the coal and open the chute and once when those great packing cases had come from the West. He had gone down and arranged where they were to be put. There had been several of them, more it seemed to her memory than had appeared when she went through the cellar with the young officer. They had probably been split up for kindling wood long ago, or else her memory had made more of them than there were. And—oh, yes—she could remember when Father went down to superintend the fixing of the wall where they said a part had fallen down. She hadn't been down herself—but she was sure her father could not have known of those packing cases in the cellar filled with bottles. Now she remembered—the man who brought them worked a long time unpacking the boxes and bringing up those specimens, and her father had been busy in his office, arranging them as they were brought up. Very likely he hadn't known a thing about what was going on. Whoever was employing him had just kept things camouflaged, and, of course, it was all the better screen for them to have her father unaware of what was going on down in his cellar. No one would have dared suspect a respectable man like her father! She would tell that detestable young man about it in the morning if he dared come near the house again—or, no, she preferred telling someone who would have more authority. She would go to the Judge's secretary and explain it all out and ask them to see that the impertinent young man was told. Of course her father was all right!

Having convinced herself bravely she got up from the bed and washed the tears from her face. By and by, reconnoitring to see that all was quiet below, she stole down the hall to her father's door again.

Softly she turned the knob, opened the door and stepped inside. The nurse sat silently by the window, looking out into the deep midnight sky. Long afterward Romayne remembered the impression of stars against the midnight blue of the sky as she stepped inside that room, and then went to look at the white twisted face on the pillow, her heart breaking with the agony of thinking how he lay there unable to speak for himself. But *she* would speak. She would clear his fair name! And she would go back now and spend the night in praying.

Lawrence might have gone wrong, but Father, *never!* She would not believe it.

She went back to her room after a little while. It was too terrible to stand there and watch that living death of her beloved.

She changed into a little plain house dress that had been her work dress before the rise in their fortunes. Somehow she felt more honest and strong in that than going about in her pretty new things that might have been bought with doubtful money. Not that she was going to believe that they had yet, but she felt better and more like her old self in the old dress.

In almost a business-like way she knelt beside her bed when she was dressed and began to pray that God would help her to vindicate her father. But when she tried to frame the sentences the words would not come, and it was just as if a preventing hand had been laid upon her soul forbidding her prayer. How strange! And then she set about it again, in a fury of anger that anyone should suspect her father—yes, and her brother—her dear brother! Surely there must be some mistake about him, too. That note—well—there would be some explanation. When day came she would go again to the prison and find out from Lawrence and get the thing straight. Why had she not made Lawrence realize their father's condition? Now she remembered she had been dazed herself.

Again, for the third time, she tried to pray that everything would be set right in the morning.

So through the night she struggled to pray, framing sentences which her inner consciousness told her did not fit the case, yet trying to reach the gate of heaven with a petition that was more a demand than a prayer that the Most High would work a miracle and undo all the sin that had been committed.

When the first crimson streak of dawn sent a faint rosy light across the window, making half visible the furniture in her room, Romayne suddenly rose from her knees with set face, and started downstairs. She realized that she was fighting to believe what her good judgment told her was a lie; trying to believe a thing because she wanted it to be true. She had to clear away these doubts that were in her own heart before she could pray to be heard. She had always believed in prayer from her childhood, but never practised it very continuously. Still, she had prayed in faith many times and received a comfortable feeling in return that now all would be well because she had given it into the hands of God. But this time it was different. It was as if her prayers reached no higher than the ceiling and then fell in broken fragments about her feet. It seemed that if it were possible to see the invisible, she would be able to see her vain words lying in useless unaccepted heaps about the room.

Romayne found a light in the lower hall, and went on past the arched doorway toward the back of the hall to the cellar door. She was going down to investigate for herself without any curious eyes upon her.

She had opened the door and snapped on the cellar light when she was suddenly confronted by a blinking officer who had evidently been dozing in the front room.

"Is there anything I can get for you, Miss?" he asked courteously.

"No, thank you," she said in a small tired voice "I was only going down cellar."

"Certainly," he said as if going down cellar in the middle of the night were quite a common occurrence. "I will go with you."

"Oh, it isn't necessary," said Romayne, looking as if she were going to cry again. "I'm not afraid."

"I'd better go," said the man.

Then she remembered that they were all under surveillance.

"Very well," she said coldly. "I'm only going down to look at something. In the morning I'm going to someone and explain all this. I'm sure my father knew nothing whatever about it. I'm quite sure someone else has been carrying on all this, because my father was in the *oil* business. Why, I've helped him send out his circulars! My father almost never came down cellar."

"Yes?" said the officer as if he were trying to be kind to her. There was something condescending in his tone that offended her. She walked on down the stairs determinedly and began her inspection of the cellar. She went over to the big box that Evan Sherwood had shown her earlier in the evening, and examined it carefully.

She saw now, what she had not noticed the first time, that the box had been made in compartments, and evidently there had been a shelf or top layer separated from the rest. Perhaps this was the way they had deceived her father to get their wares into the next house. They might have packed the upper compartment with specimens of ore, and then employed the man to open the box. She felt sure her father had not remained in the cellar long enough to have unpacked the whole box. He probably merely inspected the top of the box, and ordered the things brought upstairs, and very likely the man reported that the rest was all alike.

She turned from the box with a sigh of real relief, and with more assurance than she had felt since she entered the house the evening before. She began to investigate the remainder of the cellar. If she could just prove that her father had known nothing about it, that he had been duped, it would make all the difference in the world. But she would have to prove it to herself. If only she might go about alone without an officer at her elbow!

The back of the cellar was dark, and she peered into the shadows furtively, wondering if there was anything more she had not seen. But the officer, noticing her glance, stepped to the wall and touched a button under the edge of the stairs which she did not know existed, flooding the back of the cellar with light, and revealing a door which she had never noticed before, which apparently led into a vegetable store closet, at least that would be the natural conclusion of a housekeeper.

In surprise she stepped to the door and tried to open it, but found it locked.

The attendant, however, stepped forward and selecting a key from a bunch he carried opened the door quite as if it were not the first time that night that he had done it, and pressing another button filled the room beyond with light.

Romayne stepped within and looked about. Instead of the rows of shelves for canned fruit and the potato bins she had expected to find, there was a tall desk and stool, and on the desk an open ledger with a pen lying beside it as if it had been hastily dropped.

At one side of the desk stood a safe, and beyond were shelves filled with bottles labelled with the names of every known kind of gin and whiskey. On a long table and piled about on the floor against the wall were brown paper packages carefully done up and addressed, and one apparently recently broken open showed a dozen bottles packed in straw. She stepped nearer and saw the address on one, "E. A. Krupper, Earnheim Building—" but the thing that made her heart stand still was that the address was *in her father's handwriting!* Could he possibly have addressed them without knowing what they contained?

As if to answer her unspoken question her eyes turned to the pile of labels and revenue seals lying on the table. Of course she did not know that they were counterfeits.

Sick at heart she turned and walked over to the desk, struggling to keep back the tears and forced herself to read several lines of the entries all in her father's clear unmistakable handwriting:

" 7 Quarts Gin ....
"12 Quarts Rye Whiskey................
" 5 Quarts——"

She did not follow them out to the end of the line. She was not concerned with the price they brought nor the people who bought them. She was convinced beyond a doubt that her father knew what he was doing and that he had done it all deliberately. She was trembling and would have fallen if she had not steadied herself by the desk. The man who was awaiting her convenience stepped back in the shadow. His heart was aching for this frail bit of a girl and the burden that had been handed her to bear. His jaw set sternly over the father who had so far lost his fatherhood as to leave a sorrow like this for his girl to bear. Suppose it had been his little Nannie?

Romayne, forcing her trembling lips to steadiness, stepped to the opening in the other side of the room where the wall had evidently been pulled down hastily and the stones flung to one side, perhaps to make room for some bulky object to pass through.

She did not go over there to see anything more. She had her answer. There was no further doubt. She went there to be unobserved for a moment until she could control the overwhelming tears that threatened to engulf her.

But when she stood at the opening she saw beyond a big room filled with packing boxes like the one that stood in the front of their own cellar. It almost looked as if it reached through two or three cellars, it was so long. And there was a glimmer of light at the far end as if there were a door beyond. Why! Could it be that the business included more of the houses in the block? One, two, yes, there were three houses beyond them, two occupied and one next door vacant. The corner was occupied by a baker,—and—yes, there was a big door opening from the back of his house to the side street. She had seen it open once and a big truck hauled up to the sidewalk being loaded with wooden boxes of all sizes. Could it be? Oh, how *horrible!* Her father had always en-

couraged her to go to that store, even though things were
expensive there, rather than to go a little farther where they
were cheaper.

Suddenly she turned and fled up the stairs, her lips quivering, her eyes streaming, her heart fairly smothered with
surging emotions. Back to her room she fled and locked the
door, buried her face in her pillow and prayed. But now the
prayer was not for deliverance for herself. She prayed for
her father.

"Oh, God, forgive him! Forgive him! He did it for me, I
know he did! He always wanted me to have nice things. He
used to say I ought to have the things my mother had when
she was a girl! Oh, God, please forgive him! Won't you
please, please to forgive him, and not let him have to suffer
for it? He was not well, you know, and he had tried so long
to get a position! Oh, dear God, help me somehow to make
up for the wrong he has done, and don't punish him. My
poor dear Father!"

Wildly she whispered the petition into her pillow, sobbing
her heart out between gasps.

"Please forgive my father, and make him get better somehow so he will know You love him yet. Mother loved him,
and Mother loved You. Won't You forgive him for Mother's
sake? I know Mother is in heaven with You. Won't You
forgive him. Oh, forgive him, for Jesus' sake——"

There seemed to come a calm into her heart after that,
and she crept upon her bed and slept from pure exhaustion.

The sun was shining brightly across her bed when the
nurse tapped at the door with a tray.

There was toast and poached eggs and a cup of tea set
forth appetizingly. The nurse had a kind voice. She told her
she must eat or she would be sick.

Romayne did not feel hungry. The thought of food was
revolting. She felt as if she had been dead and buried a long
time and she wished this strange nurse would go away, this
woman who kept on saying things that she had not listened
to.

"You will have to eat something," she was saying, "because
they have sent for you to come down and see your brother
again. And before you go you must come and sit with your
father while I straighten up. The day nurse will be here
presently."

"Oh," said Romayne with sudden responsibility, "but I do
not need to eat. I will come at once. I am not hungry."

"You *must* eat!" said the nurse with an air of finality. "See, I have made breakfast for you!"

It seemed a matter of courtesy, so she ate what was on the tray, wishing the woman would go away.

"Did you say the doctor had got another nurse?" she asked, trying to make talk because it seemed she just could not endure having the woman stand there watching her silently.

"Not the doctor," answered the nurse, "the young gentleman. He arranged it when they sent me. He said there was to be two nurses, a day and a night, as long as was needed. And he said you was to eat and rest——"

"The young gentleman!" repeated Romayne with dignity. "Whom do you mean? Was my brother able to send word about our comfort?"

"Oh, no, him that was here—Mr. Sherwood. He gave me my orders. They do say as he has done more for the cleaning up of this town——"

But Romayne was on her feet with the tray in her hand, her eyes full of protest.

"What in the world does he have to do with it? It is not his business!" she flashed indignantly.

"He has all to do," said the nurse a bit importantly. "He's in charge here, and you're lucky he is. They say he is wonderful. He called up himself and insisted I should come for the night. He said it was an important case and he wanted me because he knew me. I've nursed in his family, took care of his father when he died and took his mother through double pneumonia last winter, and he knows me. You don't need to worry about anything earthly because he just thinks of everything. He was the kindest son——"

"That may be all very true," said Romayne coldly, "and I'm sure I'm obliged to whoever sent for the doctor and the nurse, but this young man is an entire stranger to me and of course I do not care to be under obligation to him. If you see him again please tell him that it is not necessary for him to do anything further. I will look after everything from now on. I couldn't possibly let a stranger."

"Don't be a fool!" said the nurse bluntly. "Don't you know this house is under control of the police and they're guarding it? Nobody can't come in or out without he says so, and you better be thankful you've got such a jailer. Now, drink the rest of that tea and then I'll let you go and sit with your father while I slick up the room. I'm old-fashioned and I like things in their places before the day nurse gets here."

Romayne had sunk back upon the bed again with a helpless despair in her face at the announcement of the police control, but now she realized that she must obey this kindly dictatorial woman or be further tried by her, so she hastily swallowed the hot tea, and went to her father's room.

It was all very quiet except for that strange breathing of the patient. Daylight gave even more of a ashen look to his face than the evening had done. Romayne dropped awesomely into the chair that the nurse placed for her beside the bed and watched him, terror like a steel hand gripping her heart.

What, oh what, was to be the outcome of this terrible situation? And yesterday had been so sweet and fair in its beginning! Oh, if they all could have died before any of this happened! And in a few minutes she was to go to jail again to see her brother! To *jail!*

CHAPTER IX

THERE was no one else but Lawrence in the room that morning when she went for her interview. She overheard the warden say to an attendant: "It's all right. Sherwood ordered it," and again she felt the steel of obligation enter her soul. Somehow it seemed so terrible to have this young man mixed up in her affairs. His gray eyes seemed to have seen clear through her life and stripped it of all its sweet reserve. She felt she could never forgive him for continuing to take care of her in this way. He had promised to get out of her life and he had not done it! Surely he might have turned the whole affair over to some other official She would rather suffer a few hardships and go less well cared for than to all the time feel his protection and know that he had thought out every inch of the way through which she was to pass and anticipated it for her She resented his right to care for her. He had hurt her father and brother! Much as he was in the right and they were in the wrong, it yet seemed disloyal to them to accept any favors from one who had been the cause of the family disaster.

Yet she was glad to have this brief freedom from watchful eyes and listening ears, as the guard withdrew and left them alone. She wanted to throw herself into her brother's arms and weep out all her sorrow on his loving breast, but somehow he seemed strangely separated from her since the occurrences of the day before. As she looked at him now, haggard and white from his night's vigil, somehow she saw only the desperate face that had gleamed for a moment behind her father yesterday and then disappeared. There had been and was still a strange lack in his face of something which, had she been a little older, she might have called principle. She felt the lack as she studied his face now while he seated himself across the little white pine table from her. It seemed like something that had suddenly disappeared out of him, something familiar that had always been there, and had dropped out, leaving a blank, as if it had been a color or a shading in the flesh.

Lawrence's manner was gay. He was making a good bluff he considered. He felt it was only a matter of time before some of the gang would help him out. His sister was not the only one who had carried notes for him. He had been busy all night. He had been able to fix up one or two little shaky matters, and to get several pieces of evidence destroyed or hushed up, and he was feeling happier.

"Well, Kid, how's Dad?" he began. "Don't look so woebegone. We can't afford to let them think we're down and out. That never pays. Is Dad better?"

"He's like death!" Romayne shuddered.

"You don't mean he hasn't come to yet?" the young man asked anxiously. "I thought he'd be on deck by this time. But perhaps it's just as well he shouldn't till the Freemans get back. They've got to straighten this whole thing out. They will, too, don't you worry. I've got a pretty good handle on them and they don't know it yet. I took care for that. I didn't go into this business with my eyes shut, Little Sister, and I've got something up my sleeve that will make them squirm. You'll see the whole pretty machine turning turtle just as soon as I get a chance to talk to the Judge."

"Then you knew it all the time?" exclaimed Romayne as if the last straw had been taken from her.

"Hush!" said Lawrence roughly, glancing fearfully toward the door. "Don't talk so loud! You never can tell whether you're alone or not in a place like this. You don't want to make things worse than they are, do you?"

"How could they be worse?" moaned Romayne, dropping her head down upon the table.

"Don't be a fool!" said her brother in a low tone. "I guess it would be worse if I got a long sentence in prison, wouldn't it? Cheer up, Little Sister. I'll soon be out and then I'll make a few people smart for this. That dirty sneak of a Sherwood will be the first one, too. He thinks he's so holy, and so wise, and so righteous! I'd like to rub his nose in some of the filth that he talks about! He says he's cleaning up the city, but he's really cleaning up a lot of notoriety and you'll see him spreading himself in one of these offices he's never done prating about, and getting a bigger rake-off than anybody else in a few months. I'll bet he's been as bad as the rest of them himself or he wouldn't be so sharp to find out things."

Something seemed to be choking Romayne. In spite of herself she did not like to hear her brother talk this way about the young man. Somehow the memory of the steady look in his gray eyes reproached her for even listening to it. She sat up straight and looked keenly at her brother, as if she were older than he; as if she had a right to question his actions.

"Stop!" she said sternly. "We have not time for such talk. They may not let me stay long. Tell me. Did you know all about this beforehand? Were you really breaking the law? Did you know what Father——"

"Shut up!" said Lawrence, rising angrily. "I told you you *must not talk* about things like that. That has nothing to do with it, anyway."

"Oh, don't!" said Romayne wearily with tears rolling down her white cheeks. "It has all to do with it, whether you are guilty or not. Oh, Lawrence! How can I ever respect you again?"

"Oh, rot!" said the young man, flinging away from her and glaring across to the other side of the room. "You're a nice one to come to see a man in trouble and begin to charge him with all sorts of things and say you don't respect him—bah!"

Romayne was sitting in troubled silence with bright tears chasing down her cheeks. She felt as if her reasoning powers were taxed beyond their comprehension with the problem before her. She wanted to say something to comfort Lawrence. Two natures were striving within her, one that loved her brother with a deep and agonizing love and longed to help him at all costs, and one that loathed the thing he had done, the person he had become, and could not rally to regard his personal trouble at all while he had shut himself away from respectability by his own act. At last she looked at his angry back and said timidly:

"Lawrence, what did you do it for? Why did Father do such a terrible thing?"

Lawrence laughed an unpleasant desperate laugh.

"That's a great question for *you* to ask! As if you didn't know that Father was desperate to get money for *you*, position for *you*, clothes and automobiles and good times for *you!* And you sit there in your self-righteousness and ask *why* we did it!"

"Oh, Lawrence!" Romayne collapsed in misery once more.

The young man let her cry for a moment without attempting to comfort her, and watched her speculatively, with frowning brows. He had a problem of his own right here in moulding this little sister of deep ingrained principles into an implement fit for his questionable uses. Yet he must use her.

"Now look here, Romayne, this has got to stop!" he said at last, touching her lightly on the arm. "Of course I know you didn't realize all this, and it isn't in the least your fault, but now that you know it was for you, don't blame Father and don't blame me. Get to work and help us out of our scrape. That's your work, and you mustn't be too darned particular and sentimental about things either. This is serious business, and you forget all your finicky little ideas about right and wrong for a while and do as you're told. Did you deliver my note last night?"

Romayne lifted eyes large with a newly remembered trouble.

"Lawrence, what have you to do with Frances Judson? You haven't surely ever *gone with* a girl like that, have you? No, I didn't deliver that note! I *couldn't* when I found where it was. I had just been there in the afternoon to see her little crippled sister who is in my Sunday-school class. I couldn't take a note from my brother in prison! I *couldn't*! Not until I understood what it was about. I knew you wouldn't want me to do it."

"There you go again with your foolishness!" said Lawrence angrily, rising and taking a furious step away from her. "I thought I had a *sister!* It seems I have *nobody!*"

Romayne was sobbing once more, softly, with a desperateness about the sound of it that showed him he was going too far. He remembered that Romayne as a child had never been able to stand fault-finding. It seemed to unfit her for doing anything. He sat down and took a different tone.

"Listen, Little Sister, you have made a mountain out of a mole hill. That girl is nothing to me. One of the fellows brought her along the other night for the ride when we were taking a load down to ship it for Dad——"

Romayne shuddered at the easy way in which he spoke of the business which seemed to her the depths of disgrace.

"She's not a bad sort as girls go nowadays, but I had nothing to do with her, only she had some evidence, and I had to ask her to keep dark about it."

"I read the note, Lawrence; I thought you would want me to," said Romayne sorrowfully. "You promised her rides——"

"Oh, well, forget it! She's nothing to me, of course. Say, Romayne, are you going to help me to get out of this or are you not? We have no time to waste like this. Come out of this silliness and let's get down to business. Can you possibly rouse Dad enough to ask him a few questions? They are mighty important and I've *got* to know them or everything will go to the dogs. I've written them out here so I won't have to waste time talking about them. When you go home you see what you can do to get an answer out of Dad. Better memorize the questions so you can get them off at a moment's notice if he rouses. It's most important. I sha'n't know how to manage my case if it comes up in court without knowing just what Dad did in that meeting. Ask him if he signed the papers. Be sure to get the answer to that even if you don't get the other two."

"Lawrence, Father is just like one dead. His face is all twisted out of shape. He doesn't look in the least like Father."

"A stroke, I suppose! But he may rally, even if it's only a minute or so, and you've *got* to watch out and be ready. It might mean everything for me if you don't."

"Oh, Lawrence!" Her head went down, and she sobbed softly. "Lawrence, have you done something else—something —even—worse?"

"No! No! No!" said Lawrence crossly, flinging himself around in his chair. "Of all things! I didn't think you'd go to pieces this way. Of course, I know you've had a shock, but you ought to pull yourself together, and be able to help a little—you're all I've got to depend on, and you seem to be worse than nothing."

"Oh, I'll help—Lawrence—I'll do anything I can—but I don't honestly believe Father'll ever speak again! If he does, Lawrence, it would be *terrible* to trouble him with things like that!"

"H'm! You'd rather have me in prison all my days—or worse perhaps——"

Romayne drew a deep shuddering sob, and the door opened into the next room. The attendant had come to tell them that the time was up!

She started up with a frightened look at her brother, shrinking from his reproving eyes that taunted her with having wasted precious time. But it was not his wish to appear before the warden as being out of harmony with his sister. He forced a smile.

"Never mind, Kiddie," he said kindly, "you'll come again, and anyhow I'll be out of here in a day or so if all goes well. You just remember what I told you."

"Oh, I'll try!" she trembled forth, and then flung her arms about his neck once more to kiss him good-bye, and whispered:

"I'll do what I can, dear, but oh, *you don't know* how desperately *sick* he is!"

He patted her on the shoulder with another smile for the attendant's benefit, but he whispered fiercely in her ear:

"*Make* him answer those questions *somehow*, Kid; there *must* be a way. If I was home I would find out! You *must find out for me.* It is the only way to get us out of this hole!"

Romayne went home feeling more depressed and horrified than when she came. Here was her brother not only acknowledging his crime, but even treating it lightly! Now that she was away from him her forebodings concerning the girl Frances returned in full force. Somehow he had not convinced her. She felt sure that he had known Frances pretty well or he would never have written her such a note. It wasn't, of course, important in the present situation only as it revealed what her brother had fallen to, and gave her a sense of utter alienation from him, a feeling of being entirely alone in the world with this awful trouble. Was ever any other girl in a place so awful as this, she wondered, as she went wearily up the steps and let herself into the house. No one in the world to turn to for help! No friends that she cared to call in, now that the shame was assured. No relatives whom she knew well enough to fall back upon, no one to take charge of her poor little affairs and see what could be done for the brother and the father! In fact, now that she was positive that it was really so, she preferred fighting it out alone rather than to have to acknowledge the truth before any relative she knew, even if they were near enough to be of any service.

She went upstairs at once to the sickroom, but the same monotonous breathing showed her there was no change here. A new nurse was in charge who looked at her with cold eyes, and in answer to her few wistful questions assured her that her father could not hear anything that went on and would probably never rally from his present state, although it was quite possible that he might linger for days and even perhaps weeks. Such cases had been known.

Romayne went from the room almost glad that it was so. Never would she wish to disturb her father with the questions her brother wanted asked, yet even as she thought this her heart gave a great wrench to think she was deliberately wishing to save him at the expense of her brother, who was young and whose life would be ruined if he had to begin his young manhood with a record of imprisonment.

She waited for the doctor that afternoon and bravely asked him what the prospect was. The doctor shook his head. He had read the papers, which had highly colored versions of the story, of course, in spite of Even Sherwood's earnest efforts to hush it up.

The doctor felt it would be the kindest thing in the world both for the man and for his daughter if he never rallied from his present state, but he admitted that there was a possibility that he might. Yes, he said, it might be possible if he rallied that he would be able to understand them. It was hardly likely that he would ever regain his speech. There were certain indications—but he did not wish to commit himself even on this point at present. They would just have to wait and see.

So Romayne settled herself as best she might to "wait and see." Where had she read something like that? "Sit still, my daughter until thou know how the matter will fall." Her mother had read it to her once. Could it have been out of the Bible? Was anything ever harder to do than to wait?

The days that followed dragged like centuries. Her agony of mind was intolerable. She spent hours going over the situation vainly seeking a ray of hope. It seemed to her that she compassed the entire universe with her futile struggles to find a way out of this maze. And ever was growing in her heart a settled purpose, that if those waxen eyelids should open again with recognition in them she would be ready with something to say. She might get no answer herself, but she must get something across to her father, some word of comfort, or hope or cheer. For if her way was dark and hard how much more must be his, who had brought all this upon them all? And another thought was growing along with this determination and that was that if he should rally and get well he would be under the condemnation of the law.

She had never realized before what it would be to be under the law. To have freedom taken away and to be shut up and ordered what to do, even when to eat and sleep. She had never sensed before the shame that would attend a man and his family through the remainder of life after he had once broken the law.

Of course, there were those who could commit crime and slip through somehow by that amazing mystery they called "pull" and get free and enjoy themselves. But her father was not one of that sort. He would feel the shame and disgrace to the end of his days. If she needed any proof of that she had the memory of his look that moment he stood in the door before he fell.

It was, therefore, the one object of her life now to find something she might say or read which would convey hope of some sort to her father.

Her mother's little Bible lay always on her desk, more as an ornament or a testimonial of her faith in her mother's religion than because she read it much. She carried it to Sunday-school and studied her Sunday-school lessons with it, of course, but outside of that she seldom read it. Still it represented to her her faith, vague though it was, and it was to this little old Bible that she turned in her distress, opening it at random, here and there, but never finding anything that quite satisfied her. There was much about sin and the condemnation of sinners, but nothing that seemed exactly to suit the case. It must be something definite and clear and comforting. That was her idea. But though she had not as yet found anything to suit an emergency should it arise suddenly, she nevertheless carried the Bible with her always when she went to sit in her father's room for a little while and relieve the nurse. It seemed somehow a talisman.

Oftener, too, she read over the paper containing the questions her brother wanted asked, puzzled and troubled, wondering how she could ever bring herself to ask them if her father should suddenly open his eyes. Would she dare distress him with business? Would it not mean another stroke, and probably instant death? What a responsibility, and what a terrible strait!

"No. 1 (to be asked instantly if he is conscious)," the paper read:

"Did you sign the papers?" She sighed as she read it over again one day. Why should it matter now whether he had signed papers or not? What could they possibly have to do with Lawrence's well-being? Or what would a man care when he was dying about papers belonging to earthly affairs?

"Does Krupper know that Freeman is in on it?" That was the second question. It bothered her a good deal because she remembered seeing that name Krupper on the outside of one of those bundles of whiskey bottles. Surely Judge Freeman could not be connected with any of this business. Surely it must be another Freeman.

The third question was more puzzling still.

"Whose car did Halsey have Thursday night?" Now how could that possibly have anything to do with bootlegging? She had heard, of course, that people stole cars, but surely, surely her family would not descend as low as that. It somehow seemed out of the question. This surely was a question wherewith to catch somebody else.

There were two more.

"Where did you put your revolver?"

"Does Barney know?"

All so puzzling and all so irrelevant. So utterly impossible to bring to this chamber of death. She folded the paper, put it back in her pocket, and took up the little Bible, opening it at random. She looked down and began to read, and the words she read were these:

"There is, therefore, now no condemnation to them that are in Christ Jesus."

Ah! Here was something! No condemnation! That would tell her father all he needed to know. He understood about salvation. It had been an old story always in their home. "In Christ Jesus." That meant believing. That would be a little sentence that could be quickly spoken, and could be said over and over if need be.

She looked toward the bed speculatively, and tried to imagine herself saying it in the event of her father's sudden awaking.

Then something in the look of the still form caused her to get up quickly and come nearer and look again. Surely there was something different—something that had not been.

She came and stood close by the bed, and saw with frightened comprehension that the waxen lids were no longer closed, but open wide and watching her alertly, as if he knew her, as if he understood all that had happened!

She clasped the little Bible tightly over her frightened heart, and tried to think what she should do, what she should say. The other hand moved involuntarily toward her pocket and grasped the little piece of paper, and in that instant it was as if she halted between two great things. Should she ask the questions and save Lawrence, or should she give the message, the talismanic message?

"Father!" she spoke softly. "Father, dear!"

It seemed to her that something in his eyes responded, a light, perhaps, or was it merely her imagination?

Then the door opened and the nurse entered and spoke in her even monotonous voice.

"There's a girl down at the door says her little sister's dying. Her drunken father struck her and she wants you. You better go. I'll sit here now."

CHAPTER X

ROMAYNE lifted a protesting hand, flashed an agonizing glance at the nurse and then brought her gaze back once more to the face upon the pillow, but the eyes that had been open gazing at her were closed again!

It had only been for the flicker of an instant, but her chance was gone. Was it over forever? Her only chance? Would she never have opportunity to speak to him again?

And suddenly with this piercing thought she flung herself upon her knees beside the bed and cried out to him in an anguished voice:

"Father! Father dear! Can you hear me? Won't you open your eyes again and look at me?"

It had been like a blow in the eyes to see that face again so blank and still, the eyelids lying without a quiver upon the waxen cheeks, and the memory only of that wistful anguished eagerness in his gaze, that seemed to be piercing through and through her soul.

The nurse with stolid pity in her experienced face walked over and laid a hand upon her slender shoulders.

"It ain't a bit of use carrying on like that, Miss Ransom," she said kindly. "He can't hear you. He really can't. I don't believe there's a chance in the world he'll ever open his eyes again. They hardly ever do when they're like he is."

"But he *did!*" cried Romayne earnestly. "His eyes were open when you came into the room. He was looking straight at me and he *knew* me. I'm *sure* he did. Oh, if you only hadn't spoken. I think it startled him! But of course you didn't see——"

The nurse looked at her as if she thought she were crazy, then realizing that the girl really believed what she was saying she walked closer to the bed, examining the patient with practised eye, pulling down the lower lids, feeling the pulse, and then stepped back shaking her head.

"You only thought you saw it," she said. "It's because you've been under such a strain. It often happens. You haven't had much sleep and you've scarcely eaten enough to keep a bird alive since it happened. You ought to get out more. It ain't natural for a young thing like you to stick in the house and just bear pain day in, day out."

Romayne swept her a glance of futility and turned back to her father.

"You didn't see it of course," she said firmly. "I did. *Father!* Can you hear me? If you hear me won't you please open your eyes again? It's your little girl, Romayne. I've got something to tell you, Father!"

Even as she said the words she wondered which it was she would say, yet she cried on again, "*Father!*"

"Say, now, Miss Ransom, I wouldn't ef I was you," protested the nurse. "If he could hear it would only distress him because he couldn't answer you. He hasn't got the use of his muscles, you know. He can't open his eyes even if he does hear you, which he doesn't. I *know.* I've had case after case. He's just pure and simple unconscious, and it's a mercy indeed that he is. You ought to be thankful he is."

"Oh!" moaned Romayne, with her face in the pillow. "Oh, if I had only told him while he had his eyes open!"

"Well, now don't distress yourself. If he opened his eyes once—*if he did*, I say,—why mebbe he'll open them again. But it won't be right off soon again. It might be several hours. It might be to-morrow. It might be a week yet. Ef I was you I'd go out and walk. It's a lovely day and it'll do you good. Why don't you go and see that child that wants you? It ain't a very cheerful place to go, I know, but they said the little thing was crying and taking on the worst way for you, and sometimes doing something for somebody else kind of takes your mind off your own troubles, you know."

Romayne shuddered as she rose from the bedside just to get away from that perpetual voice of the nurse.

"Wouldn't you like to go and walk yourself?" she said with sudden inspiration. "I would rather sit here by Father."

"No," said the nurse shortly with a keen glance at her, "I'm not being paid to take walks. I'm not that kind of a nurse. Besides, it's time for his medicine in a few minutes, and it's against orders to let you stay here too long. You better go see that girl, the sister. She's waiting for you. I said I'd call you down."

"Oh!" moaned Romayne, turning sadly toward the door. "How can I? Why didn't you tell her I couldn't leave my father?"

"Because you *can*," snapped the nurse a trifle impatiently. "You've been in here too long already, and I was ordered to see that you didn't stay but a few minutes at a time. Now *go!*"

Romayne went slowly out the door, intending to send Frances on her way with a quick excuse and get to her room to think. But Frances arose as Romayne came down the stairs and faced her eagerly.

"I knew you'd come," she said with relief. "The nurse said she didn't know if you would, but I just knew you would. My mother says if you'll come and talk to Wilanna and quiet her she'll do anything in the world for you afterwards. The doctor says if Wilanna can get quiet for a while she may pull through; she's got an awful fever, you know, but he says if she takes on like she's doing now she'll die before morning. You'll come, won't you?"

"Why, I'm sorry," began Romayne, "but you know my father is lying very low."

"Oh, yes," spoke up Frances quickly, "but the nurse said he wouldn't be any better nor any worse, and it wouldn't hurt you a bit to get out a while. And we won't keep you long, we really won't, if you could only talk to Wilanna a little bit and quiet her. She thinks you're so pretty and so nice, and she keeps talking all about the Sunday-school lesson and how you get to heaven and all, and we can't answer her questions. You see she heard the doctor say she might die and she keeps saying she ain't ready, and if she could only see you and ask you one question she'd be happy. If you'll just come home with me I'll do anything in the world for you. You see I know your brother——"

Romayne turned a startled look on the girl. Yes, of course! She had forgotten! This was the girl to whom Lawrence had sent that note! Oh, how could she go through the humiliation of going to that house again now that she remembered?

"Yes," went on Frances, "I knew him real well. We went out together a lot. I was to've gone with him the night he got pinched——"

"Oh!" breathed Romayne sharply as if a pain had darted through her heart.

"Yes, I knew all about it, and I know some things I could tell that would make it all right for him, I guess. I haven't been saying anything about it 'cause I didn't wantta get in bad with the gang, but if you'll come to my little sister and help her I'll go to the Judge and tell him what I know I guess Lawrence will get out then."

Romayne did some swift thinking. There was no use trying to ignore this humiliation. It was here and it was hers, and she was beginning now to feel that there were so many more things that mattered than just that Lawrence had been keeping company with a girl far beneath him, perhaps she should put aside her natural feelings and do what was right. It was right, of course, to go to this little Sunday-school scholar and help her to die if she could. But how could she help anybody? She had never died herself. She had never been with anybody who was dying. She did not know what needed to be said. Just to soothe her probably. But, oh,—to leave that silent face upstairs with the closed eyes and go away, when they might open and search the room for her any moment! Still, the nurse would put her out if she went up again so soon. She had been told not to let her stay in the room long at a time Who told her that? The doctor, probably. But—why should he care? *Who* told her?

Frances meanwhile was rattling on, babbling a trifle proudly of her friendship with Lawrence. Romayne had not heard half she said.

"I will go with you," she said suddenly. "But I cannot stay long. My father really is very low. He might at any time now become conscious and ask for me. I must be here."

"Oh, sure! We won't keep you long," gushed Frances, obviously relieved that her task was so easy.

Romayne did not hear the remainder of her sentence. She was on her way upstairs to get her hat. She stopped again at the sickroom door.

"He hasn't opened his eyes again, has he?"

"No," said the nurse with that half-amused smile.

"Will you be kind enough to sit right where you can watch him all the while?"

"I always do," interrupted the nurse offendedly. "I never desert my duty."

"Of course not," said Romayne, "but I mean will you take particular notice, and if he should happen to open them again will you say over to him quietly: 'Romayne will be here in a few minutes. She wants to speak to you,' just like that, and try to keep his attention till I get here? I won't be long."

"Oh, sure!" said the nurse obligingly, and settled herself for a nap as Romayne closed the door.

The two girls walked down the street in the pleasant spring sunshine, and no one, to watch them, would have known that they carried under their bright dresses two of the heaviest hearts that girls ever carried.

Frances really looked very nice. Her dress was perhaps a trifle too bright of stripe for good taste, but out of deference to Romayne she had left off all rouge, and only applied the powder most sparingly, so that Romayne did not feel any embarrassment at the appearance of her companion. Indeed Romayne was not thinking of appearances just then. Her problems were too many and too varied to leave room in her mind for trifles.

"How long have you known my brother?" she asked at last, feeling suddenly that this was a question she must know before she went further.

"Oh, about a month," said Frances guilelessly. "We went on a joy ride, a party of us, and had a real swell time. The fella that was taking me seen a man he was keeping outta sight of, and he just turned me over to Larry, and we had the swellest kind of a time. He's a Jim Dandy, Larry is. He certainly can show a girl a nice time when he tries to."

Romayne succeeded in controlling a shiver that threatened to seize her very soul, and tried to think of something to say

in a conversation like this, but she had no need, for Frances
rattled on, proud to show how intimate she was with Larry.

"He's a peach, he is. The girls in our gang are all crazy
about him, and when the word came that he was pinched we
all felt awful sorry. But I don't guess he'll be in long. In fact,
if I tell what I know, I'm sure he won't. And I'll tell. There
ain't anybody I know I'd sooner help than Larry. He's always
so free with his money and showing a girl a good time and
all."

"Then you went out with him again?" asked Romayne,
trying to steady her voice so that Frances would not suspect
that this revelation was horrible to her.

"Yep!" Frances responded gaily, "a lotta times. We went
to the roof-garden, oh, a lotta times and had dinner and
danced. Larry can dance! I'll say he can dance! I feel zif I
was just floating on a cloud into heaven when I dance with
Larry."

She glanced admiringly at Romayne's trim little feet as
they walked along.

"Say, I guess you can dance too. With a foot like that!
My, but you've got pretty feet. You're an awful pretty girl,
you know," she said. "Say! Don't you never use no rouge?
You look awful pale to-day! I sh'd think you'd put on just a
darling little bit, it would make you look sweet. Say, whyn't
you get Larry to bring you along sometime with us. I'd be
proud to have ya. Say, ain't it funny you should a ben
Wilanna's Sunday-school teacher all this time and I going
with your brother and I never knew it? See, 'twas this way.
The fella that interduced us didn't say his name right plain
and I never knew till the day Larry was pinched what was his
right last name. I mighta knowed he was a relation to you
though, you look so much alike. I'm awful glad it turned out
this way. It's real romantic, ain't it? I was telling Ma it would
be funny if we was to be——"

But Romayne interrupted her flow of terrible words hastily.

"What did you say was the matter with Wilanna? Did she
have a turn for the worse? Are you sure she is not going to
live?"

"Oh, I didn't explain that? Why, you see Papa got out.
Krupper did it. He went hisself and gave bail. You see he
didn't want Papa to give evidence against him, you know.
He's got too much at stake. He's the one that owns the place
at the corner where they've kept open right along, law or no

law. That's the place that always gets Papa, it's so handy to home, you see, and somebody's always just coming out when he goes by and inviting him in and treating him. Krupper he don't exactly run it hisself. He has a big place up at the Earnheim building lots sweller than this and only for real classy people. E. A. Krupper, you know. It's a kind of a tea room, but there's rooms behind. I've been there myself," she preened. "Larry took me."

Romayne caught her breath, and her white teeth came sharply down on the crimson lower lip. How was she going to stand any more of this?

"Have you ever been there?" asked the bright-eyed Frances eagerly, keen to have some experience in common with this beautiful girl by her side.

"No," said Romayne in a cold little voice that she could hardly hear herself. She felt as if she were freezing inside.

"Well, you oughtta get Larry to take you sometime," Frances said blithely. "It's great! There's real velvet curtains and lace on the table-cloth, and lady waiters, awful pretty girls. They do say you can't get in there to wait unless you are awful handsome and Krupper likes you. Well, Krupper, he spends a lot of time in the back room over the place at our corner, and Papa has done one or two things for him, and so he didn't want Papa talking. So I guess that's the reason he come hisself and took Papa out. But you see he took him around to the corner first to talk to him a bit, and he treated him while he was there, give him some pretty fierce liquor, I guess, for he come home crazy. He wanted his dinner right away and Mamma hadn't a thing in the house to cook. He'd left her without any money, and when he saw the table wasn't set nor nothing he shook Mamma till she couldn't speak, and flung her against the wall. He tried to hit me, but I run out the door, and then he went raving upstairs, and he dragged Wilanna right out of bed, yes sir, cast and all, and hit her over the head, and she just screamed and lay there all still."

"Oh!" exclaimed Romayne, her eyes large with horror. "How terrible! Poor little girl!"

"Yes, ain't it?" went on Frances glibly. "Mamma heard her scream, and she went right up and saw him standing looking at Wilanna like he was going to strike her again, and she just took a pitcher of water off the washstand and threw it in his face so hard it dazed him, and he slid down on the floor. He laid there a few minutes while we was getting my sister back

onto the bed, but the water kind of sobered him, and after
while he got up and looked at Wilanna and began to cry.
He's cryin' now like a big baby with his head down on the
bed. He ain't all hisself, but he seems to know he done it. He
was awful fond of Wilanna when he was hisself."

"Did the doctor come?" asked Romayne, wondering why
she had to be mixed up with any more horror than had fallen
already to her own lot.

"Oh, yes; I run after him, but he can't do nothing. He says
Wilanna is awful bad again and he don't think she can live.
She's just screamed for you ever since she got back into bed
again."

They were nearing the little brick row now and Romayne
began dreading the scene that was before her. How could she
go in and talk to that dying child? What was there to say that
would help her? And how was she to rise beyond the awful
things in her own life and help a little human soul who was
passing into eternity? What a terrible thing life was!

But Frances was talking again.

"I wouldn't wonder what I can get Krupper to help Larry
out if I watch my chance. He might. You know it was in his
tea room that the man that was killed had been drinking.
They had a post-mortem, and Krupper, he's all up in the air.
If I tell him Larry and I was in the same car and saw what
happened——"

Romayne turned a ghastly face toward her persecutor, and
tried to exclaim, but the power of speech seemed to have
departed from her ashen lips. Her look almost startled the
voluble Frances.

"Oh, you don't need to look like that! Nobody don't know
we was there, and I went to the jail this morning to see Larry
and we got it all fixed up. I'm to tell Krupper we got
evidence that won't be very nice for him, but we'll keep mum
if he lets Larry out, otherwise Larry'll come out with the
whole story and get 'em all in Dutch. He wouldn't really, you
know, because that would give him and me away, but they
don't know that and we don't intend they shall. I'm just
a tellin' you because you're his sister, and it's sort of in the
family——" she giggled consciously. "But you don't need to
worry. Krupper'll get him out. I'll see to that."

Romayne put out a trembling hand to the girl's arm.

"I wish you wouldn't, please," she said in what she tried to
make a commanding voice. "I wish you would just let things
alone. We have a very powerful friend, Judge Freeman, who

will probably be home to-morrow, I am told, and when he gets here everything will be all right. You may only make more trouble if you get this Krupper into it. It is better to leave it to Judge Freeman."

"Oh! That's a good one!" laughed Frances. "Why, Judge Freeman is one of the gang hisself, and Krupper does all his dirty work. Didn't you know that? That's why he's gone away. You won't see him round these parts for a while now. He'll leave it all to Krupper. Well, here's our house, and now you go up to Wilanna's room and I'll just stay down here in the parlor and wait for Krupper to come. Don't you worry. Leave it all to me."

And because she did not know what else to do Romayne walked bravely up the stairs, her heart beating wildly, and tears struggling with her eyes and throat. She felt as if she had entered a great sewer of filth and could never find her way out of it. She felt as if her life's happiness was already soiled beyond any hope of redemption, and nothing mattered any more. Oh, Life! Life! How terrible to be alive! How had she ever dared to think that to be alive was good? And where had she heard that name, Krupper?

Then as she was about to enter the shabby little room where the sick child lay moaning on her bare little bed and her father with his unshaven face buried in the sheets and his mop of greasy hair lying over the child's hands, moaning beside her, it all came back to Romayne.

"E. A. Krupper, Earnheim Building."

It had been the address on one of the bundles that lay in the cellar—those bundles of bottles of liquid poison. And her father, her dear father, had been dealing out this poison, some of which had helped to bring this little child to her death-bed.

Then, as if a voice had spoken to her, Romayne knew what she meant to say to that father if he ever opened his eyes again and looked at her intelligently. "There is, therefore, now no condemnation to them that are in Christ Jesus," that was the message she must get across to him before he went from this world with sin upon his soul.

Honor, nor riches, nor happiness, nor nothing else mattered, not even whether her brother was exonerated and set free to live his life, none of these mattered, if only her father might have his soul purged from this awful sin that was worse than murder or crime of any sort because it included all crimes, and worse to her because it had been done for her sake.

And suddenly strong to bear a message to the little passing soul, she entered the death-chamber, and slipped to her knees beside the bed opposite the half-drunken father, and took the little hot hand of the child in her own.

"Wilanna," she said softly, "listen. You needn't be afraid. Jesus loves you. He died to save you. He said, 'Suffer little children to come unto me and forbid them not, for of such is the kingdom of heaven.' "

Wilanna turned her wild fevered eyes on her beloved teacher.

"Yes, but, Miss Ransom, I've been awful bad. I've told lie! A lot of them. I used to tell Mother I hadn't been away from home when she was gone out working. And I had. I'd been lots of places she said not. And our teacher in school says if you told a single lie you had to go to hell for it. Ain't that so?"

"But Jesus took your lie on Himself when He died on the cross, Wilanna. He died for your sin in your place! All He asks now is that you will just give yourself to Him and let Him take care of you. If you are sorry for your sin He will forgive it. He died for all sin, and your sin is all paid for."

"And won't He punish me, and turn me out of heaven if I die now? The doctor said I was going to die. I heard him."

Her voice was high-keyed almost to a scream. Romayne tried to quiet her.

"Listen, Wilanna, aren't you Jesus' child? Didn't you tell me once in Sunday-school that you wanted to give yourself to Jesus and do what He wanted you to do?"

The bright eyes were upon her face, and the child nodded.

"Yes, but I ain't done it," she sobbed.

"Then do it now," said the girl's quiet voice.

The little girl looked in her face for a moment and then turned her eyes toward the ceiling, speaking in a shrill strange little voice, slightly raised as if she addressed some one at a distance.

"Jesus, I wantta be your child. Won't You fergive me right now quick, because I'm going to die?"

"There!" said the child, looking at her teacher, "I done it. Is that all?"

"Yes, that's all, if you really meant it, Wilanna. He heard and He has promised that there is no condemnation to those

that are in Christ Jesus. The blood of Jesus Christ cleanses us
from all sin."

A moan from the man on the other side of the bed broke
into her words, but the little weak hand of the child patted
his matted hair, and Romayne marvelled at the love of the
child that could forgive the man who had struck her to
death.

Romayne knelt beside the child's bed for an hour or more,
pointing the way to the little passing soul, and when at last
she went down the stairs and out into the bright spring
sunshine once more she found that her own troubles had
been strangely lifted from her shrinking shoulders. Nothing
seemed to matter save one great thing, to be "in Christ
Jesus." She hurried back to her home with the great thought
before her of how she might get the same message to her
father, shut in as he was from the world to a living
death.

Her father knew the way, even better than she did. He had
lived as if he believed it all his life,— and yet—he had done
this! Well, she must just remind him of the way of life. Her
father could not have loved to do this evil that had wrought
havoc in so many homes. He had done it from a mistaken
sense of love to her. She must show him before he went away
how to be clean of his sin, or she never could live out the
days that were left to her. And suddenly, as she went up the
steps, a new strength came to her, and she was no more a
child, but a woman with a great message to give. How she
was going to do it she did not know, but there would be a
way.

The nurse was coming down the stairs as she entered the
front door.

"There's been a lady here to call on you," she said. "She
left her card and said she'd come again. Her name is Sherwood. She's a very nice lady."

"Oh!" said Romayne, shrinking involuntarily. "I don't want
to see her! If she comes again please tell her I'm not seeing
visitors now, not while my father is so sick."

"Well, you're foolish, but I can't help it. There's a telegram
for you, too. It came over the telephone. I wrote it down. It's
just sympathy and it's signed 'Judge Freeman.' "

Romayne looked at her a moment with sorrow in her eyes,
and then walked silently up to her own room and knelt
beside her bed. There was only one in all the Universe that

could offer her sympathy now, and that was God Almighty. All others seemed to have failed.

CHAPTER XI

THE SEA was calm as a mirror of silver and the moon shone down with almost the brilliance of high noon as the great ship slid evenly along, over the glassy surface.

It seemed like a fairy world to the girl who sat on the deck beside her father watching the rippled pathway of jewelled light from the ship toward the moon. It was as if that pathway of scintillating gems out there on the water led to her own future that lay awaiting her, the future that had lain so long behind the rosy curtains of her imagination, and to which now she seemed to be fast travelling.

Isabel Worrell had not been abroad since she was quite a small child. She had been kept in school, and in summer camps, and well out of the way of the social activities of her gay, handsome mother, who did not believe in being hampered with children until they were old enough to make a début in the world and take care of themselves. It was, therefore, not with jaded appetite of the modern young society girl who has travelled the globe several times before she is out of her teens that Isabel came to the trip which had dropped down into her scheme of living so unexpectedly but the day before, and she was fully prepared to enjoy every moment of it. Her only regret was for the house party which had been so unceremoniously broken in upon—her first house party where she would have had all the responsibility and everything just as she wanted it; for her mother was away in the mountains with a party of friends and she had been promised full sway, with only an ancient cousin, who didn't count, for chaperone.

But what were parties compared with a trip to Europe with her indulgent father, who of late had not seemed to care how much money he spent upon her, and was willing to gratify her every whim. She only felt sorry for one girl, that sweet Romayne Ransom, who was so shy and had been so pleased at the invitation. She had a fancy that Romayne and she were destined to be great friends. When she came back home she would send for her and have her stay with her for several weeks. She was just the kind of girl who would be likely to fit in with all her plans, and be willing to take the background when she wanted her to. Besides, she had grown very fond of her during their last term of school together. Romayne was awfully handy when it came near examination time; she always knew just what to study up, and what subjects would be likely to come up in the questions. And Romayne really had a lovely disposition. It was a shame she didn't get the word in time and had all that journey for nothing. Isabel wondered whether, after all, she had really written that note to Romayne when she wrote the others, or had she only promised herself she would write it? She distinctly remembered trying to call her up and failing, and then starting upstairs to write the note, but she wasn't sure it had ever been written. Well, never mind. The water was a sheet of silver, the gemmed pathway to her vague sweet future was flecked with gold, and the night was perfect. There was music in the cabin, floating out in the most enticing strains, and there were dozens of interesting-looking young people aboard. Presently, when Daddy had his smoke, she would go inside and dance, and then perhaps she and—some one else—who would it be?—would come out for a walk on deck. Why worry about poor little Romayne Ransom? There would be time enough to make up to her after she returned in the fall. What if she hadn't written the letter?

Her father's secretary came across the deck briskly, as he always came when he approached his chief with a bit of business. How tiresome! Now Daddy would begin another cigar, and she would have to wait until that was finished, for it wouldn't do to go in alone this first night on board.

Several young men and girls strolled by and she watched them eagerly, impatient to be of their number and begin her good times. The jewelled pathway on the water had lost its charm. Her head was turned toward the music and the lights, and the moving figures.

But the low tones of the men beside her went steadily on, and somehow the words drifted to her ears and caught her attention, for the wind was just right for her to hear everything they said.

"And what about Ransom?" her father was asking. That

was what attracted her attention first. Ransom was not a common name.

"Did they get him? I'm afraid he's not a man who knows how to act quickly in an emergency. He's too elegant! He feels his own importance. I felt that from the first."

"Ransom had a stroke of apoplexy!" announced the young secretary in a dry, hard tone that was used to dealing out facts that were in themselves nothing to him.

"You don't say!" said the elder man, startled. "Did he die?"

"Judge Freeman thought not. His last message was that the man was still alive, but unconscious. Had not rallied at all."

"Well, if he dies we're safe. Dead men can't tell any tales," said Mr. Worrell speculatively. "If he lives I'm not so sure of him under pressure. His aristocratic ego couldn't endure humiliation, and he'd be very likely to blab, I'm afraid. It's best if he dies. A lot will die with him, and things will straighten out a great deal sooner. What of that rat of a son? It was all his fault anyhow, getting mixed up with that gang, and letting us in for a lot of suspicion. That murder was a most unfortunate thing for our plans——"

Isabel sat listening and trying to piece things together. What could it all mean? Was it Mr. Ransom, Romayne's father, about whom they were talking? That handsome man with the elegant bearing and the silvery white hair? She had seen him but once, but had admired him greatly. He seemed to her like a fine old portrait of a southern gentleman. She had been greatly impressed by him, and by his smile and his courtly ways. And what was this about a murder? And, why, *how heartless* they were! Saying it was best if the man died! Poor Romayne! But then, of course, it must be somebody else. It couldn't be Romayne's father who was stricken. She would ask as soon as they were through with their business talk.

So Isabel sat watching the silver sea, and turning impatient eyes toward the sounds of music and wishing her father would hurry.

The secretary went away at last and Isabel turned to her father with questions.

"Who were you talking about, Daddy? You said 'Ransom.' That wasn't Romayne's father, was it?"

"Romayne? Who is Romayne?" asked her father, a trifle annoyed, she thought.

"Why, Romayne is that lovely new friend of mine that I

met last winter at school—the girl you said you thought was so charming, the one that didn't get the word about the house party and was at lunch with us yesterday."

"Oh, why, to be sure! Was her name Ransom? I hadn't connected the two."

"Why, yes, Daddy, you told her you knew her father! How tiresome you are sometimes with your old business! Who is her father and was it he you were talking about? He's a splendid-looking man, with white hair and gold glasses with a chain."

"Yes," said Mr. Worrell, "I'm afraid it's the same man. Why, yes, we were talking about him. He's been stricken with apoplexy, Parker tells me. There's just been a wireless from Judge Freeman. It's very sad, of course. I'm sorry for your little friend. It will go hard with her, I'm afraid. You must write her a letter of sympathy."

"Oh, how terrible!" said Isabel in a shocked voice. "But, Daddy, what did you have to do with Mr. Ransom? I heard you say it would be a good thing for you if he died. What on earth could you have meant?"

"You shouldn't try to get in on business talks," said the father shortly. "You wouldn't understand, of course. Mr. Ransom has had an under position with a company in which I am interested. He is too much of a gentleman to be a very good business man, and I'm afraid he has bungled things badly. He has a son, too, who is a bad. egg, I'm afraid. He has made a mess of things and got us misrepresented. I was utterly against taking either of them on, but it seems Judge Freeman was an old friend of the mother, who is dead, and he would have it."

"But I can't understand why it would be better for any man to be dead."

"Well, you wouldn't, of course, child! You haven't any head for business."

"But I want to understand, Daddy."

"Well, you see it's this way. There are some people in town who think they have been divinely appointed to stick their noses into other people's business, and they have been nosing around and trying to cheat our company out of a good deal of money, trying to make it appear that we are illegal in our dealings."

"You're not, of course, Daddy?"

"Of course not!" said the father in a vexed tone.

"Then why did you say it would be best for Mr. Ransom to die?"

"Well, because he knows too much about our affairs, and might say something unwise. I have discovered that he hasn't much tact or diplomacy. Besides, these cranks that are making us trouble have a lot of antiquated notions and are determined to put us back in the Dark Ages and hamper our rights, and I don't feel that this man is at all fitted to cope with the matter. It is to our advantage to have him out of the way just now."

"But *Daddy!* To wish a man *dead* just *for that!* Oh, Daddy! Suppose it was you! Suppose it was my daddy instead of Romayne's! How awful it would be. Is just business worth a man's *dying?*"

"Good heavens! Isabel, what's come over you? Of course I didn't mean that except in joke. Come, you're getting morbid. Do let business alone. I have enough trouble just now without having to explain it all to a child. Little girls were made to have a good time and not pry into matters that don't concern them. It's my business to earn the money for you to spend, and yours to have a good time spending it, not to worry about the details of how it's made. Come, let's go in and see what's going on. That music sounds good and there are plenty of nice young people for you to frolic with. You can go and send some flowers to your friend Romayne by wireless if you want to, and then *forget her!* You can't bear the troubles of the world. Run along in and dance now and have a good time!"

Isabel arose only half convinced and went with her father, solacing herself by giving earnest directions about the wireless message to the florist, and presently was in the midst of a gay chattering group, her feet fluttering to be off to the music, forgetful of everything else but the joy of living.

Outside the jewelled pathway of the moon on the silver summer sea, and far away her friend suffering and sorrowing, but Isabel had forgotten it all and was doing what she called "living."

A few miles farther up the coast on a white-winged yacht whose appointments were perfect, and whose company most select, Judge Freeman was seated in a luxurious cabin discussing with three other partners the situation as it had been reported in several successive wireless messages received since they had left New York.

"If the man dies of course we sha'n't have any immediate

necessity for worry, as I see it," said a large, flabby man whom they called Steinmetz. "The papers were all destroyed at the time the new company was formed. Our names are not connected with the affair in any way. And with Ransom dead that lets us out completely."

"You forget the son," said Judge Freeman significantly.

"I didn't know that he was a factor in the matter," frowned the flabby man. "I thought the man Ransom was sworn to absolute secrecy. I thought you were so sure you could trust him."

"Yes, but the son was taken into the matter, you know," put in a little wiry fellow named Dodd, who seemed to be a sort of henchman or mentor. He kept notes on all that was said and put each man in mind of any point that seemed to be forgotten as the argument progressed. It seemed to be his function in the group, for which he was probably well paid.

"When?" glared Steinmetz. "Why wasn't I told?" and he glared at Judge Freeman.

"He was taken in because we found he was onto some things already, and being much too bright to put anything over on, we decided to put him under such strong obligation that we could use him also," answered the cool voice of the Judge, looking at the other man with a keen little eye of hate. One could easily see that here were two who would have injured one another if they had not been partners in crime and had to stick together. The Judge was the keener and cooler man of the two.

"Well, then, why isn't he safe? Isn't he still under obligation? What was the obligation?"

"A big running salary and a chance to make his own pile on the side," rumbled Freeman, still eyeing the other contemptuously.

"Well, then, why isn't he safe?" snapped Steinmetz.

Another well-fed member with the name of Goldsmidt spoke up.

"Because he was fool enough to play around with a crowd that stole an automobile and got mixed up in a murder. It's what I said in the first place. We got too many in on this. Now he's got himself arrested, and there's bound to be a lot of questions."

"Let him stay in jail then," decided Steinmetz loftily. "His word won't be worth anything against us if he's in trouble himself. Freeman, you c'n fix that up."

"The trouble is," said Judge Freeman slowly, looking the

other man straight in the eye as if he were preparing to send a missile, "the trouble is the kid has got hold of some papers that should have been destroyed. Apparently his father didn't know it or if he did he didn't report it. Anyhow, he's written a letter threatening to turn state's evidence unless we get him out right away. The letter was brought on board an hour ago by airplane. It came to Horton and he thought it important enough to send a special messenger with it. I guess he's got us all right! He has the papers that contain all the evidence in that Blatz case. I could have sworn they were in my safe, but Horton has searched and they are not there. Something's gone fluey somewhere. I'll have to investigate when I get back. Meanwhile I've had Horton take special measures with all the other papers. But the fact remains that the fellow has all these papers and seems to know just how to use them. We've got to do something about it and do it quick! He's set a limit of to-morrow night before he shows them to that Sherwood crowd. We can't stand for that! We've got to act."

There was an ominous silence in the cabin for a whole minute, and the swift flight of the birdlike vessel across the bright water seemed suddenly a tangible thing, a part of them. They were fleeing from danger themselves, but their interests were in jeopardy.

"This comes of taking up poor relations!" roared Steinmetz, glaring straight at Freeman. "It's the last time I'll consent to taking on seedy aristocracy."

"They are no relations of mine," spoke the calm voice of the Judge. "They were only acquaintances in youth, but I felt no obligation to help them, and merely suggested the possibility that shabby gentility would be a better screen than anything else we could get, provided we had it under entire control. You said yourself that it was a great idea, the fine old house, and the girl and all. There couldn't have been better cover for our work!"

"Yes, but you didn't have it under entire control."

"We certainly did. The man Ransom was down and out. He had borrowed until he couldn't borrow another cent. Then he was up to his eyes in debt everywhere and his creditors ready to pull down his house around him. Added to that, he idolized that girl of his and wanted to give her a chance in the world. We couldn't have had a better hold. Besides, he had a conscience, such as it was. He did it to death nearly when he took up with our proposition, but the conscience was still alive enough to be working somewhere, and since it couldn't work in the old lines, he set it to work for us to salve its hurt. He was doing good conscientious work, and getting results, too. Then, besides all that, he had something bigger than his conscience, and that was his pride. We had more trouble to break down his pride than we did his conscience when we first put up our proposition to him. And when he saw his conscience had been crossed he put the stress all the harder on his pride. He would have died rather than have it found out that he was connected with the liquor business. That's the kind of a guy he was, or is, if he's still alive. His god is his pride."

"Seems like a pretty strong proposition. What's the trouble then? Why did it fail?"

"The trouble was we didn't take into account the young fellow. He was too sharp. And somehow he got onto things and had to be let in."

"Well, isn't he just like his daddy? Can't you work him the same way as the old one?"

Judge Freeman shook his head.

"Another generation," he said. "Been badly spoiled! Hasn't got a conscience, never had one, and would sell his pride any day for a good time. He's in the game for himself and doesn't hesitate to say so. We've got to do something about it at once."

Another silence while the men thought with anxious faces, and smoked furiously.

"What about that South American project?" asked Steinmetz finally. "Couldn't we work him in on that? He can't do much damage away off there?"

"I've been thinking of that," said Judge Freeman. "The trouble is that Sherwood gang have got him good and tight and it isn't going to be any easy job to get him free. If I were at home I might be able to work it. But it's got to be done somehow. Read that letter. You can see he's not going to be easy to handle, and the worst of it is he knows if he hands all these papers over to Sherwood the mischief will be to pay for us. He's got the nicest little bunch of evidence against the crowd of us that any enemy could care to have. There's the bills of those furnishings for the school board, and a lot of other stuff that'll play havoc with our plans for election. The tax-payers are all sore now and suspicious about us, without anything like this. I tell you that young Ransom is a sharp one all right. He seems just to have cribbed a lot of those little things from time to time with a view to getting us in a hole when the time came that he needed our help. If this all comes out we might as well head this boat to some desert island and stay there ourselves, for we won't ever be able to go back to the States again."

Long they sat in troubled conclave, hatching out a new set of evil plans, and before morning a wireless in code had gone to the henchman back at home with orders to get Lawrence Ransom out of jail at all costs and off to South America by the next possible boat; or, if that couldn't be done to hurry a trial and fix a jury and somehow get him a sentence of "Not guilty."

Then another wireless went to Larry to assure him that his interests were being cherished and cared for and that he was to keep a cheerful patience, for he would soon be free.

Before the council broke up a third message was also framed, to the daughter of the stricken father, expressing sympathy and offering financial aid in the present trying situation.

Then those five mighty noblemen went to their luxurious couches and slept the sleep of the just, having by their own cunning worked a way out of their difficulties, and set their troubled minds at peace.

CHAPTER XII

EVAN SHERWOOD had ordered an elaborate breakfast brought to his bachelor apartment of two rooms and a bath in honor of his aunt, Miss Patricia Sherwood, who was spending a few days with him in the city.

The breakfast was set forth from the caterer's container by Aunt Patty herself, on the old leaf-table that used to belong to Evan's own mother. Aunt Patty had drawn it into the front window where the spring sunshine brightened the room, and spread it with linen from the chest that Evan had kept in his bedroom since he came away from the old homestead and all the familiar surroundings that he had held dear from childhood.

There were daffodils in a blue bowl in the centre of the table, also in honor of Aunt Patty, and Evan neglected his morning paper to watch his white-haired aunt with her springy steps and her gentle ways move about his rooms and seem to give grace to what had before been a dreary and desolate apartment.

There was grapefruit carefully prepared in the first container, oatmeal nicely cooked with fairly rich cream in the second, French chops, French-fried potatoes and griddle-cakes in the third, besides rolls and butter and a pot of coffee. Evan had ordered it from the best caterer he knew. He often had meals sent in this way when he grew tired of restaurants or wanted to read or work. But somehow the layout didn't seem altogether up to his hopes. He surveyed it critically as he sat down opposite Aunt Patty.

"It doesn't smell like your cooking, Aunt Patty," he said wistfully, looking at her with eager eyes, "but it's the best I could do. And anyhow it's great to have you here sitting opposite to eat it with me."

"It's wonderful!" said the little old lady, sliding spryly into her chair. We don't get chops like that up in Melgrove. But my! What a lot you ordered! You don't expect me to eat half of all this!"

"It isn't half good enough for you, Aunt Patty!" laughed the young man. "When I think of your buckwheats, and the doughnuts——"

"Well, aren't you coming up for a good long vacation this summer and eat to your heart's content? I know it isn't right to have buckwheats in summer, but I've been keeping a little buckwheat flour very carefully for you, and there isn't a bug in it yet. And we'll have corn cakes, and waffles besides, and new maple syrup. From our own tree, you know."

"I know," he said a little sadly. "I'll try, but I don't see my way clear this summer. Maybe in the fall, but it's not likely till after election anyway. You see I'm up to my eyes in this League business, and the bootleggers and politicians are giving us all kinds of trouble. We mean to defeat them if we can, but it's going to be a hard pull to clean up the town."

"Well, it's a great work," said Aunt Patty, with a gleam of pride in her eyes. "How your father would rejoice over you! He would be so proud and happy that you were in such work! And your mother! It seems too bad they couldn't have lived long enough to see what you've turned out to be, when there are so many fathers and mothers who have to go sorrowing all their days over the way their children are turning out. But maybe yours are allowed to look down——"

Evan smiled.

"I like to think they can," he said. "Sometimes when I get downhearted and lonely I like to remember that Father and Mother were doing things like this, and would be pleased to have me going on with it."

"I'm sure they are," said Aunt Patty briskly, "and now, tell me about it? Has it been a big fight?"

"Oh, yes. At first they didn't think we were in earnest and everybody was sneering and saying we were making a great ado about nothing. The officials smiled and agreed that it was just what they wanted done, to keep the laws, and that they were doing it with all their might. But when we began to show them up, when we gave sworn testimony about the places that were open and running a regular business, when we began to give names and dates and to ferret out the owners of these saloons and immoral places that were doing business openly without regard to the law; when we let them know that we knew about the bribes they were taking and the salaries they were handing out to their friends with money they got from a stuffed budget of expenses; when the city taxpayers began to learn how their money was being spent, and misrepresented in the reports, then the beast began to snarl and show his teeth. Then the anonymous letters began to come in threatening our lives, and the poor women and children whose husbands were coming home drunk with empty pay envelopes began to come to us with evidence; then the real fight began."

"Anonymous letters!" said Aunt Patty, looking anxious. "I suppose really you are in great danger."

"Oh, no," laughed Evan, "not real danger, not any more than any man who really does his duty in the world ought to be. Of course, when the enemy is at work anywhere against righteousness there is danger, but it's all in the day's work, and I figure that we'll be taken care of while we're needed for the work. Anyhow, we've got to die when the right time comes. Besides, you know, Aunt Pat, a man is a coward who will take refuge behind an anonymous letter, and there really isn't anything to be feared from him. Here's one for instance," and Evan took a somewhat crumpled envelope from his pocket and handed it to his aunt. She opened it with curiosity and read:

"Mister Shurwud:

"You are a good lawyur if you wud sticke to yur job, but when you go out of your way to stick yur knose into uther mens bizness I have kno yuse fer you. This here is to knotify you that ef you dont qit this monkey bizness meddlin with uther mens rites I will blow yur brains out and this here is the last notus fer we wont stand fer kno moor. A Friend."

Aunt Patty laughed as she handed back the letter, yet there was a troubled look in her eyes.

"I wish you would be careful, Evan," she said. "I know you are awfully courageous, and I'm afraid you take unnecessary chances sometimes. You ought to have some one with you when you go out late at night. These people may be cowards, but even cowards can be brave in the dark when they know they have an advantage."

"Aunt Pat," said the young man, looking into her troubled eyes with steady earnest ones, "there's a Bible verse that Father taught me when I was a little shaver that stands by me a whole lot these days. I guess you know it. 'No weapon that is formed against thee shall prosper; and every tongue that shall rise against thee in judgment thou shalt condemn. This is the heritage of the servants of the Lord, and their righteousness is of me, saith the Lord.' That's the passport I travel under now, Aunt Pat, and I figure I couldn't have a better."

Aunt Patty's eyes were bright with proud tears as she looked at the young man tenderly.

"You're right, Evan. I needn't worry!" she said. "How I wish I could help in some way."

Evan's face sobered thoughtfully.

"I'm not so sure but you can't," he said. "I only wish you could make it to spend the winter with me. There's a lot you could do for some of the victims. If only Aunt Martha could spare you. But I know she can't."

"No," said Aunt Patty, shaking her head sadly. "Poor Aunt Martha. She's all crippled up with rheumatism and suffers terribly. It was almost wrong for me to run away for even these few days; if it hadn't been for the papers that had to be signed, and her feeling that nobody but you could attend to the business for us, I wouldn't have left her even with Hannah Hartzell, good as she is, for Martha misses me. But I do wish you were located so you could live with us."

"You couldn't persuade Aunt Martha to let us bring her down here to live? We could get a wonderful apartment where she could lie and look out of the window and watch people all day long. It would be cheerful for her and might do her a world of good. Then perhaps some great specialist ——"

"No, Evan, no. It wouldn't do any good. I tried all that five years ago. Martha nearly broke her heart. I believe in my soul she would die of the break. You know she's over eighty and has lived all her life in that one little town. She was married there, and her children were born there and married, and both of them died and were buried there, and her husband too. No, she would feel that she was leaving behind everything and every one that belonged to her. I've tried reasoning, but it does no good. Martha will have to live out her days in the old homestead. It's the only comfort she has, and I'm glad I kept it for her to come home to when she was widowed and childless. It's my work, Evan, and I must do it, but I certainly would love to be down here with you, too. What did you mean by 'victims'?"

"I mean the people who have been crushed under this Juggernaut of drink."

"The families of those who drink, you mean?"

"Yes, and the families of those who make them drink. I was thinking just when I spoke of the daughter of a bootlegger."

"Oh!" said Aunt Patty with a little gasp of surprise, "I scarcely see how any one could help them. I should think they would probably be benefiting so much by the business that they would be in thorough sympathy with it."

"This one isn't," said Evan sadly, "she is simply stricken! She wouldn't believe it when she first found it out, was very angry and indignant that any one would charge her gentleman father with any such deed. But when I took her into the cellar and showed her the stuff stored there, and the secret entrance into a private cabaret where drinking orgies were carried on, she was simply crushed."

"Poor child! What a heritage!" said the kind-hearted woman. "But surely, the daughter of a man who would go into a business like that would not have as fine feelings about things of this sort as you would."

"There's where you are mistaken, Aunt Patty," said the young man earnestly. "Her father is a southern gentleman of the old type, and has always lived on pride and family. But pride and family don't keep a man and his family from starvation quite as well in these days as they used to in the old time, and it came to be a question of letting his pretty sheltered daughter go out with the common throng to work, or accepting the proposition of an unprincipled politician who was an old friend of the family and saw a chance in the weakness of this old patrician nabob to screen his own interests and get an abject slave to do his dirty work. It was put up to him in such a way that the old Southerner accepted the proposition, and such immediate prosperity followed that his conscience and his pride were lulled to sleep. If it hadn't been for his rascal of a son perhaps he wouldn't have been found out yet. The son was utterly unlike the father. The old man really was getting along famously from the standpoint of his employers. He and his lovely daughter made a perfect camouflage for the business, and the daughter was absolutely unaware of the whole thing. You could see he just adored the girl, and wouldn't have dared lift his head before her if she knew what he was doing. She seems to be quite an unusual girl, is a Sunday-school teacher, interested in church work and that sort of thing."

"You know a good deal about her?"

"No, Aunt Patty. Don't look at me like that. I'm not in love with her nor even interested in her beyond the fact that I've been the means of bringing great sorrow upon her, and I hate myself for having to do it."

"But you didn't do it alone——"

"No, of course not, but I was in charge when the raid was made on the house, and we were waiting inside the house for the man to come home. Everything was all set. The girl was supposedly off in New Jersey at a house party, and the time had been carefully calculated to catch both father and son, and hold them until we had evidence for the real owners back of them. Everything went off well till suddenly the girl walked in on us and wanted to know what we were doing in her father's house. Of course I had to answer her, and when I found I couldn't put her off I had to tell her the truth. She was simply furious at first, and then when I showed her the evidences which she couldn't doubt she was stricken. It was terrible, Aunt Patty! I felt like a murderer! And right in the midst of it in walked her father with the brother behind, and when he saw her, and saw us there in his house, he just crumpled up and dropped as if he had been shot, a stroke of apoplexy, and he hasn't roused at all, probably never will."

"How terrible! Poor child!" Aunt Patty was beginning to take the right point of view now. Evan went on.

"The brother disappeared, but our men outside got him,

and he's lodged in jail now. The girl, meanwhile, has all that to bear, and not a soul apparently of kith or kin to help her bear it. She looks like a wraith."

"The poor little girl!" said Aunt Patty. "And what have you done about it? I know you haven't been idle."

"Done! I haven't done a thing. She won't let me! She asked me if I wished to do her any favor would I please get out of her sight and never let her have to see me again. I don't blame her, of course, but it's tough luck, for there are a lot of little things I could have done——"

"And you've done them anyway without letting her know who did it. I know you, Evan Sherwood. You're your father all over again. But go on. What can I do?"

"I don't know, Aunt Patty," said the young man, letting the real misery for the situation show in his eyes now. "I've thought and thought. I can't bear to have her going it alone through all this. It's horrible! And she's such a little flower of a girl!"

"I'll go and see her!" said Aunt Patty briskly. "I may get in and I may not, but I'll try."

"You won't get in, I'm afraid," he said. "She's as proud as Lucifer, and she hates the very name of Sherwood. I represent humiliation, you see."

"I see. Well, I'll try what I can do. Give me the street and number and I'll find my way. Now, Evan, you mustn't bother about me. You've got important things to do, and I'll take care of myself till evening. I'm going to see those lawyers this morning and get that off my mind."

"I'll take you there," he said. "I have to go right by the door. How soon will you be ready?"

"In half a minute!" said the spry little woman, springing up. "Oughtn't I to wash up these dishes first?"

"No, the janitress looks after those when she comes to clean. I often have meals sent in this way, and they just stack the dishes back in the container and the caterer's man calls for them. Just leave them as they are."

Aunt Patty disappeared into the bedroom and came back in a very brief space attired in small gray hat and wrap and looking like a little gray dove with her silver hair and delicate bearing, and they went off together in Evan's shiny little car that was waiting down in front of the apartment.

Aunt Patty had much and trying business to look after that day and it took hours longer than she expected, but she did not forget her nephew's commission, and before she went back to the apartment in the afternoon, she rang the bell of the brown stone house where Romayne lived and was admitted to an interview with the nurse, which was later detailed to Romayne.

The good lady went away from the brown stone house baffled, but not conquered. She was greatly troubled in her soul that she had had to reveal her name. She knew that was a false move, but her New England conscience had not been able to elude the direct question of the nurse, and now she felt she had lost ground rather than gained it. Nevertheless she meant to try again. She meditated whether it would be wise to send some flowers without any card, but decided against it. It might look as if Evan had sent them and be an offense to the girl. She must walk wisely and ask counsel of heaven in this matter if she could hope to be of service.

About that same hour or a little later Romayne received a mysterious note from her brother which greatly disturbed her.

It was not written on prison paper nor sent by the same messenger who had brought his other communications. It arrived by the hand of a grubby little boy, who demanded a receipt for it written by Romayne herself.

After he was gone she took the letter up to her own room and locked the door before she read it.

It was a request that she would pack certain of her brother's clothes and personal property in a suit-case and take it herself to the downtown station and check it, keeping the check carefully until he should tell her what to do with it. He explained that there was going to be a way for him to have some of his things, and that she must be ready to hand out the check quickly at any time if he should send some one to her for it. She was troubled that he had no message for her in her sorrowful situation, and no word about their dying father. Lawrence seemed to be entirely engaged with his own perplexities. It was so unlike the character that she had, through the years, built up around the thought of her adored brother. She sat a long time on the bed staring at the hasty note, and trying to excuse Lawrence for his seeming selfishness. Of course he was in a terrible strait himself, yet they were all in it together, and it would have seemed natural that he should have had some little word of comfort for her somewhere.

By and by she arose and washed the tears away from her troubled face. She remembered that the nurse was busy with

her father at this hour and that the guard, who usually stayed
somewhere downstairs all day, would be gone to his supper,
leaving only a young substitute down in the office. She could
more easily now than at any other hour during the day or
night go into Lawrence's room and get his things without
exciting suspicion or question.

She put on her soft slippers and went directly down the
hall, opening the door of his room and leaving it ajar that she
might hear if any one came up the stairs or the nurse came
out of her father's room. She hated such underhand ways,
but there seemed nothing else to be done, and she dreaded
any interference by the officers, who had since the first
entrance been most considerate for her feelings.

She hastily gathered an armful of clothing from bureau
drawers and closet, and went back to her own room again to
go over Lawrence's list once more and see what she had
missed.

She made three silent trips to his room before she had
everything, and she carefully arranged what was left in his
closet so that it was not noticeable that anything had been
taken out. While she was doing this her cheeks burned with
shame. She felt as if by this act somehow she were being
implicated in the illicit business that had brought disgrace
upon her clean, proud family.

The suit-case was in a hall closet under the third-story
stairs, and she had no difficulty in getting it into her room
without noise. When she finally locked her door and turned
her attention to the packing of it she drew a deep breath of
relief. It only remained to get the suit-case to the station now
and checked, and then her part would be over. The anxiety
of it all wore upon her as if she had done a hard day's work.
She found herself working with nervous haste.

When it was all packed and fastened she threw her kimono
and a bath towel over it, lest the nurse should suddenly come
out of the door as she passed, and carried it down the hall to
the bathroom.

She had provided herself with a ball of stout cord, and,
locking herself in the bathroom, she carefully let the suitcase
out of the window and lowered it to the ground. It was quite
dark outside and there was no light in the bathroom, so she
felt reasonably safe about this, but her heart was beating so
wildly when the suit-case finally settled into the grass below
the window and she could shut the window and draw back,
that she could scarcely get her breath. She resolved then and

there that when this business was finished, and the suit-case checked, she would never again resort to stealthy means. It was terrible. She felt like a thief.

By this time the regular night officer was on guard in the office downstairs, and it was quite dark outside.

Romayne went downstairs to the kitchen, where she fussed around washing the few dishes that had come down from the sickroom on a tray, washing out a dish-towel and hanging it on the line on the little back porch, and then slipped quickly down the wooden steps and around to the area at the side of the house that was under the bathroom window. The only way to get that suit-case out without the officer noticing it, and Lawrence had been quite insistent about that, was for it to go over the back fence into the alley.

Romayne recovered the suit-case from the ground, made sure the cord was still fastened to it securely, and, carrying it to the back fence, arranged it carefully, with the cord thrown over the fence into the alley, so that she could easily pull it up from the outside. Then she made her way back to the kitchen, closed and locked the door for the night and hurried up to her room for her hat and hand-bag.

She stopped in the front hall to say to the officer:

"I am going out on an errand. If any one calls me on the 'phone please tell them I will be in by ten o'clock," and then hurried out. So far there had been no embargo placed upon her movements, and she might come and go as she would.

She hurried around to the alley, had little difficulty in finding the cord and pulling the suit-case over the fence, and was at last on her way to the station.

She felt it was safer to walk than to attact any attention by getting into a lighted car.

The suit-case was heavy, the way was long. She was almost worn out when she reached the station. With the check finally in her purse, she hailed the first car for home. She was tired to exhaustion and was glad to go straight to bed.

Hours later she was awakened by a firm hand on her shoulder, some one stooping over her, a whisper in her ear:

"Hush! Don't say anything! Somebody is coming up the stairs!"

CHAPTER XIII

IT SEEMED to Romayne that she could hear her own heart beating, as she lay still and listened to the steps coming up the stairs. Awaking out of her exhausted sleep, she scarcely knew where she was, for she had been in the midst of a dream whose scene was laid in the cellar of her own house with rows and rows of whiskey bottles waltzing all about her and encompassing her to the voice of the drunken man of the police station singing raucously:

> "If a body meet a body,
> Comin' through the rye——"

And now she had a curious feeling that the bottles were marshalled in orderly ranks, all marching up the stairs, or was it the drunken man coming step by step toward her door? She had an impulse to scream, but a hand came over her mouth and the whisper was in her ear again:

"Hush, Romayne, don't stir! They mustn't find me here!"

Suddenly she knew that it was Lawrence, and a cold fear possessed her. What had Lawrence done now? Had he escaped from jail? What would they do to him for that? Imprison him for life? Or perhaps shoot him if they gave chase! She lay like marble, feeling as if she had utterly lost the power of speech and of movement, and heard those steps come on to her door and stand and listen.

It seemed hours, while she and Lawrence held their breath, before the steps turned and went back down the hall, pausing on every door. They could see the flashlight like a moving sprite dancing through the crack under the door fitfully, growing paler as the officer receded, and finally disappearing as he went back downstairs. Then the tension relaxed. Finally, Lawrence put his lips down to her ear again:

"Listen, Romayne, don't speak nor stir! I've only a minute, and this is dangerous, but I had to have the check for my suit-case. No, wait till I finish! We mustn't make a noise! Freeman got me transferred to another jail, see? And I'm supposed to be on my way. But I've got a *double*. The Judge fixed it all up, and he's sending me to South America. I make my getaway to-night. If you want to go with me you'll have to sail on a different ship. There's directions in this letter——" he pressed a paper into her cold, trembling hand. "Will you come? I've got to know to-night, because I can't have you writing letters to me."

"And *leave Father?*" she managed to whisper in a frightened voice. "Why, Lawrence! How could I?"

"Hush! Don't call me by name! You can't tell who's listening. Father's as good as dead. Judge Freeman said the doctor said so. No one can blame you for coming. And it's no one's business anyhow."

"Lawrence! How *horrible!*" said Romayne, unconsciously using his name once more, and raising her voice to an excited whisper. But her brother's hand was placed firmly over her mouth again till she almost smothered, and his voice in her ear whispered:

"Shut up, can't you! You'll can the whole thing! Don't be a little fool! You don't have to come if you don't like. I can get on much safer and easier without you. I'm only offering. It's likely Judge Freeman will be kind to you and you won't suffer, but I've got to beat it right away. Now, will you be sensible and shut up and do what I tell you or have I got to stuff something in your mouth?"

Romayne signified by a relaxed nod that she would do his will.

"All right, then. You get up as still as you can and get me that check for the suit-case and all the money you've got. I'm short. Do it quick, and don't speak! Then you open your door, rattle it good and loud, as if you'd just got up, and go out into the hall and call down to that officer to know if it was he came upstairs. Say you heard some one come up and did he want anything? While you're talking I'll beat it back to the bathroom and swing out the window the way I came. No, don't speak! Just do as I tell you. The mischief will be to pay in no time if you make any mistakes. Now, *go!*"

Cold with anxiety and trembling so that she could scarcely move, Romayne slipped out of bed to her bureau, where she had pinned the check to her pin-cushion. She groped for her purse. There was a five-dollar bill and some change in it. She emptied it into his hands mutely, and, with her kimono wrapped around her, opened the door and went out to the hall, calling downstairs as her brother had bade her. It was all dark in the upper hall, and she scarcely knew when her brother slid by her to the bathroom door. Her heart seemed almost smothering her as she tried to conduct a reasonable conversation with the officer.

"No, ma'am," he was saying, "there ain't no one around. I just was stepping up through the halls to make sure all was right. I do it regular every little while. Yes, I did think I heard a noise, but I reckon it was only a rat. They sound awful human, and, you know, these here old houses always has 'em. No, ma'am, don't you worry, lady. I stay awake all night and I'll look after the house. It's my job."

Romayne thanked him in a small shaking voice and crept back to her room, feeling like a criminal herself. To think she had had to descend to subterfuge to help her brother! Oh, had it come to this? And was it right, what he was doing? Wasn't it cowardly to get out of facing the law? She had always been taught to believe it was. Was it honorable, what Lawrence was doing, slipping away to South America this way? And what was that he had said about a double? She ought to have asked him more, only he had stopped her mouth, and she had been only half awake. Had she been a party to something dishonorable, helping him to escape? Yet how could she detain her own brother to face a possible charge of murder? Oh, how complicated and awful life was getting to be! The simple rules of right and wrong by which she had been brought up seemed not to apply at all any more. Nothing was as it ought to be and the people you thought you could depend upon had failed. It was as if the foundations of the earth were shaken and she was tottering with them.

She crept shivering into her bed and tried to go over the whole experience sanely, but the more she recalled everything, word by word, the more disturbed she was, and when she finally came to the end and realized that there had not been a single word of loving or kindness to her beyond that cold-blooded suggestion that she leave their dying father and escape from it all into another land, the tears smarted into her eyes and a sharp pain darted through her heart. Lawrence was gone! Her only dependence gone far away; without leaving any address, and without even a good-bye kiss!

The tears came in a flood then and relieved the terrible pressure on her heart. She felt so alone and utterly desolate.

"Oh, God!" she cried, "I've nobody but You! Won't You please help me, somehow?"

Sleep was driven utterly from her. She found herself listening to every sound in the house and on the street. She wondered if Lawrence had succeeded in getting safely out of the bathroom window. There was a bay window out from the dining-room, to the roof of which he might possibly manage to drop, although it would be a dangerous feat even in the daytime. How had he possibly managed it in the dark? Of course, Lawrence had always been a great climber, but as she continued to think about it her flesh grew cold with horror. Perhaps even now he was lying unconscious on the brick-paved court below. She wanted to fly down and see, or at least to go to the bathroom window and look down to be sure he was safely out, but she dared not attract the attention of the officer again. He would surely think something unusual had happened and perhaps begin an investigation which would put Lawrence in jeopardy. Anyhow, Lawrence was her brother, and perhaps he was doing the right thing somehow. Only if it was right why did he have to come to her so secretly?

Morning brought relief of one kind in that she could go openly to the window and look down. And glad she was that she had gone before any one was astir, for there she saw a heavy rope fastened firmly to the leg of the radiator and going out the open window. Lawrence had not hesitated to leave behind embarrassing evidences for her to erase. With a quick gasp she locked the bathroom door and looked out the window, half expecting to see a huddled form lying below. But to her relief there was nothing but the rope dangling ten or twelve feet from the ground. Lawrence had managed the difficult ascent by way of the dining-room bay window, likely, but he had come prepared with a rope for descent. Well, she must get rid of that rope at once. It was in full sight of the upper part of the dining-room window. If the officer should chance that way he could not fail to see it.

She pulled it in quickly, hand over hand, and soon had it coiled on the bathroom floor. The difficult task was to untie the complex knot that fastened the other end to the radiator.

She worked and tugged with her frail fingers. The rope was heavy, and the time was short, for at any moment now the nurse would be coming down the hall to get water for her father. She must have the rope hidden before she came. She dared not go back to her room for scissors or knife lest the nurse come in while she was gone.

Frantically she looked for some implement to help her, and at last discovered a nail-file on the shelf of the medicine closet. It was not large nor strong, but it had a stout little handle, and she managed at last to insert it into the knot and so loosen it up. Little by little, such a very little that it scarcely seemed any at all, the stubborn rope yielded. Her fingers smarted and burned and rubbed into blisters, but she finally got the knot untied. It seemed to her when it finally yielded the last inch and she pulled it free from the radiator, that she must sink down and cry for relief, but she did not. Instead she gathered it quickly into the smallest coil she could manage and, enveloping it under her kimono, hurried with it to her room, hiding it far back in the depths of her closet behind some big hatboxes, and dropping a big cloak carelessly over the whole as if it had fallen from the hook. Nobody would probably go to her closet in search of a rope, of course, but it made her feel easier to hide it utterly.

Her next act was to dress hurriedly and rush downstairs to examine the ground under the window to make sure there were no footprints nor anything else dropped that might look suspicious. She also went out to the ash-barrel with some papers, and gave a careful furtive look in the yard and the alley where Lawrence must have climbed the fence. Then she came back to her room and sat down to think. She felt like breaking down utterly and weeping, but she knew she must be strong and brave, not a cry-baby. Whether or not Lawrence had done right, even whether or not *she* had done right in helping him, was not any longer the question. Lawrence was gone! She had herself and her father to look out for and she must not go to pieces.

The nurse was sorry for her that morning as she went about her little daily household duties and came and went in the sickroom, with great dark circles under her eyes and a deep look of sadness about her firm-set mouth.

A special delivery letter reached her midway of the morning. She set her teeth in her trembling underlip and took it up to her own room. Always now when anything new happened, even the most commonplace things, there was that clutch of terror at her heart. She knew this letter was from Lawrence even though the handwriting was disguised. What could he have to say now? How her heart hungered for just one loving word from him.

She tore it open hurriedly and read:
"Dear Kid:

"Sorry I upset you so last night, but it couldn't be helped. I had to beat it so quick I forgot the most important thing. You *must find out the answer to my questions somehow or other!* Read them out loud to him even if he doesn't waken. It may rouse him. I *must know* what happened that last morning at the meeting. It means *everything* to me. Keep reading them every time you go to the room when nobody's around. *Don't let anybody hear you,* and *don't tell!* Make up some way he can signal yes or no to you; tell him to close his eyes if it's yes. You fix it, kid; I'm depending on you! It may mean a whole lot of money to us. Get it on your mind so you're ready any minute to ask him if he should become conscious.

"When you get any answer at all send it at once special delivery to Kearney Krupper, Van Dyme Building, Room 66. *Don't delay!* It's the only way I can get back into things. If the answer is what I think it is I've got my enemies by the throat, so don't you fail me, kid!

"Tough luck you've got to weather this all alone, but I guess we'll sight blue sky again sometime. Keep a stiff upper lip. So long. As ever."

There was no name signed and when she had read it slowly through twice she dropped upon her knees beside the bed and hid her face in the pillow.

She did not cry. She just lay there trying to get strength to face the hard facts. Lawrence was engaged in trying to save himself at the expense of their father. Yes, and at her expense, too. He did not seem to care what became of her nor how hard things were for her. No endearing epithets, no tenderness, no thoughtfulness. Just that hard, cold expression, "tough luck," which might have been the solace of the slums. How could he be her brother and write like that? Not a word about their father, not an expression of anxiety about either of them!

Of course he was in a terrible situation himself, and for the time that might have effaced all other emotions. She had never been in prison or in danger of her life. She could not tell how she might act under similar circumstances; and of course perhaps he was taking all these gentler things for granted. Yet she could not hide the fact from her inmost soul that Lawrence was thinking of no one but himself; and that he had laid upon her a command that she could not fulfill.

Never could she go into the sickroom and bombard her father's stricken consciousness with matters of business. Not even if she could call him back would she use such things wherewith to do it. If he were getting well again and strong enough to bear references to matters which obviously had been the cause of his trouble, there might come a time when she could tell him about it all, but not in his present condition; no, not even to save Lawrence! There was something innately basic about her decision that made it seem final. She knew that this was right.

But Lawrence's letter had given her another idea.

When she stayed in the room alone with her father again she would read aloud to him those words from the Bible. She would give him a hope out of his living death. If her words could reach his dull ears and his submerged consciousness at all they should be words of forgiveness and life. She reasoned that her father, if he were conscious at all of his situation, must be troubled that he had done wrong. His whole life had been spent in an atmosphere where wrong-doing meant a cutting off from eternal happiness. She could not think of her father as being content to be a wrong-doer, a law-breaker. If he really had done the thing that they were charging him with, then he must feel condemned in his soul. That, and that alone, must be the important thing now for her to do, to let him know that she believed he could be forgiven for what he had done, and to remind him that God had promised to forgive if one would ask.

With such a purpose in her heart she took her little Bible that afternoon and went to sit with her father while the nurse slept. As soon as the nurse was gone to her room and all was quiet she began in a gentle voice, very low but clear:

"There is, therefore, now no condemnation to them that are in Christ Jesus."

Over and over again she read it, with a pause between, speaking distinctly, saying it each time as if it were a new sentence. For who could tell which time it would reach the deadened brain and stir the heart?

She had repeated it over and over again perhaps for an hour to the motionless figure upon the bed, when suddenly the sick man's eyes opened, as they had done once before, and he looked at her as out of the dark, hungrily, eagerly, a great longing in his look.

Romayne's heart almost stood still, but somehow she controlled her voice and went steadily on in a conversational tone as if she were telling him something they both knew was true, reminding him, reassuring him, with a smile of comfort on her lips:

"There is, therefore, now no condemnation to them that are in Christ Jesus."

Suddenly there came other verses as if they were sent to reënforce this one, verses she had not thought of for years, had not known she had ever committed to memory, verses she must have learned at her mother's knee.

"He that believeth on him is not condemned: but he that believeth not is condemned already, because he hath not believed in the name of the only begotten Son of God."

"God so loved the world, that he gave his only begotten Son, that whosoever believeth in him should not perish, but have everlasting life."

"If we confess our sins, he is faithful and just to forgive us our sins and to cleanse us from all unrighteousness."

"The blood of Jesus Christ, his Son, cleanseth us from all sin."

"The wages of sin is death, but the gift of God is eternal life through Jesus Christ our Lord."

"As far as, the east is from the west so far hath he removed our transgressions from us."

"Like as a father pitieth his children, so the Lord pitieth them that fear him, for he knoweth our frame, he remembereth that we are dust."

"Come now and let us reason together, saith the Lord: Though your sins be as scarlet they shall be as white as snow, and though they be red like crimson, they shall be as wool."

The eyes in the twisted face upon the pillow were bright with a kind of light of comprehension. They seemed to be hanging on her every word, or so it seemed to her.

Romayne marvelled that somehow strength came to keep her voice steady, and give her words to speak. It was wonderful. How was it that all those verses spoke themselves through her lips for the need of the soul in agony? It was as if God Himself were speaking through her. And there seemed to have come a change upon the face of the sick man—a softened look, an eagerness, not so stricken, not so twisted as before. She arose and stood beside the bed and his eyes distinctly followed her.

The door opened suddenly, quietly, and the nurse stood

beside them. The sick man's eyes looked at the nurse and went blank and shut as if a door had been closed One looking at him could scarcely realize that his eyes had been open but an instant before.

The nurse put out a practised finger on the pulse, and said, "Ummmmh! You better let him rest now!"

And Romayne went out of the room and dropped upon her knees beside her bed.

CHAPTER XIV

THE NEXT day there was a big raid in the city and more than seventy-five thousand dollars' worth of bonded liquor was seized in an apartment house on one of the finest streets.

A few minutes later Evan Sherwood was shot in the left shoulder as he was crossing an alleyway not far from the scene of the raid, and was carried to his rooms in a serious condition. The bullet, which was evidently intended for his heart, passed through the fleshy part of the left arm and lodged under the shoulder blade, and the best surgeon's skill in the city was summoned to remove it.

Meantime the assassin escaped and the city was agog with excitement. Wireless messages were sent to the white-winged yacht that carried Judge Freeman and his gang, and the cabin was rife with speculations and plans. Here was another man, it appeared, with whom they could gladly dispense. Evan Sherwood had given them more trouble than all the rest of the city's population put together. He was absolutely fearless and absolutely unbribable. He seemed to be gifted with uncanny powers and could scent out a plot as fast as it was hatched. He was never off his job, never seemed to rest nor play, and apparently had no family or close attachments whom they could kidnap or otherwise strike him through. The gang had been driven to sea to get out of his way, and now, just when they had hoped that things were quieting down and they might return, here had happened this double blow. The biggest enterprise they had, that had been bringing in goodly returns daily, was revealed to the light of day and their henchmen scattering like rats from a burning building. It was disgusting. It was unbearable! And now this damnable young upstart had got himself shot like a hero and was in the limelight more than ever. If he would only die of his wounds and get out of their way finally they might go home and bring flowers, and attend his funeral, even sympathize with anybody who pretended to care about him, if afterward they might get to work to repair the damage he had done to their fortunes. But if he got well he would be more than ever a hero, and folks who had smiled at the dramatically inclined leader of a lot of fanatics would begin to admire and then to follow. Oh, Judge Freeman and his gang knew men, and they understood what an advantage it would be to them if Evan Sherwood were to die.

There were other people who understood that also. There was a mean little rat of a saloon-keeper, whose place had been among the first raided, who went so far as to offer his services as nurse that he might make *sure* that Evan Sherwood did not live. But that was a thing that would never have come out if Chris Hollister hadn't happened to be hid, for purposes of his own, behind the fence of the dirty junkyard where the saloon-keeper and two of his cronies hatched out the idea. But, of course, the League was not doing things with its eyes shut, and no strange man with an eye and a jaw such as the would-be nurse owned would have got within a hundred yards of their beloved hero.

Besides all this, Aunt Patty was on guard, doubly alive to dangers both from without and within, Aunt Patty, who had nursed Evan through chicken-pox and scarlet fever and whooping-cough, and then in later years through typhoid fever and pneumonia, and no one, neither friend nor foe, need hope to get by Aunt Patty.

So the saloon-keeper slept in the jail that night along with his two cronies, thanks to Chris, and the town was out hotfoot after the man who had shot Evan Sherwood. The newsboys were calling special editions of the paper, and Romayne, going out sadly to mail a letter, wondered what it was all about, and why people cared to read papers and gloat over other people's troubles. She had enough of her own without reading about others, and how did it happen that her family had not been cried about the streets? Poor child! Little she knew how much they had been! But she had mercifully been spared all that. At the next corner the newsboy yelled it in her very ear:

"ALL ABOUT THE SHOOTING! EVAN SHERWOOD SHOT!"

It was the first time she had heard the name, the hated name that was connected with her father's disgrace. She stopped short and listened while the boy cried out once more: "EVAN SHERWOOD SHOT IN DE HEART!"

Romayne walked very fast away from him, a sick feeling at her heart. Then he was gone, dead! He would trouble her no more with his officiousness!

His fine, strong face came back to her clearly as he stood looking down at her that first night, begging her to sit down, assuring her that no harm should come to her personally.

She tried to conjure his look of superiority when he had told her that the house was under suspicion, and the white anger that had overspread his face when she mocked him and tried to use the telephone, and when she had called him a coward. Oh, he wasn't a coward! She knew that now. The things that had happened since, the respect he was held in by the officers who had been about their house, all showed her he was not a coward. And he had been right in being angry at the things she had said. They had been contemptible—if she had realized what she was doing.

But try as she would, she could not remember his face in anything but the expression of kindness when he had offered to help her in any way in his power.

She had a depressed feeling that it was somehow her fault that he had died—as if her own feeling had been a part of a great unfriendly force that had killed him, and she, though unconsciously, had helped it on. Were things like that in the world? Were there perhaps forces in the air of evil and of good, just as there were sounds lying about stored up in the atmosphere, which the radio set free? Was there perhaps some way in which unpleasant enmities combined into a great force which something let loose against a fellow-being to down him? What a queer idea! She must not think such things. Perhaps she was losing her mind. Of course, this young man was nothing to her—only—she had asked him never to let her have to see him again—and it seemed now somehow as if that wish of hers had gone into the assassin's bullet and helped to send it on its way.

She tried to throw off all thoughts of the young man It

was nothing to her, of course, his death. Her contact with him had been brief and sharp, and at least she need have no more fear of being humiliated by meeting him again. She walked toward the park, and tried to be rested by the evening sounds of the little city birds gossiping in the twilight. She sat down on a bench and endeavored to carry out the suggestion of the doctor and nurse and detach herself from her situation, just to rest her mind and body from the awful burden she carried day and night. But there was over her a feeling of catastrophe, of depression that she could not shake off.

And when she tried to analyze it she found that it was because she had heard that Evan Sherwood was dead. Why did that make the world seem even a drearier place than it had been before? He was less than nothing to her. Yet the thought of his young face lying dead seemed unspeakably sad. The thought of his strong, true personality gone from the world made it seem less safe than it had been before.

Had she then been relying half unconsciously on his promise to help? Why, it had never occurred to her before, since he made it a condition of leaving her that she would call upon him if she ever were in need of his help. Had somehow the vague sense of his being there if stress came, helped her any? She could not tell. She only knew that she felt in a sense bereft—as if the world had been robbed of one more thing that had made living possible.

Well, it was ridiculous! She would go home and sit with her father again. He was her responsibility, her life. The only thing worthwhile living for now was to watch for his eyes to open once more with that look of hungry eagerness.

Since the nurse had found him with his eyes open she had scarcely left him, and Romayne had had no further opportunity to repeat the wonderful verses to him again. She somehow felt she must not do it with the nurse in the room. The fact that her father had closed his eyes both times when the nurse came made her feel that she could only communicate with him when he and she were all alone. Perhaps she could coax the nurse off to a nap during the evening and then she would sit with him once more. It gave her a warm feeling of comfort to think that perhaps her father would open his eyes again and look into hers.

But when she reached the house and went upstairs she found the nurse in the lower hall weeping with the evening paper in her hands, and for one awful moment she thought it was all over and her father was dead. She did not stop to realize that her father was nothing to the nurse and she would not be likely to weep if he were dead.

But before she could cry out or ask, the nurse turned toward her, wiping the tears away.

"Miss Ransom, would you mind setting with the patient for a while? Mr. Sherwood's been shot and I feel I must go and see if there's aught I can do. His mother was one of the best patients I ever had and I can't be content without knowing all about it. I'll not be gone long, for I promised him I wouldn't leave you, not without letting him know, leastways, but I can't keep my thoughts going till I know how it fares with him. I'll ask the officer to set up in the hall if you should want anything, and he can 'phone for me if there's any change—not that there will be, of course."

"I'll be glad to stay," answered Romayne quickly, "and you needn't speak to the officer. I'd rather he stayed downstairs. I like to be alone with my father, it comforts me."

"Well, I'll not be long then, for I promised Mr Evan faithfully I wouldn't leave you——"

"You promised who?" asked Romayne surprisedly.

"Why him! Evan Sherwood. Him that's shot!" answered the nurse with a suppressed sob. "He was always one fer caring fer other people and he wanted you should be looked after real constant. He said you was fine as silk."

The nurse, with another semblance of a sob in her voice, vanished up the stairs, leaving Romayne with a strange sensation of mingled amazement and pleasure, albeit mingled with irritation. He had presumed then, in spite of all she had said, to keep a guardianship over her. It was kind of him, of course, but unnecessary, and a part of his dominating character probably that could not bear to have anybody else plan anything or do anything without his surveillance.

Yet—he had said she was fine as silk. And somehow her pride was soothed by that.

She went upstairs, took off her hat, and went straight to her father's room. He lay sleeping as usual in that deathlike trance. It was very still in the room after the nurse had shut the front door. She could hear the soft plunk of her rubber heels on the pavement as she hurried along. It seemed to the girl as she stood by the bed and watched her father that he scarcely was breathing at all, and she found herself putting up a prayer that he might waken once more and give her some sign that he was comforted from that terror that had been in his eyes before he fell.

Softly she began in her quiet voice to repeat again the verses in the order that she had repeated them before—very quietly at first, for she did not wish to arouse the attention of the officer downstairs. On and on, verse after verse, again and again, watching with tense strained nerves for some sign that she was heard.

Once it seemed to her that there was a slight fluttering of the eyelids, but it passed and did not come again.

Yet she stood still in the shadow by the bed, ready if he should open his eyes once more. She repeated the verses until they began to bring a message to her own tired heart, and she began to pray, "Oh, God, forgive him!" And then by and by she changed it and said in her heart, "Oh, God, forgive us!" It was like one of Isaiah's prayers for his whole household. It was as if she were confessing sin which her household had committed, and pleading for forgiveness for them all, including herself among the guilty.

While she stood there with bowed head the door opened and the nurse came back.

Romayne could see even by the dim light of the night-lamp that the nurse had been crying. She motioned to the girl to follow her into the hall.

"I came back to see if you would mind if I'd get another nurse to take my place just for to-night? There really isn't a thing to do but give him his medicine and his nourishment at the right time. I'd fix him all before I left. I wouldn't ask it only I promised Evan Sherwood's mother long ago if he ever took sick I'd nurse him if I had to turn heaven and earth to get away from a case. Of course, his aunt is there and that makes it different, but she ain't a trained nurse, and the doctor says he's pretty serious and a great deal depends on to-night. They ain't sure if he's going to pull through till morning. The doctor said it took an experienced nurse, and if I could come to-night he'd try and look around by morning for somebody that would do if he lived that long. But, of course, I wouldn't leave you if you don't like it. There's a little probationary nurse down to the children's hospital I could get you for to-night——"

"Then he's not dead!" exclaimed Romayne, with a strange feeling of elation that her soul had a reprieve from a personal crime. "I thought you said he had been killed."

"No, he's living," sighed the nurse, "but he's awful bad. The ball just missed the heart and they had a turrible time getting it out. It was too near the vital parts. It seems he was all run down working so hard with all these raids, and he's been up nights a lot running the whole gang while the rest of 'em were off on their vacations. He ain't the kind that takes vacations fer hisself when there's something needs doing. But I promised him I'd look after you and I won't go if you think there's anything out of the way in my doing it. I could phone that little nurse, you know, and have her here in ten minutes— she said she was off duty to-night—but it's just as you say."

"Why, of course, go to him. There is no obligation for you to stay here. And you needn't get the other nurse. I can perfectly well stay with my father to-night. It won't hurt me in the least to sit up. I want to be with him all I can anyway."

"Well, I'm not leaving you alone in the house with a strange man downstairs, anyhow! That's not the way I keep my promises. I'll get the nurse! Thank you! I'll be back in the morning as early as I possibly can. Now, I'll go call up Helen. She said she'd be right by the 'phone waiting and would be here in fifteen minutes."

The nurse disappeared and left Romayne with a strange deserted feeling. She had not known she would feel that way. She had wanted to be alone with her father and care for him and now she was, and all sorts of forebodings assailed her.

She could hear the distant murmur of the nurse calling up her substitute, and presently the front door closed, and silence followed. The house seemed very still. A minute dragged out to a long period of time. She began to wonder what she should do if a crisis arrived. Suppose her father died. Would she know it? She had never been alone with death. It suddenly seemed terrible to have such a weight of responsibility upon her. The thought of Lawrence, far away, somewhere intent on saving his own life, stabbed her like a sword.

She began to repeat, like an incantation against her fears, the verses she had said the day before. She did not hesitate nor have to think what they were. They seemed to follow in the same logical sequence that they had come to her at first, and the majesty and greatness of their purport, as before, lifted her out of the darkness of earthly fears and made her strong once more.

She slipped her hand in the clasp of the cold, inert hand of her father and began to pray softly, in a whisper, over and over, "Oh, God, forgive my father, and help him to take hold of Thee." Over and over, her warm hand in the cold one, till little by little the hand seemed to warm to hers. Was it wholly fancy that her hand-clasp seemed once to be returned gently, feebly? Her heart leaped at the thought, as she lovingly covered the cold hand, and went on whispering her prayer.

By and by the assistant nurse stole in cautiously and signified that the lady might leave everything to her, but Romayne shook her head, and whispered with a sad little smile:

"I'd rather stay here, to-night. I have a fancy he likes it."

The nurse brought her a low rocker and arranged pillows so that she could lay her head back, and so she rested, her father's hand in hers, her head against the pillows, and fell asleep.

She was still asleep when the morning sun slanted in at the window, while the substitute nurse went deftly around doing all the early-morning things that nurses do, no matter what awful thing has happened or is about to happen. She did not waken until the regular nurse returned, somewhat noisily, perhaps, on account of her excitement.

"Mr. Sherwood's better," she announced in a husky whisper. "He come to and knowed me, and sent me piling right back to you. Beats all how he never thinks of hisself. He said I was not to leave you again, not as long as you needed me, not even if he died. He said if he died that was his last will and testament. So I come. I couldn't do otherwise. Everybody does as he says. But his temperature is down some and the doctor says he thinks he'll pull through. He's got clean blood and good living, and a spirit like noon sunshine, and that's more than two-thirds of any battle in sickness. My soul, child! You're white as a ghost! You don't mean to tell me you set there all night! My land, Helen! Why did you let her?"

Then she stepped nearer to the bed with her professional air and put her finger lightly on the pulse.

Her face grew grave. She scrutinized the patient more keenly.

"There's been a change here," she whispered very low. "Did he open his eyes again?"

Romayne shook her head, the clutch of fear gripping her heart once more.

"There's been a change," she repeated with a kind of awe in her voice. "Can't you see yourself, child? His face is more peaceful, not so drawn looking. The twist is going out."

Romayne stood up and looked down on her father, and as she drew near suddenly his eyes opened again, with a look as if he had just awakened and were searching for something. His gaze came to rest upon her, and a relief dawned in his eyes.

Romayne had hold of his hand, and now she distinctly felt a quiver in the hand she held.

"Father!" she cried, her voice full of the thrill of his knowing her.

And then there seemed to pass a struggle over the poor father, the lips moved, the eyes still desperately upon her face as if there were something she must say.

Something told her that now was the time for her to speak. This was the time that Lawrence had begged her to be ready for, but her own voice seemed paralyzed, all her vitality struggling with him to frame the word he was trying to give her.

The lips had opened and formed a sound!

She bent nearer and caught its precious meaning:

"Forgive!"

It was mumbled and half inaudible, but she was sure of it

"Yes, Father!" she answered in a clear, triumphant voice "Forgive! It's all right!"

And again the lips struggled and the hand gave a feeble clutch, the eyes lifted with just a flutter in a significant glance above and back to her face again

"F-f-f-r-*given*!" and he searched her face eagerly to see if she understood.

"Yes, Father It's all forgiven. God forgives. We forgive."

The tortured eyes rested on her face for a long moment, a kind of content grew in their expression, and a wistful tenderness. Then slowly there dawned on the white face a look of peace, a straightening of the twisted muscles, a smoothing out of the care and horror. The eyelids closed. A slight, almost imperceptible, movement passed over the whole frame, and he was gone!

CHAPTER XV

It is a terrible moment when one has to turn away from the death-bed of a loved one. But when the nurse gently drew Romayne from her father's bedside, though there was a smart of tears in her eyes, and a great sense of sudden overwhelming loss, yet there was in her heart a joyful triumph.

She had got her message across to her father's poor numbed senses that there was forgiveness for him, and he had been able to grasp the hope held out to him, and to give her assurance that he did so. What else mattered? That was enough to lift her above the catastrophe of the moment. He was gone from her, but he was gone home! It did not occur to her to think just then of her own desolation. She was rejoicing for her father in that he had found peace.

The nurse looked for her to break down in hysterical weeping, but she gave her a little trembling smile and walked quietly away to her own room, coming out again presently, with tears upon her cheeks, it is true, but with a look of calmness and strength about her that made all those with whom she had to do marvel.

"Of course," they said with wise looks at one another, "she must know it is better for all concerned that he didn't get well."

Still, that didn't quite seem to explain the look on her face. The word "exalted" described it better than any other. The nurse was trying to find words in which to give her report to Evan Sherwood. But exalted was not a word with which the nurse had familiar acquaintance. "She looks kind of as if somebody had give her a great unexpected gift and she can't be thankful enough," was the way she finally put it.

It seemed that there were so many appalling questions to settle all at once, details of death that had never entered her consciousness before, and she all alone to settle them! Why had Lawrence gone out of her life in this way? If he had only remained in the jail where she could have consulted him! And yet, he had been so filled with his own troubles that he had not seemed to realize about their father. Some word should be sent him, of course, though naturally after the manner of his departure it would be out of the question to expect him to come, or to hope to consult him about arrangements. She felt so helpless and so young. And then the matter of money suddenly loomed before her as a tremendous question. Things must be done right, of course, and she had no idea how much money she had to depend upon. She knew only that her father had put five hundred dollars in the bank to start an account for her the day she went to the house party. She had not touched it as yet. It occurred to her that there must have been expenses, and yet no one had come to her for money. Probably the colored girl in the kitchen had charged whatever she got at the stores, and there would be big bills to pay. She ought to have been watching, but how could she, with her mind so full of trouble? And there would be the nurse to pay, and the doctor——

She sighed sorrowfully and wondered why all this awfulness had to come upon her, and where she should begin to try and take up the burden of life on her own responsibility? It seemed incredible that, after all was done that had to be done for her father, she still must go on and live by herself with all of a natural life likely before her. It was unthinkable! It was appalling!

There appeared, quietly, unobtrusively, a little white-haired woman in gray who entered with some lovely flowers in her hands and made no fuss nor asked any questions, just went about doing little helpful things. Romayne took her for one of the people with the undertaker at first, but later when she asked her name she said:

"Oh, I'm just a neighbor near by. I heard you were in trouble, and I came to see if I could help. I'm not really a neighbor, either, for I live away up in New Hampshire, but I'm in the city for a little while on business, and I heard you were alone. Just call me Aunt Patty. You won't need to feel any obligations toward me. I'll be gone back in a few days."

Romayne smiled wistfully at her and felt a sudden relaxing of the tension of her nerves. Somehow it was good to have a motherly woman around who understood and didn't bother with questions. She didn't say whether she knew the whole story of shame or not, but it didn't matter. Romayne somehow felt she would have been just as kind if she had known, and it was a relief to accept the gentle sympathy and not have to think about the shame.

This same Aunt Patty helped to settle a good many puzzling questions, just by being there and letting Romayne talk them out to her. It somehow seemed to clarify the atmosphere and help her to decide on the natural thing to be done.

It was Aunt Patty who helped arrange about the service. "Your mother? Where is she buried? You will want your father to lie beside her, of course?"

And Romayne suddenly saw that that was the natural thing to be done. The undertaker had been talking about lots, and the whole thing had seemed so terrible, and so impossible, and expensive!

It was Aunt Patty who arranged with the undertaker to telegraph to the little Virginia town where they had lived before Romayne's mother died, and make everything ready for their coming, and Aunt Patty who went to see Dr. Stephens, the minister, and arranged a simple service at the house before they left for Virginia. When she asked if there was anything special that Romayne would like to suggest for the service, the girl shook her head at first, and then thoughtfully said: "Wait. Yes. There are some verses——"

She wrote out the verses in their order as she had repeated them to her father and handed them to Aunt Patty.

"Just those," she said, "and a simple service with a prayer. I don't know much about funerals, but I want those verses to be read——"

She paused and looked at Aunt Patty shyly.

"He—*spoke* to me—at the last, you know——" She paused again as if it were hard to go on—— "He said one word! It was 'Forgiven!' "

She swept the elder woman a quick keen glance to see if she understood, and Aunt Patty's face lighted up with instant sympathy and understanding. Yes. Aunt Patty understood and was glad. Romayne was satisfied, and glad she had told her, and went away quickly to her room, leaving her new friend to perfect the arrangements.

It was while Aunt Patty was gone to see Dr. Stephens about the funeral that another visitor arrived, and Romayne, thinking the minister had come, opened the door herself.

It was a woman, ferret-faced and important, who stood there staring openly up at the house and the surroundings, taking in obviously the "vacant" house next door as if it were Exhibit A, too noted to miss. When Romayne opened the door, she stepped inside with that "Now-I've-come-to-settle-everything" air that some women can assume so offensively.

She pinned Romayne with her first glance coldly, condemningly, appraisingly, and then began to talk:

"You're Romayne, I suppose," she said, dropping her gaze disapprovingly to the little pale-blue muslin dress the girl happened to be wearing, and had not thought to change to one of a quieter color.

"You won't remember me, of course," she went on, while her little ferret eyes seemed to be jumping around the room, taking in every object and searching out each corner as if she had known about it all before she came; pausing to inspect the fine old console in the hall, then the office desk, the silk curtains, the alabaster vases, and lingering again on the panel-door beside the mantel.

"You were only three when you were at our house last. I'm your third cousin, Maria Forbes. My mother was Charity Jane Harkness before she married my father, and she was your mother's second cousin. I suppose you've heard your mother talk about us?"

She paused and brought her ferret eyes to Romayne's face once more with an added disapproval.

"You don't look much like your mother, do you? She was always said to be a beautiful girl. You favor the Ransoms. They were all scrawny and light. It's a pity, especially now. Well, of course, we saw in the paper he was dead, so Mother thought I'd better come right down and see you."

Romayne looked at her in a dazed sort of way. She was herself so far removed from the ordinary things of every day that the frank insults that were being offered her did not make much impression upon her. She was only annoyed that some one had turned up who would have to be talked to. She was so tired it did not seem as if she could talk about things now. And a relative! That was harder than a stranger, because one couldn't really put a relative off as you could a stranger. If only Aunt Patty hadn't gone away yet! She made everything so much easier when she was present!

"Won't you come in and sit down," she said wearily, "I've heard Mother speak of a Cousin Maria, of course, although I don't remember the visit very well. It was kind of you to come. Do you live far away?"

"Why, yes, it's quite a piece. It's beyond Millville. Are those the secret wine closets the newspapers told about?" she asked, suddenly pointing to the panel beside the fireplace.

A flood of crimson went over Romayne's white face and her eyes grew stern and haughty.

"I would rather not talk about those things," she said coldly. "We will go into the dining-room and sit. We shall not be disturbed in there."

"Well, that's a foolish way to feel!" declared the new relative. "You have to face facts as they are. You can't wash out dirt by shutting your eyes to it, and since your father has committed a crime, of course, everybody knows about it. *You* couldn't help it, of course, as Mother says, but you're not in a position to be proud, and you might as well acknowledge that first as last. I take it that I, being a relative, have a right to know the *facts*. In fact, that was partly what Mother sent me down for, to see just how it all was. If we are going to do anything about it, of course, we've got to *know* all about *every*thing. You couldn't expect it otherwise."

"*Do* anything?" asked Romayne puzzled. "What could you do?"

"Well, I'm not prepared to say just what we'll do until I hear the whole story. We live in a town where everybody knows everybody else's business, and we couldn't take you without being able to feel that we understood the whole matter from A to Z."

"Take me?" said Romayne, again quite uncomprehending.

"Why, yes, of course? We're the nearest living relatives; in fact, we're the only relatives you have on your mother's side—and, of course, if there are any of your father's they don't count, for you wouldn't want to go to *them!* Mother and I are willing to take you to live with us. Mother is getting on in years, and I'm not so spry as I used to be, and there'll be plenty of work you can do to pay your board. Besides that, there's a vacancy in the post-office we can probably get for you that'll net you a small salary—enough to clothe you economically. Of course, there's the disgrace on the name and all, and there may be some trouble getting you in there. Government officials are mighty particular, you know, about having people who have a good honest name, and it's right, of course, because they have to handle thousands of dollars' worth of stamps, and money orders and all, and, of course, they've got to be sure who they employ. Both Mother and I figure everybody knows us, and if we vouch for you there won't be any trouble. But we can't do a thing till we know everything about this miserable business. You've got to make a clean breast of it. Did you know about it all along, and couldn't you stop it? It's terrible on us having a disgrace like that come in the family, even though it's only by marriage, and Mother getting on in years, too. But we can't have folks saying we didn't do for our own, even though we have to suffer."

Romayne stood still with her back against the wall and looked at her persecutor, her eyes large with a kind of helpless terror. She could get no words wherewith to answer this creature. Somehow, all the spirit with which she would have protected herself a few weeks ago had departed from her. She could just stand and take it. It was like being caught out in a deluge of fire.

"And what's all this about your brother Lawrence running away from jail?" went on the tormentor. "Did you help him to get out? Because if you did that ends it! We can't have anything to do with *him*. You'll have to drop all communication with him if you come to live with us. Bootlegging's bad enough, the dear knows, for a woman who's been a W.C.T.U. president most of her life to put up with in the family, even by marriage, but a *murderer* isn't to be thought of! And you must understand from the start that you will never see or communicate with Lawrence again. Of course, you wouldn't want to, anyway, if you really want us to help you be an honest respectable girl again———"

Romayne's eyes seemed to be growing larger and darker with horror and her face whiter. She looked as if a moment more of this harangue and she might crumple into a little heap on the floor.

Neither of them had heard the front door open quietly until suddenly Aunt Patty stood beside them and slipped an arm about Romayne's waist.

"My darling child," she said tenderly, "you shouldn't be standing here like this. You look done to death!"

Romayne turned and flung her arms around Aunt Patty's neck, buried her face in the soft gray shoulder, and burst into a flood of nervous tears. She did not know how long Aunt Patty had been standing there, nor how much she had heard, but she had a feeling that she would understand everything and that a refuge was found.

"I'm her cousin, Maria Forbes, from Millville," explained the indomitable relative. "I've come down to take her home with me and try and see if we can't bring back her good name——"

"And I'm her Aunty Patty Sherwood from New Hampshire," spoke up the little dove-gray woman firmly, "and you've somehow made a mistake. It's very kind of you, of course, but Romayne hasn't lost her good name and never will! You've been misinformed! But she *has* been through a great sorrow and she's not able to be up, so if you'll excuse me a few minutes I'll just get her to bed, and then I'll come down and talk with you."

"Sherwood? Sherwood?" said the ferret woman sharply. "I don't seem to remember any Sherwood connection. New Hampshire, did you say? Mother has the family tree. You don't mean that you're on the Ransom side?"

But Aunt Patty and Romayne were halfway up the stairs.

"Just sit down in the hall a minute, will you," called back Aunt Patty commandingly from the first landing. "I'll send the maid with a cup of tea for you while you're waiting for me to come down."

And Aunt Patty gently and firmly propelled the stricken girl up the stairs to her own room and pressed her down upon the bed.

"There, precious child!" she said soothingly, arranging the pillows and smoothing back her hair from her hot face. "Just cry as hard as you like. It'll make you feel better. But she isn't worth noticing, she really isn't, you know! There are always people like that in the world, only they don't often dare come to the surface. But you're not to think a second time about anything she says. And you don't have to go and live with her and her cruel old mother! The whole world is before you, and plenty of nice people will want you. I want you myself just as hard as anybody could, only I know you don't belong to me and oughtn't to be hidden away off in New Hampshire. But if you'll say the word, I'll just tuck you in my pocket and take you home with me."

Romayne managed a sobbing little smile at that, and was cheered in spite of herself. But the tears were in full tide and could not be stopped so easily.

"But she knew all about us," wailed Romayne with sudden

recollection. "It must have all been in the papers! All about those secret panels by the fireplace and everything! Oh——how can I ever look anybody in the face again?"

"Look here, child!" said Aunt Patty tenderly as she swiftly unfastened Romayne's shoes, and tucked her up under a light blanket. "What's in the newspapers is the least of your troubles. To begin with, every right-minded person knows that more than half they read in the papers isn't so, and the other half has a lot of explanations. And there's so much in the papers, that people don't remember for more than a week what they have read. So you can just forget that part of it. It's annoying, of course. I don't discount the hurt it gave you, and that little cat downstairs ought to be gibbeted for talking to you that way; but, after all, what is she? I'll give her a cup of tea and tell her a few things and send her on her way a sadder and a wiser woman. Trust me! Now, look up some of the things you've got to be thankful for. Take that word 'forgiven,' for instance. Isn't that bigger than all the rest? I take it that's what it meant to you. There's coming a time by and by when all these things are going to be evened up and everybody's going to know it. And that word 'forgiven' is going to cover all the things that anybody has to be ashamed of. If anybody has a right to that word he can go rejoicing and not be afraid. I reckon that 'the sufferings of this present time are not worthy to be compared with the glory that shall be revealed.' Ever hear that verse? Well, think about it, and don't let your faith be dimmed by a sour-faced woman who doesn't look as if she knew what it meant. Now, you're going to sleep for an hour till I get rid of that old raven downstairs, and then I'm going to bring you the nicest little lunch you ever ate, and we're going to talk about pleasant things and be happy. There's sorrow enough in the world without making more. Will you go to sleep?"

Romayne nodded her head, mopped the tears from her eyes, and Aunt Patty stooped and kissed her tenderly; then, pulling the shade down, Aunt Patty went out tiptoe and down the stairs, her face growing formidable as she went.

She found the visitor endeavoring to pry open the panel by the mantelpiece with a hair-pin, and she turned to Aunt Patty nothing daunted.

"Have you got the keys to this place? I want to see everything while I'm here. Mother will want to know all about it."

"No," said Aunt Patty grimly, "I haven't the keys, and if I had I wouldn't use them on other people's property."

"But I'm a relative!" stated Cousin Maria as if that covered any multitude of sins.

"I guess you don't know that this house is under police protection," said Aunt Patty quietly.

"Protection!" sneered Cousin Maria sarcastically.

"Yes," said Aunt Patty, "an officer is stationed close by to see that Romayne is not annoyed by any one, and I'm here to see that he does his duty whenever occasion arises."

"Oh," and Cousin Maria turned her sharp eyes on Aunt Patty, "how did *you* get that office? I don't really see how you *can* be related. Did you say you were on the Ransom side?"

"You might call it that," said Aunt Patty serenely. "Suppose you step into the dining-room now. I think the tea is ready."

"But I never heard that George Ransom had a sister!" said Cousin Maria, reluctantly following into the dining-room.

"Didn't you?" said Aunt Patty. "Do you take cream and sugar or lemon? Excuse me while I give directions to the maid."

"You didn't tell me how you came to be here," began Cousin Maria, turning from a survey of the back yard through the bay window the minute Aunt Patty returned.

"Just take this chair," said Aunt Patty graciously. "Why,— the Chief who had the house in charge sent for me. I came here because he wanted me to come, and I stayed because Romayne wanted me."

"H'm!" said Cousin Maria coldly, "I don't see what a chief of police had to do with it."

"He has a great deal to do with it," said Aunt Patty calmly. "Will you take some of this cinnamon toast? I've just been teaching the maid how to make it."

"I should think there would be enough to do in a house like this, and at a time like this, without trifling with fancy cooking," acridly remarked Cousin Maria, taking two pieces of cinnamon toast on her plate.

"I don't consider anything trifling that gives an appetite and a little comfort at a time like this," said Aunt Patty serenely. "What time does your train go back? Will you have to hurry?"

"I'm not going back till I've seen Cousin Romayne again.

She ought to be awake pretty soon, oughtn't she? I'll just go up when I've finished my tea."

"Oh, no," said Aunt Patty firmly, "she won't be awake for an hour and a half at least, and she doesn't feel that she can see you any more to-day. If you are staying at a hotel, I can telephone for a taxi for you."

"Really!" said Cousin Maria with her chin up. "I think you take too much upon you. I certainly shall go up and see my cousin. If she isn't awake she'll have to wake up, that's all. I have to get back to Millville to-night and I've got to make my proposition to her. Mother is expecting me to bring her with me."

"Romayne has no idea of going with you. If that's all, you can save yourself the trouble. But it will be quite impossible anyway for you to see her. It is against the doctor's instructions that she be disturbed. She has been under heavy strain and must rest. Were you intending to stay for the funeral? Because the service proper is to be held in Virginia, you know."

"Service? Mercy no! I wouldn't think they'd have the face to have a service after what he has done! *Nobody'll come.* I certainly wouldn't want George Ransom to have that much satisfaction out of me. Let him *understand* that he had *disgraced* the family!"

"Oh, do you really think it would give him satisfaction? *Now?*"

The sharp-tongued Maria looked at her keenly, suspecting that she was being made fun of, but Aunt Patty's tone was quite quiet and sweet. "It seems to me he is wiser than to care for such things now, even if he ever did."

"You surely don't think George Ransom has gone to *heaven,* do you?" said Cousin Maria excitedly. "You *can't think* he was *saved,* surely?"

"The thief on the cross was saved," reminded Aunt Patty gently. "You and I are not his judges."

"Are you *upholding* bootlegging?" Cousin Maria's voice was almost a scream.

"Not consciously," said Aunt Patty. "Can I give you another cup of tea? I'm afraid you'll be late getting home."

"I expected to have to sacrifice something. What makes you so sure Romayne won't come to us? I'm sure I don't see where she can go. She hasn't any property, has she? The paper said she hadn't a cent. It would be tainted money if she had."

"I'm sure I didn't enquire," said Aunt Patty. "But Romayne has no idea of being dependent on any one, and if she had she has plenty of places to go. She certainly is not coming to you, although I am sure if she were able just now to speak for herself, she would thank you for offering."

"Well, she's going to have a *chance* to speak for herself in about a minute," said Cousin Maria, swallowing the last of her tea, and reaching for another piece of cinnamon toast, "for I'm going up to see her! It's ridiculous, babying her like this! She's got her own way to make in the world and she'll have to stand on her own feet!"

She had risen while she was speaking, and walked toward the door, but Aunt Patty had risen also and taken up the telephone, speaking into it quietly under the rattle of Cousin Maria's threats.

"Is Mr. Hollister there? This is Miss Sherwood. Will you please send him around to Ransom's *at once* with a taxi for duty?"

She hung up the receiver and followed the visitor into the hall. It had all been done so casually that Cousin Maria had not realized.

"You have been in close touch with Romayne and her mother and father during the years, I suppose?" asked Aunt Patty, pausing in the hall and stooping to straighten a rug, as if she were merely making polite talk.

"No," said Maria, caught by the bait of a bit of gossip, "my mother never approved of Cousin Caroline's marriage into the Ransom family. George's brother used to go with me for a while, but mother broke it right off and sent me away to school! And afterwards he jilted the loveliest girl, from New York! She died of consumption. They were all alike, those Ransoms, not a good one among them! Handsome and wicked! All they could do was spend money they hadn't earned! Well, I suppose I might as well go look at him, now I'm here. Mother will want to hear all about it. Which room is he in?"

"No," said Aunt Patty firmly, "I don't think Romayne would care to have you go, feeling as you do about him. Romayne loved her father tenderly."

"How *could* she!" exclaimed the visitor angrily. "That's just what I said when Mother suggested my coming after her.

'Mother,' I said, 'they're all tarred with the same pitch, those Ransoms! Romayne will be just like them. Why, how could a good respectable girl *love* a man like that? But she'd have to *give them all up* if she came to us!' "

The door opened suddenly and Chris Hollister in full uniform appeared for duty, his hat in his hand, a respectful look upon his nice young face. Cousin Maria turned a sharp look of curiosity toward him, but Aunt Patty forestalled anything she might have said by giving her directions.

"Mr. Hollister, you will please take Miss Forbes to her train at once. She will tell you which station."

"But I'm not *going*, I tell you, till I've seen Romayne!" blazed Cousin Maria. "And I'm going to see George Ransom, too. I always do my duty by the dead, even if they are criminals!"

"I'm sorry," said Aunt Patty firmly, "but you'll have to go at once. Mr. Hollister is in charge of this house this afternoon and he has orders to see that Romayne is not disturbed. Anything you wish to say to her you can write. The undertaker has the key to the room where Mr. Ransom is lying. I will bid you good afternoon, Miss Forbes," and Aunt Patty, with a meaning look at Chris, swept softly up the stairs, a lady to the top.

"I'll see that you pay for this," screamed Cousin Maria, white with rage and starting to follow up the stairs, but somehow Chris stepped between her and the stairs.

"Just step this way, Miss Forbes. The taxi is right outside," he said in his deep bass voice.

Cousin Maria looked at the solid young giant before her with his Sam Brown belt and pistols and paused.

"Step right this way!" repeated Chris once more with his best football roar.

And Cousin Maria stepped.

CHAPTER XVI

AUNT PATTY came up to Romayne's room several hours later with a tempting tray, and to say that Chris Hollister was downstairs with a request from the officers who had been stationed in the house during Mr. Ransom's illness. They wanted to know if it would trouble Miss Ransom if they attended the service in a body. They all felt deeply sympathetic with her in this most trying situation, but they were afraid that perhaps their presence might be unpleasant to her.

Romayne lay still for a moment thinking about it, and then she said:

"No, it wouldn't trouble me, I'd *like* them to come! I want them to know, somehow, that he was forgiven." She paused a moment and then looked up earnestly.

"I would like them *all* to come—" and Aunt Patty folded that look away to tell Evan about it.

The service was in the evening after it was quite dark.

It was held down in the office where the tragedy had begun. Aunt Patty, prompted by Evan, suggested otherwise, but Romayne shook her head.

"No, I'd like it to be there. It seems as if he would want it to be there—where—" she hesitated—"where the other thing had gone on. It seems as if it was the only way it could be wiped out. I don't suppose you will understand——"

But Aunt Patty brushed the bright tears away from her eyes and said: "Yes, child, I understand."

For to Aunt Patty Romayne had confided the story of her father's last moments.

So the big desk was rolled to the back of the room, the heavy silk curtains drawn, and the alabaster vases filled with roses that the officers who had guarded the house brought.

There were other flowers, an overwhelming amount of them, great pillows and wreaths and costly sprays, sent by

Judge Freeman, the Worrells, and members of the "gang" at sea. The fact that they knew to a minute what had happened and when to send flowers, and that the flowers came in such profusion, made the display offensive to Romayne. She had them all put in the hall, and only the roses of the officers were near the coffin.

She bought no flowers herself and would not allow Aunt Patty to bring any.

There was one other magnificent spray of roses and lilies bearing the card of Kearney Krupper. Romayne had asked Aunt Patty to call him on the telephone the night before and ask him to inform her brother, if he knew where he was, that his father was dead. The flowers had arrived early the next morning.

Romayne regarded the flowers mournfully as she came down the stairs for the service. She shunned touching them as she passed into the front room. It seemed to her they represented her father's shame.

The officers were lined up in the front of the room, gloved and uniformed, looking dependable and uncomfortable.

At the last minute, as Dr. Stephens was opening his Bible to begin the service, a stranger arrived. He was a young man flashily attired, and he stood in the hall looking at Romayne with hard, interested eyes as the minister read the service. The flowers were banked behind him, and he seemed a part of them. Romayne did not look at him after the first glance. It annoyed her that a stranger should be present. She wondered why he had come and if he were another of the "business associates."

Romayne sat with Aunt Patty near the casket and listened to the words of the burial service. It seemed so strange that these words were being spoken there in their home, for the father who had, but a few short days before, been going about well and strong. The words seemed to give her the vista of the desolate future more distinctly than she had yet seen it. Down through the years, separated from her father by this burial service, she must walk alone to the end! The triumph was still in her heart when she thought of the end and the glory of it, but the years between loomed dark and long.

But when the minister came to the verses she had selected and began to read them, she lifted her head and took courage. Now was her father being made right before the representatives of his world here in this room where he had sinned.

"These verses," said the minister, "were read and re-read many times to Mr. Ransom during his last illness. It is perhaps not known by all present that he roused, at the end, and spoke; and that the one word which he uttered was 'Forgiven!' Let us pray!"

It was a tender enfolding prayer that followed, and Romayne felt as if it brought the promises of God right up to the throne and used them as a plea.

During the little hush when the prayer was over, after the undertaker had announced that the burial would be private, Romayne still sat apart, a look of peace on her white face. She lifted her eyes once and saw across the hall the honest, troubled face of Chris Hollister beaded with perspiration, uncomfortable in his dress uniform, trying to do all he could; and somehow it came to her that it was not all for his own sake he was doing it. His Chief's orders were back of all this quiet helpfulness and decorum.

Then the flashily dressed stranger came over to speak to her, and she shrank back and wished she had gone upstairs at once.

"I'm Kearney Krupper," announced the young man in an undertone. "Is there any place where I could speak to you in private?"

"Oh, no! It isn't necessary, is it?" said Romayne, shrinking back. She could not bear the intrusion just then, and it would would be about Lawrence. Oh, she couldn't talk about Lawrence, now!

"Well, perhaps not," said the young man, squaring his back impolitely to Miss Sherwood and encompassing Romayne by seeming to spread himself widely and shut her off from the others in the room. "So sorry I couldn't have come to you right away last evening, but I had a date, you know. Glad to do anything I can for you!"

Romayne lifted her eyes to his face and gave him a perfunctory "Thank you," wishing he would go away quickly.

The young man was studying the delicate features, the clear eyes, the exquisite curves of cheek and brow and lip, the fine texture of the white skin. Such things were his specialties. He was always collecting new specimens.

"So sorry you had to go through all this!" he waved his

hand effusively toward the casket. "But of course you know it's much better so. Saves a lot of trouble for everybody."

Romayne cast a startled glance at him and turned coldly away, answering nothing. She had a strong desire in her heart to strike him. There was something offensive in his voice.

"I sent your *message*," went on the unpleasant voice nothing daunted. "Of course your *friend*—you understand what I mean?—your *friend*—expected this before he left. He fully agreed with me that it was the best thing that could happen ——"

Romayne felt that she was going to scream if this went on, and she turned sharply away once more and found to her relief that Chris Hollister stood formidable and glowering by her side.

"Oh, Chris," she said appealingly, "can't you get me out of here—upstairs? I—can't stand any more!"

Chris gave her his arm and led her proudly toward the stairs and Romayne never knew that by that small appeal to his chivalry she had soothed many hurts that she had given him on the day the house was raided.

But a man like Kearney Krupper was not to be shaken off so easily. He was at the stairs as Romayne put her foot upon the first step.

"By the way, what time is the interment? Virginia, I understand. I'll be there——"

"Oh, *no!* Please!" said Romayne. "No one is going. It is to be private——"

"But I represent your—ah—'*friend*,' you know, Miss Romayne. He would wish it, I'm sure. Good night! I'll be there to-morrow. Let me know if there is anything I can do in the meantime."

If Chris hadn't been absorbed in the act of assisting the lady up the stairs, it is very possible he might have forgotten himself and knocked Kearney Krupper down right then and there. As it was, his honest face got fairly black with rage and he looked toward the door threateningly. If he could have hoped that he would ever again have the privilege of escorting Romayne Ransom anywhere, he would have followed the cad into the street, and had it out with him, but he hesitated, looking from the lady to the enemy and back again, and went on up the stairs with Romayne.

"Thank you, Chris," said Romayne earnestly. "Oh, I wish

that man wouldn't go with us to-morrow! I wish he *couldn't!* There isn't any way to stop him, is there?"

"Yes," said Chris. "Don't you worry, Romayne, he sha'n't go!"

Romayne thanked him again and Chris went downstairs to find Aunt Patty, feeling as if he had just been handed a wreath of olive leaves for his brow.

It was Chris who found another earlier train on another road, and told Miss Patty and the undertaker about Romayne's wish; and Chris who took the flowers from the hall in a big car at Romayne's request and distributed them among the children in a hospital down near the slums.

So the funeral cortege started from the house very early in the morning, before the residents of the street were up, and with only the officers' roses lying on the casket.

It was Chris again who put Romayne and Aunt Patty into their chairs in the parlor car, gave Aunt Patty the tickets, touched his hat and left them just as the rain started, leaving Romayne with a curious sense of loneliness to know that he was gone. His kind perspiring face had been always there, ready to respond to her slightest wish, during the last two days, and it had comforted her not a little.

But when the train drew into the little station in the Virginia town that was their destination and Romayne and Aunt Patty arose to get out, it was Chris again who appeared as naturally as if he had been there all the time; Chris in his Sunday-best citizen's clothes, ready to pick up the small hand-bag they had brought and put them into an automobile.

And when they came to the quiet cemetery on a hilltop above the town and got out to walk to the newly dug grave, there at its head in a body, grave and kind and impressive, in citizen's clothing and no hint of "officers" about them, stood the entire force who had guarded the house during George Ransom's illness.

There were a few old friends there, too, Virginia friends of the family. It had been several years since Romayne had seen them, and she scarcely recognized some of them. She was grateful to them, of course, for coming to do honor to her father, or to the family, though she could not help being conscious of all they must have read in the papers. But she felt a warm glow of gratitude toward that body of splendid strong-faced men with Chris at their head, who had come all the way from the city with her, riding in another car, and coming as friends and citizens rather than as officers They were giving her father the honor of their respect, and showing the people in the old home town that he still had some friends to follow him to his grave.

The old minister was there, too, and as Romayne stood on the hilltop in the morning sunlight watching the play of light and shadow over the grassy mound where her mother's body lay buried, looking up to the sky with its cloudless blue, with the birds in the trees singing their spring songs, she could not help a little feeling of triumph. Her father, too, had gone home, forgiven! And what a place for resurrection day, if such things mattered then!

It was when they were seated in the returning train at noon, and just as they were pulling out, that the later train from the city came in and halted at the station in full sight of Romayne's window. There had been a freight off the track, and it was two hours late.

Kearney Krupper hopped blithely off and looked around him. It is possible, if the train to the city had not at that moment begun to move pretty rapidly, that it would not have carried Chris Hollister back with it; for he spied his flashy enemy just a moment too late, and he would have loved to have taken him away off in the fields and given him a good lesson. But he reflected as the train got into full motion and rounded a curve, giving a last glimpse of the indomitable Kearney, that perhaps to spend a few hours searching for a funeral that was already over would be as good a lesson as any that he could teach.

Late in the afternoon they got back to the house and Aunt Patty tucked Romayne into bed and made her promise to go to sleep a little while. Then she made sure that the colored cook was in the kitchen and a tempting little dinner well under way, before she hurried off to her neglected nephew, intending to be back to eat dinner with Romayne.

But instead of eating dinner with Romayne at half past six, as she had planned, Aunt Patty was sitting in a parlor car, rushing on her way to New Hampshire.

She had found a telegram at her nephew's apartment saying that Aunt Martha had been taken suddenly seriously ill and she must come immediately.

"You'll have to go at once, of course, Aunt Patty," said Evan anxiously. "It's ridiculous for you to think you have to stay with me! I shall be out on the street in a few days more."

"Yes, that's just what I'm afraid of," said Aunt Patty wiping away a furtive tear. "You've had me out on duty so much I haven't been able to do anything for you, but I had counted on helping you convalesce and seeing that you did it gradually."

"Well, I'll promise to be good if you'll promise to come back again as soon as you can."

"Of course," said Aunt Patty shortly, trying not to cry. "But what are you going to do about my little girl? She can't sleep in that great house all alone to-night."

"That's true, too," said Evan, looking serious. "Well, I'll get to work on that right away. Now, you'll have to hurry, Aunt Pat, if you want the express. It leaves the downtown station at six. Phone for Chris to come right up. He'll look after everything for you and at the same time do some things for me. And then you pack! Don't bother about anything you don't need at once. I'll have the rest sent after you. Just take things easy, and don't worry about Aunt Martha. She's been pretty sick before. She'll pull up out of this as soon as you get there. I know her."

"Yes," sighed Aunt Patty. "Poor little Aunt Martha! I ought not to have left her."

Then Aunt Patty flew to her packing.

She did not stop for many details. She folded things and stuffed them in and in a few minutes had her belongings marshalled into her suit-case, her hair brushed and everything ready for her journey. Then she sat down to write a note to Romayne.

Chris meanwhile had arrived and done efficient service with the telephone. In half an hour a man from the League office came up with Aunt Patty's ticket and reservation, and shortly after that a taxi arrived to take her to the station. Chris escorted her, put her on her sleeper, and gave the porter a special care over her. On his way back to the house he stopped at the hospital and brought back a night nurse that the doctor whom he had called up had grudgingly recommended. The doctor did not like Evan Sherwood to have any but the best, and why couldn't Nurse Bronson stay with him now that the Ransom patient was dead? He couldn't understand.

Chris didn't explain. He simply said she couldn't be there that night. Chris had learned early to keep his mouth shut.

Meantime, Evan Sherwood's supper-tray was brought up,

and while Nurse Bronson was feeding him, for they wouldn't let him move enough yet to feed himself, he told her, between mouthfuls:

"You're going away to leave me to-night, Nurse, did you know it?"

"Well, indeed then, Mr. Evan, you're mistaken," said Nurse Bronson crisply. "I'll not leave you again till yer able to be out and tend to yerself. Not till that wound has all healed! It's a nasty place and it needs careful looking after. I'll not trust anybody else to dress it. Didn't I promise your mother——"

"Yes, but you promised *me*, Nurse. You promised me you would stay with Miss Ransom as long as she needed you."

"Well, didn't I? Isn't the patient dead and buried? What more do you want?"

"I want you to go and stay with her to-night. Bronson, she's all alone in that great house with all those memories "

"Memories can't bite, can they?" snapped Nurse Bronson. "I'm going to stay here!"

"Look here, Nurse, do you want me to get well?"

"Sure I do. That's why I'm staying "

"Don't you think I need to sleep to-night?"

"Yes, and you're going to."

"Bronson, I can't sleep unless I know that little girl is being taken care of."

"But where's that wonderful aunt of yours?"

"She's on her way to New Hampshire. She had a telegram. Aunt Martha was taken worse."

"Well, this is a pretty kettle of fish! So you want me to go off and leave you alone all night, do you? Well, I won't and that's flat!"

"No, Bronson, I don't want you to leave me alone. There's another nurse downstairs waiting to come on duty while you go and have a good night's sleep over in the Ransom house, and I want you to keep your promise to me and go."

"Another nurse!" said Bronson, her chin in the air. "Well, of course, in that case I *leave!*"

"But Bronson, I want you to fix me for the night before she comes up here," smiled Evan with a twinkle.

"Aw, get out with ye, Mr. Evan. Yer the self-willed child, so ye are! What time do I have to be over to the Ransoms?"

"Oh, about half-past eight "

"Well, then! Get to work and eat yer supper before it's cold."

"I knew you'd be reasonable, Bronson. You always are. And you'll only be away at night, you know, and have a chance for a good sound sleep."

"How long does this keep up?"

"Why, as long as she needs you, I said. It's a part of the League's work, you know, and I feel responsible."

"Aw, you and yer League! You make me tired! Will you never think of yerself and getting well? Now eat them quabs. Mrs. Sam Pace sent 'em. I cooked 'em the way yer mother used to like 'em."

"They're wonderful, Bronson. And is that currant jelly? Who made that? And ice cream! I shall stay sick! Say, Bronson, you'll be sure to come back in the morning?"

"Oh, Mr. Evan, quit your kidding. You know we'll all do just what you say, you're that spoiled!"

Tenderly, as if he were a baby, she fixed him for the night, and never went near the waiting nurse till she was ready to leave for the night. She was most explicit in her directions, too, and left with a wistful look back.

"All right, Bronson," smiled Evan, "See you in the morning. Hope you have a good night's rest."

Bronson carried the letter from Aunt Patty and walked in on a forlorn little belated supper with Romayne in the dining-room all alone. She had just waked up. She didn't want to eat, it choked her, but she knew the maid had tried to please her and she was doing her brave best.

So Bronson sat down and made a second supper with her and brought some of her good cheer to the sad dining-room.

"Why, Nurse," said Romayne, looking up with relief, "I thought you were on a case. I thought you went to that Mr. Sherwood!"

"And so I did," said Nurse Bronson. "But nothing would do but I must come over and get a night's sleep. I was wondering, could you spare me a bed? It isn't so far as going to my lodging, and I thought you might be alone."

"Oh, I'll be so glad to have you!" said Romayne eagerly. "This house seems so big and terrible!"

"Oh, yes, and I brought a note from Miss Patty! She got a telegram from her sister in New Hampshire and she had to go right off."

Romayne opened it eagerly. It was good to know this new friend had not forgotten her after the stress was over.

"Dear little girl," it read.

"I'm in a great distress to leave you this way, but there's nothing else to do. My sister, who is a good deal older than I and very feeble, has been taken seriously ill, and they have telegraphed for me. I've only a minute to write, but I'll think of you and pray for you, and remember the God who forgives also loves and comforts and goes with us through hard times. I'll write you as soon as I get a chance.

"Lovingly,

"Aunt Patty."

Romayne looked up with a sad little smile.

Just then the telephone rang sharply and Nurse Bronson waved her hand commandingly.

"Sit still. I'll answer it!"

A man's voice came over the wire.

"Is Miss Ransom at home yet?"

"Yes."

"Well, tell her I'm coming to see her. I've just got back from Virginia. I'll be there in ten minutes. This is Kearney Krupper and I've got something important to tell her."

CHAPTER XVII

Every word that Kearney Krupper spoke over the telephone was audible to Romayne across the room, and when there came that quick click of the instrument, showing that he had hung up in the midst of Nurse Bronson's protest that Miss Ransom was too tired to see any one that night, Romayne looked at her aghast.

"Oh, I can't talk to him to-night!" she cried. "I simply can't! He's a terrible man! I wish I didn't have to see him ever! I can't bear the way he looks at me!"

"Well, you don't have to!" declared the woman. "Just you

go up the stairs quick and get to bed! I'll teach him to hang up on me that way! *I'll* go down and see him!"

"He'll only put it off until to-morrow," wailed Romayne, her eyes filling with tears. "Oh, I wish I could run away! It seems as though I couldn't stand any more!"

The nurse's answer was to lift the girl gently from her chair and lead her toward the stairs.

"There, child!" she said. "I'll help you to run away if you want to." The nurse's lips were set in a grim line.

"We might lock the door and turn out the lights," suggested Romayne wearily.

"But that would be all to do over again, as you say," answered the nurse. "You leave him to me!"

"He said it was about my brother," said the troubled voice hesitatingly. "He won't tell it to you."

"Do you *want* to talk to him?" asked the nurse sharply. "Do you think you *have* to?"

"I don't know," said Romayne with a frightened tone in her voice.

"Well, then, I'll tell him you said he was to say his say to me! If he don't want to he can keep it to himself. But I want you to know that whatever he says will go no farther. And when I tell it to you that's the end of it. *I forget.* It's my business to forget what people say that's none of my business, so you needn't be afraid."

"I'm not afraid," said the worn-out child. "And I'm very grateful to you!"

The nurse answered by a little pat on her hand, a sign of deep emotion for Nurse Bronson, who was nothing if not adamant.

Romayne was soon in bed with the light out, and the nurse took care there should be only a dim light down in the hall when the caller arrived.

Grimly, in an old red cotton crêpe bathrobe and night slippers, with her hair in crimping pins—which, by the way, were an addition for the occasion—Nurse Bronson never was known to crimp her hair—she descended the stairs with a thump on each step.

Grudgingly she opened the door an inch or two and told the visitor that Miss Ransom was gone to bed.

"Well, just tell her I'm here. She'll get up," he announced. "She wants to see me."

"No, she doesn't want to see anybody to-night!" said the

nurse firmly, "and she won't get up if she does, for I'm her nurse and I'm here to take care of her. She's all beat out and she'll have a fit of sickness if she don't get some sleep."

"Sorry, but this is important. It's about her brother. She'll want to know. He's in trouble."

"I guess that's no news to her," said the nurse satirically. "If all I hear's true, he's been there a good many times. He'll probably live through it."

"Look here, my good woman," said the arrogant Krupper, inserting a fashionable toe inside the door. "You don't know what you're talking about. This is serious business—a matter of life and death, as it were—and Miss Ransom has got to know this to-night."

"Very well, you'll have to send a message by me then," said Nurse Bronson. "I'll see if she's awake yet."

By this time young Krupper had inserted the most of himself into the hall.

"That's quite impossible!" said the young man. "This is private business."

"There's nothing too private to tell me if you want her to hear it to-night. She said I was to tell you you could say anything you liked to me. She doesn't have secrets from me."

"My dear lady, as I said before, you don't know what you are talking about!" said Kearney condescendingly, perceiving he could not sweep this stout lady aside quite so easily as he had expected. "I will write her a note, and when she finds out what I have to say, you will see she will get up and come downstairs."

"Write yer note," said Nurse Bronson, waving toward the desk in the office.

Kearney got out a fountain pen and wrote forcefully a few lines. The nurse took the folded paper in a contemptuous thumb and finger and went plunk, plunk, on her expressive rubber heels upstairs.

She opened a door—it happened to be the door of Mr Ransom's room—closed it softly, snapped on the light and read the note without a compunction. Nurses learn to take responsibilities sometimes when the life of a patient is at stake. She had no respect whatever for the young man downstairs. He was of a class whom she despised.

The note was blunt and written in a bold scrawl:

"Your brother needs a thousand dollars before he can get to safety. If you can let me have five hundred of it to-night he can go on his way and I can forward the rest by telegraph."

"H'm!" sniffed the nurse, folding the paper thoughtfully and putting it into her pocket. Then she opened the door noiselessly, went with her silent sickroom tread to Romayne's room, and entering, closed the door before she spoke in a whisper:

"Do you want me to follow my own idea in dealing with this young man?"

"Oh, yes," said Romayne, shrinking from the thought of him. "I don't like him."

"Well, then, answer me this. Have you got much money? Because I need to know."

"Oh, no," said Romayne anxiously, "I've got less than five hundred dollars and I owe a good deal more than that for the funeral and everything——"

"That's all right," said the nurse. "Of course you do. Now, is there any reason why you should have to give money to that scapegrace of a brother of yours?"

"Oh, I don't know——" said Romayne, bursting into tears. "I——"

"That's all right, too," said the nurse. "Let me give you a piece of advice. If you ever *do* have to, *don't* give it through that weak-chinned little monkey downstairs, because I don't believe your brother would ever get it! Now, lie down and I'll settle this. When I get rid of him, I'll come up and tell you what I mean."

So the nurse swept rubberly down the stairs again with triumph in her wake.

"She says she hasn't any money," repeated the nurse arrogantly.

The young man arose and tried to make himself tall and important.

"My good woman, I happen to know that she has five hundred dollars! Her brother told me so, and he wants it at once! In fact he *must have it!*"

"It cost more than that five hundred dollars to pay expenses here," said the nurse. "That's all spent! She hasn't got a cent for herself. A pretty pair you two are, coming to a *girl* for money! Let him get his own money! She hasn't any!"

"My good woman, you don't understand," drawled Kearney as if he were being the most patient of mortals. "This is a peculiar situation. Miss Ransom understands, and if she knew the critical need to-night she would get the money at once without further delay. Every moment is dangerous for one she loves."

"I tell you she hasn't got any money! How can she get what she hasn't got?"

"Miss Ransom knows that she has friends who will give her any amount she needs if she lets them know by telegraph how much she wants. She has only to mention that she is aware her brother has evidence against them and she will have no trouble——"

"Look here, young man! That sounds like blackmail!"

"That shows how little you understand," he said sadly. "You see, it is imperative that I see Miss Ransom herself! If you don't call her down I shall be obliged to go upstairs and find her."

He started toward the stairs, but the nurse placed herself in front of him.

"Just you set down," she said firmly. "I've got to telephone for some medicine Miss Ransom needs. I forgot it, and I'll be too late——" She stepped to the desk and took up the telephone, calling up a number.

The young man paused, watching her annoyedly. He was in haste to see Romayne. He meditated a bold dash up the stairs while the nurse was occupied, but was held listening to her message.

"Chris there? Well, why don't he bring that medicine? Yes, we need it right away. Miss Ransom ain't feeling so good and she's got a visitor. Can you hurry it right up? All right."

She clicked the telephone in place and glanced at the young man.

"I was just coming down to get a hot-water bag," she said. "I suppose you won't mind waiting a little——"

She whisked into the dining-room door but did not go far beyond the door, with an ear alert to the hall, and she whisked back again in a jiffy.

"Just set down and wait, if you must." She waved her hand toward a chair again. "I'll see what I can do."

And Nurse Bronson made a sound of bustling about above stairs.

In about three minutes' time a hoarse little Ford drew up in front of the door, somebody flung out and up the steps, a key clicked in the lock, startling the caller into sudden alert attention. He half rose, with a furtive look about him, as the door swung open and Chris Hollister's broad shoulders and round ruddy face appeared in full uniform, a heavy frown upon his straight young brows.

To say that he glared at the young man who stood in the office is putting it mildly. He seemed to be piercing the intruder through and through with his gaze. Justice fairly exuded from him, and no one looking at Chris Hollister now could possibly call him a boy. Manliness spoke in every line of his sturdy figure.

They glared at each other for a full second. Then Chris opened the argument, in a voice of authority.

"You—are waiting for—somebody?"

There was deliberation in each syllable.

The caller bowed haughtily.

"I am waiting for Miss Ransom. She will be down present-ly. *You?*" There was a nasty snarl in the word, a kind of upward inflection that was intended for a reflection upon the other. "You—seem to be rather—at *home* here!" There was insult flung with the final word.

"Yes," said Chris gravely. "This house is under my protec-tion."

"Oh, I *see!* And all its inhabitants, I suppose!"

Chris paid no attention to the sneering laugh. He strode over to the dining-room door where he could see a light from the kitchen beyond. He paused with the door half open, still keeping the front part of the house in view, and held a brief and inaudible conversation with the nurse, who stood within the shadow.

"I see!" said Chris at length in a clear voice. "All right, Mrs. Bronson. Your word is law here!"

Then he swung the dining-room door shut and strode back to the waiting visitor.

"I am told that Miss Ransom has retired and that she cannot see you to-night. She has, I believe, sent you an answer to your message, and the nurse wishes me to say to you that her answer is final. She cannot possibly accept your suggestions!"

Anger rolled hot in the face of Kearney Krupper.

"Oh!" he jeered. "So *you* have a date with her, have you? Well, two can play at that game, and my turn comes first. I'm not taking any second-hand messages from a kid like you just out of High School. Miss Ransom understands the impor-tance of my message, and if she knew I was down here, she would come down at once. I don't believe that wall-eyed woman took my message at all. I want Miss Ransom called down at once or I'm going up! It's absolutely necessary to Miss Ransom's happiness that she know what I have to tell her, and if you don't know enough to send for her at once I'll go and get some *real* police officers and have you chucked from your fancy job before you know where you're at! I know you! You're only one of those fool League men. You haven't any real authority!"

Then down the stairway came a clear voice from above.

"Chris, please tell Mr. Krupper that I have entire confidence in you, and that he may say whatever is necessary to you. I shall not come down to-night. As for extracting money by threats from any of the people who have caused my father's downfall, I would rather my brother and I both spent the rest of our lives in prison than touch a cent of such money!"

Then swift steps went into a room and the door was shut and noticeably locked with a decided click.

There was a moment's startled hush in the hall below, while the two men faced each other, and the dining-room door swung slowly open, revealing Nurse Bronson in her red bathrobe and crimping pins, a light of grim triumph in her eyes.

A wave of pride rolled into Chris's face, a great light of restored self-respect in his eyes, and a new dignity fell upon him like a garment. By those few words Romayne had lifted a cloud from his honest heart and taken away the blight she had put upon him the night of her father's arrest. She had, as it were, in the presence of witnesses, handed him a crown of honor. He was her trusted friend again! It was more than he had ever hoped to have and he accepted it humbly and joyfully.

The face of Kearney was dark with wrath, and in his eyes gleamed something like fear. It was as if Romayne's clear voice had cut through the secrecy with which he had sought to veil his errand and thrown all open for the enemy to see. He cast about for a way out of his dilemma, and smothered his anger in a semblance of condescension.

"Miss Ransom little knows what she has done," he said haughtily. "I am here to represent the son of this house——"

Chris interrupted him coldly.

"The son of this house is in prison—or ought to be! It is

his own rascality that has put him there and left his sister unprotected to face the rottenest situation a girl ever was in. I am here to represent the daughter of this house, who has had enough to bear to-day without anything else that you have to say. If you wish to discuss this matter any further, we will go down to my office and do so. My car is waiting outside——"

"I have no wish to discuss anything—*with you!*" contemptuously. "There are important things this girl ought to know, and she will be sorry if she lets them go——" Here he raised his voice louder and looked up the stairs. "But if she refuses to talk with me, she'll have to take the consequences. I see you have it all framed up to suit your own devices, and I suppose you expect to profit thereby, but the time will come"—here his voice was still louder—"when she will bitterly regret that she turned away her only brother's confidential friend and put her trust in *traitors!*"

"We will discuss those matters further at my office!" said Chris authoritatively. "March!"

Kearney Krupper lowered his eyes from the stairhead and perceived that Chris held a revolver in his right hand and that his eyes were very stern. Much too stern for a High School boy's eyes. Kearney had never realized how stern a recent High School graduate's eyes could get. He grew a shade whiter around his mouth, but he kept his braggadocio voice.

"Oh, now, don't get funny!" he said with a nervous laugh. "I have no idea of troubling you with any of my confidences. I'm going now, and I'm only sorry for poor Miss Ransom."

"March!" said Chris. "We'll finish this in my office! I've something very important to say to you if you are Lawrence Ransom's friend."

Kearney Krupper turned hastily toward the door, feeling that he suddenly had no further desire to continue the conversation, but in turning he found himself confronted with six more men in uniform and six other revolvers in evidence looking exceedingly handy.

Solemnly they opened ranks, three on a side, while Kearney Krupper, hat in hand, with Chris behind, revolver in hand, walked out the door and down the steps into the car that was waiting to take him to the station house.

During that ride Kearney Krupper endeavored to pull his usual cloak of bravado together and demanded to know why he was being taken against his will and what Chris wanted of him anyway.

"We just want you to tell us what you have done with Lawrence Ransom," stated Chris briefly, and would say no more, in spite of all Kearney's protests that he knew nothing whatever of Lawrence or his movements, that he was only acting for him in response to a note received from the prison. Lawrence was in the prison, of course, where he had been all the time, so far as he knew anything about it.

"Well, we just want you to prove that statement," said Chris quietly, as he drew up before the station house, and Kearney got out to face another cordon of uniforms drawn up to welcome him. "Also," added Chris, "we'd like to know what you were going to do with that thousand dollars after you had bullied Miss Ransom into giving it to you? If you can explain everything satisfactorily, why, they will probably send you on your way to-morrow morning. If not, you may be detained longer."

Kearney gave a furtive glance up the street and down as he got out of the car, pulled his hat over his face and made a hurried dash inside the hall of justice, while the cordon of uniforms closed up behind him. It began to look as if he had made a rather serious mistake. Who would have thought that little delicate girl could have had so much spirit? There must be some one back of it all or she never would have dared! Evan Sherwood, perhaps. Lawrence had said she was innocent as a lamb. Well, she should pay for this! Kearney Krupper had an ugly streak of vengeance in him, and when any one did him a bad turn he never forgot it. He resolved that this girl should cringe and crouch to him, should beg for her life, yes, for her very soul, to him, before he was done, just to pay for that speech of hers flung down from upstairs as if he were a cur! And it began to look as if it was going to cost him something to get out of this affair, too! Just when he had been expecting to clean up a tidy thousand on the side and nobody the wiser for it!

He began to cast about in his mind for a friend to go bail for him in case this turned out to be a genuine arrest. His father, of course, but he was in mid-ocean and not anxious to be in the limelight just now. So also were most of his father's confederates. He was not expected to get into trouble just now. He had been ordered to be most cautious. There were things he had to do for "the gang." He could not afford to get into the papers!

He was startled out of his meditations by a voice like a steel trap.

"When and where did you last see Lawrence Ransom?"

CHAPTER XVIII

"WELL!" said Nurse Bronson, arriving in Romayne's room after having double-locked and bolted every door to its utmost capacity. "That settles it! You've got to get out of here! You weren't planning to stay alone in this great house, were you? I hope not!"

"Why, no—that is—I hadn't planned!" said Romayne helplessly. "I—why, what *can* I do? I really haven't thought! There hasn't been any chance to think. Of course I'll have to do something. There won't be any money left when I've paid all these bills. The undertaker alone will be over three hundred dollars. And I haven't thought to ask you what you get a week? I should have given you a check before you left. You must excuse me——"

"There, *there*, THERE!" said Nurse Bronson. "Don't you begin on that! I may as well tell you that the League has paid all those bills! They gave me a check the day I left here, and I happen to know the doctor and undertaker are paid, too. I heard some of 'em say it was their responsibility. But I didn't intend that fox downstairs should know it. *You* didn't know it! As far as you were concerned your money was spent on those things. It's time that brother of yours knew it, if he doesn't know it now. And as for that fox that came here for him, you mark my words! If you'd given him anything your brother would *never have seen a dollar of it!* Now don't you forget what I say, and don't you ever let him fool you! I know him and his father before him. They're all alike and you can't trust one of them! Why, do you know what he did? The old Krupper, I mean. He's chairman of a committee to buy things for the schoolhouse, and they had a whole long list of things charged up to twice and three times as much as they really cost. They had a bedroom set for the High School. You know they have a fool thing they call Domestic Science, where they teach the girls how to cook and make beds—all nonsense, I say, because haven't nine-tenths of all them that goes to school got homes and mothers to teach 'em to make beds? Howsomenever they didn't ask my advice and they teach them things, and if they want 'em I s'pose they've got a right to 'em. But the taxpayers buy the stuff fer all this carryings on, and one of the things they have is a bedroom. And they bought a solid mahogany bedroom set, exactly like my cousin got for her daughter when she was married, at Blatz's department store for three hundred and fifty in the August furniture sale, and what do you think they pretended they paid for it? Fifteen hundred and seventy-five dollars! Yes sir! That's how them politicians live! That's what that man's father is. Now, when he asks you fer money fer *any-thing,* don't you give it to him! Not to *save your life,* don't you! He'll take the money and he won't lift a finger for you. You put that away and remember it. I know, fer I saw the bedroom set and I studied my cousin's daughter's set before I went, and they're exactly the same to a keyhole. And I noticed it before I saw it in the papers, or ever heard the League officers talking about it, either!"

"Oh, I'm so thankful you were here!" sighed Romayne, sinking down on her pillow, white and weak. "This has been such an awful day!"

"Yes, and you, child, had better get to sleep right away."

"I don't think I can possibly sleep!" said Romayne. "There are so many things to think about. I felt so angry when Mr. Krupper suggested my telegraphing to those people!"

"Yes, wasn't that the limit?"

"And how did Chris happen to be here? Wasn't it wonderful that he came in the nick of time?"

"Oh, we had an agreement. Evan—that is, Chris and I—that if I needed any help in the night I would telephone, so I just gave him the tip and he was here in the jerk of a lamb's tail. He certainly kept his agreement."

"I'm very grateful——" said Romayne, "I can't thank him enough. I was horrid to him the night father was taken sick—and"—more thoughtfully, "I was horrid to Mr. Sherwood, too——"

"Oh, well, he didn't hold it against you. If you only knew—he's always asked after you the kindest way——"

"Is he any better?" asked the girl half shyly.

"Yes, he's getting slowly out of danger. He wanted to get up to-day. Imagine! He said he must get up and attend to the League. There's been some big things happening——" Nurse Bronson stopped short, remembering that one of the big things that happened to make Evan Sherwood feel he must get up and get back to business was the news of Lawrence Ransom's escape, and that two of the members of the League had suggested that perhaps his sister ought to be put into custody lest she, too, were in league with the gang. Nurse Bronson could have told many things if she had not a well-trained mouth that knew when to shut tight. It certainly would not help the worn-out girl on the bed to know that she was an object of suspicion, and that Evan Sherwood had stood between her and a good deal of unpleasant publicity.

"Oh, you don't know what a fine young man he is!" finished Nurse Bronson. "Some day you'll understand and have a chance to thank him, perhaps. He did a lot of nice things while your father was sick. Wait till he finds out about that old Krupper!"

"Oh, don't tell him!" begged Romayne, her cheeks flushed with humiliation at once. "I would hate so to have him know about my brother!"

"Child! He knows! And anyhow, Chris will have had to tell him. He makes 'em bring him a report of every little thing every day. Now, you forget it. I've talked too much. To-morrow we'll set about fixing things so you can't be annoyed this way."

"Oh," cried Romayne, the weak tears running down her white cheeks, "I wish I'd died, too! Why couldn't I have died? How can I live without anybody? My brother, too! Oh, I wish I could get away from here where nobody knows me!"

"Well, perhaps you can," said Nurse Bronson cheerily. "But you mustn't talk that way about dying. I ain't much of a Christian myself, but I always sorta sized it up that

Him that put us here knowed when He wanted us to leave this place, and we hadn't oughtta fret till our time comes. Likely He's got something yet fer you to do. Say, how would you like to move to my room in my sister's house for a few days, till you make up your mind what to do? The room's there and it ain't occupied when I'm on a case. There ain't many I'd let go into it, but I don't mind you. You'd be real comfortable. It has a good bed, and two big winders, and my mother and my sister would just love to have you. My sister's husband travels and he ain't home much, so they'd like you fer company, and she has two little children. It ain't a grand street, it's Maple Street, and only a two-story house, but we got a little garden and some flowers and there's a speck of a lawn in front, it ain't right on the street. You could stay there and it wouldn't cost you anything for the room, and then you could look around."

"That would be wonderful!" said Romayne. "Could I go right away to-morrow?"

"Sure!" said Nurse Bronson. "You needn't stay here another night. I'll get you away real early in the morning and when you decide what you want to do we'll come back and pack up in a hurry and wipe the dust off our feet."

"Oh, that will be good." Romayne lay back on her pillows. "I can't really let those people in the League pay my bills, of course, but they will give me time, perhaps——"

"Oh, well, you can settle all that better when you've had a chance to rest first——"

"I'll have to sell the furniture," said Romayne, looking around the room.

"Is it furniture you've had a long time? Do you want to keep it?"

"No; Father picked it up here and there. It's good stuff, he said. I think he paid a good deal for some of it, but we've only had it a short time. There's only Mother's old-fashioned rocker and sewing-table and a little chest of drawers I'd like to keep. If I could get a room somewhere I could keep them."

"Sure you could and that's sensible," responded the nurse heartily. "My sister would let you have house-room for them till you settled where you were going. She's got a storeroom with lots of empty space——"

"Oh, I wish I could move to-night where that man couldn't ever find me again!"

"Well, you can move to-morrow, if you want to. Just pack up your clothes early, the things you want with you, and we can get an expressman. Then you can sell the things at your leisure. I know an antique man that has a little shop. They say he pays pretty good prices. Now, you go to sleep!"

But there was little sleep for Romayne that night; her brain was too excited. She lay planning ahead, thinking of possibilities that had not occurred to her during the days of her father's illness, realizing as she had not done before what a future would mean in which she must support herself.

She had time to feel grateful to the League for lifting her burden of debt for the moment, to suspect the fact that this Evan Sherwood was likely at the bottom of this kindness also, and to tell herself that she must write him a note the first thing to-morrow thanking him for it and for his other kindnesses. Now that everything was over and she would have no need of help any more, she could afford to be generous and show her gratitude. He was sick in bed and she was going to get out of the vicinity as fast as she could and would probably never have to meet him again. She really must be a lady and write that note. But she must pay that debt at once!

Five hundred dollars would probably not be enough, but she could at least send him a check for that amount and ask him to let her know how much more she owed him. Perhaps she could get enough from the furniture to support herself a while, till she could get a job. But where should she go for a job? She had never learned stenography although she wrote well on the typewriter, and had written many of her father's letters for him. She had lived a sheltered life, reading and studying with her invalid mother during her earlier years, and then away much at school after her mother's death. Never a thought of learning how to earn her living. Her father was old-fashioned and believed in a girl being brought up to be an ornament and to be provided for by the men of her family. She had never thought much about the matter, but if she had visioned any sphere it was always of the household, making a home. Well, she did not exactly want to go out to service in somebody's kitchen, and the only other way to use her domestic talents would be to get married, which was of course out of the question and out of her thoughts. It seemed to her that she never wanted to get married: that she had passed through an experience which set her apart from the rest of the girls in the world and unfitted her for the joys of life. If she had ever dreamed the dreams of youth, she put them aside now as over forever.

A few weeks ago, if her father had died, leaving her penniless, she would have had a brother to lean upon, or if he too had been taken from her, she still would have felt that there was a host of friends who would stand by her and help her to get a position where she could earn her way in the world.

To-night she was brought up short and sharp with the realization that there was not a person in the world to whom she was willing to be beholden.

Before all this had happened she would have gone naturally to Judge Freeman, next to her father, for advice and assistance, but now she knew that never again could she respect or trust him or any of his family. The telegrams and flowers and elaborate notes of sympathy seemed like hypocrisy. She was not just sure why she felt this way, but while she had been listening above the stairs to Kearney Krupper's hateful hints, she had had a revelation, and their friendship had seemed to drop away from her life and leave her standing alone.

But it was better to know where one stood.

Now, how was she to go about getting something to do? She must start to-morrow, as soon as she got moved, and she must settle it all in her mind to-night what to do.

Long she lay tossing and thinking, framing advertisements to put in the paper, thinking out things that she knew she could do, until, as the night began to wane, she fell asleep at last.

It was late in the morning when Nurse Bronson awoke her with a tray of poached eggs and toast and a glass of milk.

Nurse Bronson had a cheerful philosophy of life, that if you gave folks plenty to eat and plenty of sleep and plenty to do, they would get along a great deal better than if they lay around and moped when they were in trouble.

So now as she propped Romayne up with pillows and

threw a kimono about her shoulders, she began to talk cheerily.

"I phoned my sister this morning and she's real glad you're coming," she said. "And Chris happened in to see if all was right and I made him bring the trunks down from the third story so we could lay things in. You know it isn't as if you had been keeping house here a long time. There really isn't an awful lot of stuff to sort out and pack or throw away like there is in most houses."

"No," said Romayne sadly. "We hadn't much when we came here, and Father hadn't bought all the furniture we needed yet. He wanted to furnish this house entirely with old valuable pieces. It was a sort of a hobby of his."

"Well, I've been looking around and I see you've got some real nice things that ought to bring you in quite a sum. I called up the antique man I told you about and he said he'd run in to-day or to-morrow and take a look around to see what you had. So when you get your breakfast you better get dressed and we'll put away some of your things before he gets here. We can lay your clothes right in the trunks if you like. I had them put out in the hall where they'd be handy. I think it's best to do it now while you're rested. Then you can get away before night with a clear conscience. You won't be troubled with that Krupper fellow. He's been detained at the station house on his own business to-day, Chris says."

"You have been so kind," said Romayne, trying to eat the delicate toast and egg that had been so nicely prepared, though her throat somehow would not swallow much.

The nurse talked on of practical affairs till Romayne was able to put aside her tragic thoughts and get down to the need of the day. It was terribly soon to rush into action after her father's funeral, but oh, it would be good to get away from the house, and from any possibility of meeting that terrible man who came last night! The thought of Kearney Krupper gave her control to finish her breakfast and hasten with her dressing, and very soon she was ready to consider matters of the household.

It is marvellous what can be accomplished with a practical woman at the helm like Nurse Bronson. She marched from room to room helping Romayne to classify the various articles. She made the girl pick out in each room the little personal things she wanted to keep, first. It was surprising how quickly this was done, and how it simplified the whole matter of moving out.

"We're going upstairs now and put all your brother's things in a trunk!" said Nurse Bronson firmly. "I think it's best you should do it now. You can't tell later who will be here when you get to selling off your things, and those things ought to be safely put away."

"Yes," said Romayne with a little catch in her breath. "But oughtn't you to go on your case? I thought you said the substitute nurse only came for the night. It's almost eleven o'clock now."

"I phoned her and she said she just as soon I came at eight this evening. She was willing to stay all day, and Mr. Sherwood sent word he wanted me to help you get things straightened out here if I could; that the authorities would be taking possession of the place in a few days now, but they would give you time to get your things together before they bothered you. He said there would be an officer ready to help us if we needed any one and not to hesitate to call for one."

The color crept quickly into Romayne's white cheek. Even from his sickbed he was directing her affairs; thinking of all the kind little things to do for her! It was beautiful! But it was galling, too. She could not remain so in his debt! She must write that note and send that check this very night before she slept!

"He is—most kind——" she said in a cool little voice that made the nurse eye her curiously, and wonder if she had been just wise to say so much. Evan Sherwood had especially warned her not to talk about him. This girl was queer! Now almost any girl in the world would be proud to know that that young man was taking thought for her. Why did this one seem to cringe when she mentioned him? Well, she would get back to work, that was safest.

So they spent two good hours in Lawrence's room.

Nurse Bronson had all his coats and woolen clothing out on a line in the sunshine, brushing it with a whisk while Romayne was standing dazed and wondering where to begin.

"You clear out the bureau and chiffonnier drawers, child, and lay things in whichever trunk is his. Don't stop to moon over things. That won't help you any, and it isn' necessary. If you've any doubt about throwing a thing away don't throw it, pack it. That'll simplify things. Then some day they can be gone over again if it's necessary. Stow everything in somehow. Yes, the pictures and trinkets around the walls, too, though whatever any one wants woolen flags around in hot weather for is more than I can understand." She waved a hand indignantly at the college pennants decorating the room. "Now, come on! I'll take the things off the wall and dust 'em, and you do the clean clothes. Lay 'em in the trunk trays all nice and smooth!"

Romayne went at her task swiftly, her mind busy with sad thoughts as she worked. How happy she was the day Lawrence came home and fixed up his room. How he told her jokes and bits of stories about the college days and the different pictures. It was too bitter to linger over now. She gathered the things and laid them away. Drawer after drawer was emptied and the trunk filled up fast. It was necessary to put the pictures and books in a big box, and that too was at hand, ready. Nurse Bronson never forgot things and never did things by halves.

It was not till the trunk was locked, labelled, the keys with their labelled tags put carefully in Romayne's handbag, and the box nailed up and labelled, that they halted in their work. Then Nurse Bronson brought a glass brimful of iced orange juice to Romayne and told her to drink it.

"You've got something else hard before you," she said, "and it's got to be done. The sooner the quicker. We've got to do the same to your father's things. I know it's hard, but you'll just be thinking about it if you put it off, and you wouldn't want anybody else doing it."

"Oh, no!" said Romayne with a sharp intake of her breath as if she were girding herself to the task.

"Well, I put his things down on the line and whisk-brushed 'em, and they've been hanging in the sunshine a long time. We can pack 'em away in camphor in a trunk, unless you want to give some of 'em away."

"Yes," said Romayne with sudden lightening of the trouble in her eyes. "Yes, I would like to give them away where they will do some good. Wouldn't the Salvation Army like them?"

"I guess they would. It would be a good haul to them.

Why some of those coats are wonderful! You better go through all the pockets. I wouldn't presume to do that!"

So Romayne, with tears blurring her eyes, went through every pocket, laid away a few little things she wanted to keep in remembrance of her father and the days when everything was right and beautiful, and packed the rest in a box for the Salvation Army. Then Nurse Bronson locked the door on that room and drew a long breath.

"Mr. Evan said I was to tell you that they had to take charge of all your father's papers and everything outta the desk and them cupboards in the front room downstairs, and they would go over 'em carefully and any that didn't have to do with the business and was just personal he would give back to you when they got through with their investigating."

The color mounted painfully into Romayne's face and the tears stood in her eyes. She looked as if she had had a blow, and the nurse felt guilty, but it had to be done. It was the one thing Evan Sherwood had asked her to say, so of course it must be said.

"Now," she said briskly, not seeming to notice Romayne, "you and I are going down and have a bite of lunch. I've got two cantaloupes on a bit of ice in the refrigerator, and two lamb chops frying on the range and two potatoes roasting in the oven. There's all the rest of a quart of milk besides a cup of coffee. Can you make a meal out of that or shall I run out and get something more?"

And actually a smile dawned behind the tears in Romayne's eyes.

They had a nice little lunch in the dining-rom, and incidentally Nurse Bronson gathered up an armful of table linen and laid it on a chair ready to pack.

"You know you're really pretty well cleared up!" announced that good woman, looking around with satisfaction. "After you've packed your clothes any one could come right in and buy up the whole lot that's left without your bothering at all."

In amazement Romayne looked about her, and turn whichever way she chose, she could not see anything that she felt she could not leave behind. All were recently bought, or valueless to her.

She turned to Nurse Bronson in gratitude.

"You know you're a very wonderful woman!" she said. "It would have taken me weeks to have done this all alone. It is terrible of me to have let you work so hard! You must have begun before daylight."

"Why, child, I've enjoyed it. It's the first time in my life I ever got away with my own plans from start to finish. I woke up in the night and worked this all out. I thought it would be so nice if you could just get this done and have it over with. If it hadn't been for that nice policeman, Chris, coming over so early and helping, though, I never could have done it. He lifted all the heavy boxes and trunks for me, you know, and carried armfuls of things down to hang on the line. Now! You're going to take a nap! You're worn to a frazzle! No, it's no use protesting. I know when a person needs sleep. It's my profession. When you wake up, if you feel like it, we'll pack your trunk. If you don't we'll just pick up a few duds and run over to my room for the night and do the rest some other time."

So Romayne was tucked into bed once more, and, much to her own amazement, fell immediately to sleep.

The room was quite dusky when she awoke again, and she thought she heard some one moving softly about. She lay still with dull, cold facts coming, one by one, back to mind as they always do after sorrow. Then the light sprang up and Nurse Bronson stood over her.

"Ready for some supper?" she asked pleasantly, and looking around, Romayne saw her clothes in neat piles on chairs about the room and the door open wide to an empty closet.

"Oh, I've overslept!" exclaimed the girl, springing up. "I'm so sorry! And you've been working all this time."

"Oh, no, I rested a while," said the nurse. "I sat and folded up dresses. Do you want to pack now or shall we go home?"

"It's half-past seven!" said Romayne. "We ought to go at once. You should be at Mr. Sherwood's—and—*that awful man may come!*"

"No," said Nurse Bronson, "I phoned the other nurse I would be there till half-past ten or eleven. And the Krupper fox is still in custody, though he'll likely be out in the morning. It won't take long to lay these in the trunk."

So Romayne went to work and in a very short time had her trunk and hand-bag packed and ready to go. Her suit-case she had not even opened since the day she brought it back from the delayed house party. It seemed too much the symbol of all the joy and hope of that day. Its lovely new brushes with their silver monograms, and all her little new toilet articles; its pretty garments and ornaments; she had not had the heart to take them out and hang them up. They were probably badly crushed by this time after their long pack, but she had felt a great reluctance to look at them after all that had come to her, and had continued using her old things. Now she laid the suit-case on the top of the locked trunk ready for the expressman, and announced herself ready to leave.

Nurse Bronson went about locking up, and presently a taxi drew up to the door, and Romayne and her baggage, in the company of the nurse, drove away toward Maple Street.

From an alleyway across the street a slinking figure like a dark wraith leered out, presently emerged on a well-oiled bicycle of an ancient brand and pedaled after the taxi; furtive and shadow-like, darting out of traffic, and back again at a stretch, always keeping the yellow cab in sight, till they came to Maple Street and another convenient alley The wraith loitered out of sight till the driver was paid, and the Bronson door shut behind the two travellers. Then silently he shot away into the city once more, going like one who has done a long day's work faithfully, and attained his end.

CHAPTER XIX

Nurse Bronson waited only to see her young charge tucked into bed before she sped back to Evan Sherwood's bedside. She had worked with a will while she had it to do, but her heart had been with the boy she loved all the time, and she was jealous as jealous could be of the other nurse who had taken her place by his side.

Here this second time she had had to leave him and let another take her place, and it was only because she was doing his will that she was borne up at all in being absent from him. She had nursed his mother when he was born, and of all the babies she had held in her arms, he was the dearest, perhaps because as he grew up he had given her an affectionate return for all her care. She was proud of every hair on his splendid head, of every hairbreadth escape he ever had, and of every brave deed he had done, and though she had been touched by the girl she had been helping this day, and made tender toward her in spite of herself, in her heart she really bore a grudge toward her that she had asked this idol of hers to keep out of her sight. What kind of a girl was it that did not know a gentleman when she saw him?

Nevertheless, jealous as she was for the bairn she had nursed from his childhood, the little lonely girl in her desolate situation had somehow crept into her heart, and she was torn between two duties.

"Now, I'll come back sometime to-morrow or call you up," she said to Romayne in leaving. "The antique man said he'd surely come to-morrow or the next day, and you'll be happier when you know what you've got to depend upon. Now you're to just stay here and rest till I can get off again. Then we'll go back and see if we've missed anything and meet that antique man and go over things with him."

But Romayne did not sleep late the next morning as she had been bidden to do. Instead, she woke earlier than usual, and found that a great sense of burden had rolled from her heart with the realization that the worst of her packing was over, the part that broke her heart.

There was one duty, however, that still lay heavy on her conscience, and that was her letter to Evan Sherwood. So she rose quietly that she might not disturb the family, hunted out the writing paper and pen she had been careful to put in her hand-bag the night before, and wrote her letter.

"Mr. Evan Sherwood.
   "Dear Sir:
   "I am afraid I was very rude to you on the night when I found you and your men in our house. I thought I was justi-

fied then in treating you as I did, but I found out, of course,
that I had been most unjust, and I want to apologize.

"Your kindness to me then and since, I know, has been
great, and I cannot thank you enough for all you have done
to make things easier for me, and also for your unobtrusive-
ness. Forgive me, please, for being so disagreeable. I could not
believe that all that has happened was true.

"I must thank you, too, for meeting the bills of doctor and
nurse and undertaker, which should have come to me. I have
no means of knowing how much they are, but I am sending
you my check for five hundred dollars, which is all I have at
present. I know you must have paid out more than this, and
would send more if I had it. But I expect to have some money
soon from the sale of household goods, and if you will let me
know how much more I owe you, I will send you another
check at once. But for your kindness, I know, I cannot ever
pay. I am sorry you have been put to so much trouble and
expense for—us.

"I hope you will be willing to forgive and forget my rude-
ness.

"Sincerely and gratefully,
"ROMAYNE RANSOM."

She wrote her first check, for five hundred dollars,
enclosed it in the letter, and slipping out, mailed it in the
letter box at the corner.

It happened that the postman who gathered up the mail
was on his way then and in a few minutes it had started
toward its destination. It was brought up to Evan Sherwood's apartment that afternoon by the janitor of the
building, who wanted an excuse to enquire how "the
Chief" was getting on.

Nurse Bronson, who had been sent away to rest and
had in reality taken what she called a "cat nap," came in
and found him reading it with a light of interest in his
eyes and a smile upon his lips.

"See here, Bronnie," he said at length, handing over the
letter to her, "are you in any way behind this? Because I
thought I made you understand that *the League* paid those
bills."

Nurse Bronson ruffled her brows and lifted her chin
arrogantly, as she always did when any one found fault
with her.

"And so you *did*, and so *I* did, sir," she said as she took
the paper stiffly, half offended

"Well, she's some kid!" he said pleasantly. "We'll send it back, of course."

"Well, she's quite right!" said Nurse Bronson hotly. "No self-respecting girl would do otherwise, you know yourself! She wouldn't be worth yer notice if she didn't. She can't let a young man pay her bills!"

"But I told you I am not paying them, it's the League."

"It's all one and the self-same thing, Mr. Evan, and she knows it, and what's more, you know it, too. She's a right-minded girl, she is. I like her the more I see her. She'll not take it back, I can tell you that."

"Yes, but she must," said Evan Sherwood firmly. "She hasn't much more, I suppose. There'll be little or nothing, perhaps less than nothing, from her father's estate, I imagine. What will she live on?"

"*Much* more, did ya say? She hasn't a *cent* more, I happen to know. But she'll live. Ye needn't fear that. There's more than yerself has that firm chin, Mr. Evan."

Little by little she told him the whole story of Kearney Krupper's evening visit and its outcome, and although he had heard Chris's version before, he managed to appear surprised and glean a number of details that set him to thinking seriously along new lines the rest of the evening.

"We'll have to do something about that little girl, Bronnie," he said when she had finished. "I wish she hadn't taken such an aversion to me. You don't suppose she'd get over it enough to come and have a talk with me for a few minutes, do you? Couldn't you manage that?"

Nurse Bronson frowned. She had her views of decorum for these two.

"Best wait till yer well, and I'll try to manage it," she said. "She's not the kind of girl who goes traipsing after the men. She's had a good mother, and she hasn't got bobbed hair. They have notions when they don't bob their hair. She's old-fashioned."

"Perhaps you're right," said Evan, looking disappointed. "Of course you're right. I wouldn't want her to come, on second thought. It might make talk against her. But we must do something. This check will shut the mouths of the rest of the committee, I'm thinking. I must tell them about it to-morrow, and then I'll write her a letter and send it back!"

"Yes, write her a letter!" said Nurse Bronson with

satisfacton as she went about getting the dressing ready
for Evan Sherwood's shoulder. "She's a bonny little thing,
and that'll be far better!"

For somehow the delicacy of Romayne had so impressed Nurse Bronson that she did not want her put in a
position where anything slighting could be said about her.

So Evan wrote his letter, slowly, a few lines at a time,
flavored perhaps with just a tinge of aloofness from the
memory of her stormy brow and scornful lips as she told
him she wished never to look on his face again. But by the
time he had written a very nice, pleasant letter accepting
her apology as if there had never been anything to forgive, he decided not to ask her to come and see him, nor
to suggest that he would like to call upon her when he was
able. Why should a man force himself upon a lady who
had thrice expressed the wish never to see him again? She
had apologized, of course, but that was not saying she
wanted him for an intimate friend, much as she might feel
indebted to him.

She was nothing to him, of course, even if he did feel
sorry for her, poor little kid, and of course he could find
ways to help her without ever seeing her again. It would
be like sending money to a foreign mission. One never
expected to travel to Africa or China to personally admin-
ister one's collection envelope. As for the check, he would
simply return it, telling her that the League, not he, had
been responsible for these bills, and that they were a part
of the regular work of the League. In a sense their work
had been the cause of her father's illness and all that
ensued, and it was only right and proper that they should
pay all costs. He realized that that was a cold, practical
way to put it, but it was the logical fact, and he mentioned it to show her that she need feel no further compunction in keeping the money.

He was careful to show her check to Chris, and to two
other members of the League Committee, before he enclosed it in his letter. One of these members was also the
one who had suggested the possibility that Romayne might
be one of the conspirators.

Chris was deeply stirred by the check, and Evan allowed him to read her letter. But the suspicious member
of the committee, while he perfunctorily said it was "very
commendable of her," still suggested that this might be

only the gang's way of trying to avert suspicion from her
so that they might be able to use her again in new
schemes of their own. And at that Evan's jaw set firmly
and he told the little narrow-minded man that he *knew*
Miss Ransom had nothing whatever to do with the business in any way and had never been aware of it until the
night of the raid.

That night Evan Sherwood set his firm jaw pleasantly
and told the doctor it was time for him to get up, that he
needed to get up to attend to his business, and that
anyhow he was *going* to get up.

That night, too, Chris went away thoughtfully, and the
next day being the Sabbath, in the afternoon, he washed
and dressed with unusual care, shaved himself till he
shone, and was very particular about having the right shirt
and collar, and about the crease in his trousers, and
getting the right lick to his plastered-back hair. He tried
several neckties before he was suited, and at last he took
his way to Maple Street, where, with many honest
blushes, he asked if he might see Romayne.

The little Maple Street parlor, with its red-plush uphol-
stery, its crayon portraits, its blatant victrola and its cen-
tre-table bearing a vase of artificial flowers, seemed the
wrong setting for the delicacy of the girl he had come to
see, and only served to make Chris more uncomfortable.
He wished that he had thought of coming before she left
her old house. It would have been so much easier to tell
her what he had to say in the shadow of the heavy cream
silk curtains and the alabaster vases. Somehow Romayne
did not seem to belong here. And yet it was from this and
worse that he was about to try to rescue her.

"I guess maybe you'll think I'm presuming, Romayne,"
he began, fumbling the brim of his hat awkwardly, "but I
had to come!"

"How could I think that, Chris?" said the girl kindly.
"You have done so much for us all that I can never forget
it. I think perhaps I owe you an apology, too, for the way
I talked to you those first days. I wrote a note to Mr.
Sherwood about it. I want you to know that I appreciate
everything you have done——"

"Please don't, Romayne!" he said, putting up a big
earnest hand, on which he had spent much unaccustomed

grooming. He felt as if she were forestalling all he was about to say.

She stopped and looked at him puzzled.

"I guess you know how it is with me, Romayne. I've always thought you were the greatest girl on earth. I always will, even if you stamp on me. I know I'm not fit to lie down and let you walk over me. I'm not in your class at all when it comes to that——"

"Oh, Chris! Stop talking like that. You're just the finest of the fine! I guess I know after all you've done for me the past weeks, and I sha'n't allow you to talk that way!" broke in Romayne earnestly.

"You don't understand!" said Chris hopelessly. "I'm not just throwing bouquets. I'm trying to tell you how I feel about it. I'm making a proposition to you, and I want you to listen and understand it. But first, I want you to know that I know I'm not really good enough when you come right down to it. I don't want you to think I'm stuck on myself!"

"Oh, I won't ever think that, Chris!" said Romayne, trying to help him out of his evident dilemma, although she could not quite get at what he was trying to say.

"Well, then, it's this way. I know I'm not good enough, but I seem to be all there is, and I want you to let me take care of you! It oughtta have been somebody like Evan Sherwood, but you won't let him do anything, and of course you had a perfect right. And then I don't know as he ever thought of this way out of the trouble, and I couldn't just suggest it, you know; but I thought if Sherwood was out of the question entirely—you see, he let me read your letter last night and I knew when you sent him that check it was all up with him doing anything more—so I thought the next best thing was me. You're sure you won't be offended or anything——" Chris's face was red as a beet and he mopped his shining forehead violently.

"What on earth are you trying to tell me, Chris? What is it you want to ask? Don't be afraid to say it right out?" urged Romayne.

"I'm asking you to marry me, Romayne!" broke forth the earnest boy. "I know I ain't good enough. I don't have your class and all that, but you've gotta be taken care of and that's the only nice way I could do it. I'll love you a lot if that'll make up any way. I've always loved you.

You've been like an angel in my life, so pretty and so good, and so little! And I'll learn anything you want, and get to be the best I can——"

"Oh, Chris!" said Romayne with sudden tears in her eyes. "You dear Chris! Please don't! It's wonderful of you, but I couldn't! I *couldn't* possibly ever marry you! I'm not going to marry *anybody!* But it's not because you're not good enough! Chris, you're the best thing I know. But I just don't feel I could. I think a lot of you, but there's something more to marrying than that. You have to love people in a different way. And I don't love *anybody* that way! I don't really! It wouldn't be fair to you, you know."

"Oh, I wouldn't ask you to do that!" said Chris wistfully. "I'd do the loving, and you could have things your own way. I wouldn't mind!"

"Chris, you are wonderful! And I'll never forget it of you, never! That's the biggest sacrifice a man can make for a woman, to just put aside himself and let her have her way, and if I lived a hundred years I'd never find a greater love than that, I know. But Chris, that isn't real marriage. I'm sure it isn't. My mother has told me that. I could love you like a brother, and I will. My own brother has forsaken me, but you've done more for me than he ever did. But I couldn't marry you! It would be wrong!"

"It's *class!*" said Chris sadly. "I mighta known. But I couldn't help trying anyway. You aren't offended, are you?"

"Indeed, no! How could I be offended? Chris, I think that was a most wonderful thing! Other people gave me flowers and wrote nice notes and telegrams, and even came and helped me, but you tried to give me yourself. I think it's the most beautiful thing anybody ever did. I shall keep it in my memory like a treasure and some day when you find a dear girl who loves you and whom you love, I shall tell her what a wonderful brother you've been to me, and how glad I am I wasn't selfish enough to let you do what you offered, and saved you for her."

"There'll never be anybody else like you, Romayne!"

"There'll be somebody better, Chris! Somebody who loves you that way! Somebody God made for you!"

Chris sat staring blindly through big tears at a crayon portrait of Nurse Bronson taken at five years old, with stringy ringlets around a chubby impertinent face.

"Well, mebbe," said Chris with a long sigh, "but I don't see it now. What I'm thinking about is, how am I going to take care of you when you won't let me marry you?"

"Chris! Listen!" Romayne leaned forward earnestly. "You've not got to take care of me. God is doing that! He wants me to work my own way out, I'm sure of it. If He hadn't He wouldn't have let things come out this way and left me to make my way alone. You mustn't feel you're responsible for me just because we're old friends. I tell you, God wanted me to be in this situation for some reason or He wouldn't have let it happen."

"Yes, and He left me here to take care of you!" said Chris doggedly. "If He didn't, why did I think of it?"

"Well, you *can't!*" said Romayne decidedly. "It's quite impossible."

"If you were going to marry somebody like Evan Sherwood," said Chris sadly again, "I'd be satisfied. You'd be taken care of a great deal better than I could do——"

"Well, *I'm not!*" said Romayne shortly. "Chris, please don't mention him again in that connection. He and I are absolute *strangers* and neither of us has thought of such a thing. And I tell you I won't marry *any one,* not now, anyway. And Chris, you needn't worry about me, I can take care of myself, I really can."

"Wouldn't you come and stay with my mother for a little while?" suggested Chris after a long silent pause, while he thrummed his hat-brim round and round in his big nervous fingers. "She'd let you help her about the house, and she'd love to have you."

"Oh, thank you so much, Chris," said Romayne with a troubled face, "but I couldn't! Indeed I couldn't. Just think what people might say about me! You'll understand I couldn't do that. I must have a job and take care of myself. That's what all self-respecting girls do."

They talked for an hour and a half and finally Chris went sadly away, his broad shoulders drooping pitifully, his round face downcast. It wasn't so much that he had failed in his aspiration toward an angel, as that he was worried what might come to the angel alone in this wicked world. There are just a few men like that who can forget themselves; and such love as theirs knows no class distinction.

His dejection lasted till he went to see Sherwood for his usual evening orders.

Evan Sherwood listened to his reports of various matters that had come up that day—how Krupper had got bail at last and was out and away, but a watch was being kept on his movements because they felt sure he would try to communicate with Lawrence Ransom somehow; how nothing more had been heard of Lawrence and it was thought he was on some South American ship which had sailed within the last two days. He must have shipped under an assumed name, or else was working his passage. Search was being made by wireless and by radio, but as yet there was not the slightest clue. It was important that they get him because it was now known that he possessed papers which gave evidence against the gang and could be used to great advantage in the coming election. But as yet neither the Federal authorities nor the League had been able to get a hint of his whereabouts.

"Personally, I don't think they'll find him working his passage," said Evan. "He's too lazy, and too selfish. He'll make somebody else pay it, or he'll stay where he is till he can. Those papers are with him wherever he is, too."

Having dismissed the business matters, he turned to Chris.

"Now, what's up with you, kid?" he said kindly, as Chris stood gloomily drumming on the window-seat, staring down into the dark street.

And Chris told him the whole story.

Evan listened with a light of tenderness in his eyes and a growing thoughtfulness, now and then ejaculating:

"You said that about *me* to *her*, kid?" or "What did she answer to that?"

At last he called, "Come here, kid, I want you to know I think that was great! I know what your humility is, and how you must have struggled to go to a girl that you felt was above your class with a proposition like that. It's all nonsense of course. There is no what you call 'class' to real love. But you felt that way and you did the best you could in spite of it. Now, kid, you're not to be long-faced about the result. You're no worse off than you were before, and I take it she is more your friend than before. You can't tell what may come——"

"No!" said Chris with a choking sound in his voice.

"She won't change. She can't! She appreciates it, as you say, but she'll never feel different about me. I'm just Chris! That's ended! But what gets me is, what's going to become of her, with that Krupper let loose on the community again, and that gang coming home? They know her brother has something on them, and there's no telling what they'll do to her!"

Evan Sherwood lay still for some seconds thinking, and then he said slowly:

"Don't you worry, Chris, I'm getting back on the job to-morrow, and I'll see what I can do."

There was something in those words, and in the Chief's eyes as he smiled at Chris and gripped his hand, that comforted the boy, as he went his way. If the Chief got down to business something real would be done, he was sure.

CHAPTER XX

ROMAYNE sent the check straight back again to Evan Sherwood with a brief, decided line or two showing how impossible it was for her to let any one, be he person or League, pay any bills pertaining to herself or her family. She mailed it on her way to the house, where she had an appointment to meet the antique man.

Romayne had been very much touched, but also very much upset by Chris's offer of marriage. She saw that it went deep with him, and this distressed her, but the immediate effect of his words had been to make her feel that she must lose no time in getting a job and putting herself on a plane where people would not feel they had to take care of her. She wondered what it was about her that made people feel that way. She studied her delicate, wistful face in the glass before she started and decided she looked too babyish and unsophisticated, and her cheeks burned hot over the memory of Chris's suggestion that if

Evan Sherwood would marry her he would be satisfied. Generous of Chris, of course, to hand her around this way to be taken care of, but her natural pride did not like it.

So she stopped at two employment agencies on her way to her old home, and registered for a job. When it came to giving references she gave Nurse Bronson and Chris, and then after some hesitation she added Dr. Stephens' name. After all, he could say what he pleased about her. Perhaps he doubted her, but she could not help it, and his influence, if he cared to give it in her behalf, would, of course, count more than either the nurse's or Chris's name. Surely, Dr. Stephens would give her a good character, and he had seemed friendly.

Nurse Bronson had warned her to be non-committal with the antique man and not let him know whether she liked the prices or not until he was through with his estimates, so Romayne followed him around with pencil and paper and wrote down what he said he would give. Sometimes she remembered what her father had paid for a thing, and that helped a little. But for the most part she was utterly ignorant and knew she must trust to what he was willing to give. It was better to sell for a smaller price and get it done quickly. She longed to be out of the hateful house.

Chris sent one of the officers around that morning to hunt for some papers in the cellar, so that she was not alone, and Nurse Bronson came flying in about noon with some parcels in her hand and suggested a lunch together. That helped, for the antique man had gone away, promising to return at two o'clock with a truck in which to take the articles she was willing to sell, so she had opportunity to go over the list with some one.

But Nurse Bronson was as ignorant as a baby concerning antiques, neither was Chris, who dropped solemnly in for a minute or two, any wiser. They both agreed that the price the man offered "seemed pretty good for second-hand goods," and except in one or two cases where Romayne happened to remember just what her father had paid for something, she felt herself that she was doing well.

There were a lot of things he would not take, of course, and these she easily sold to a second-hand man for a small pittance. It was amazing how little it all amounted to, a trifle over nine hundred dollars, when all was sold. On the other hand, the bills were coming in, things her father had bought, a hundred here, two hundred there, a fifty-dollar bill for plumbing which probably belonged to the business, but as Romayne was not dealing with the "gang" she felt she had to pay it. Little by little her small fortune diminished until more than half was gone in little things that she had not known about. Then, too, she remembered that she had given away her last winter's coat because it looked shabby, and now the winter would be upon her again before many months. There would be other things she would have to have. Her face began to take on a careworn look before a week was gone.

She worked by herself in the big house with the doors locked, never daring to answer the bell without first peeping out the window, for she had an almost unreasonable dread of Kearney Krupper, and felt she would not dare meet him alone. It was only an idea of course, but she told herself that he gave her the creeps.

By the end of that week the house was nearly empty, and room by room she had, with the help of the colored woman, given it a fairly good cleaning. There remained only her mother's little rocking-chair of fine old mahogany, and the highboy and chest of drawers that had been brought from Virginia and which she hoped to keep. Nurse Bronson's sister had offered her a place to store them until she found a home again, and Romayne had decided not to part with them.

But one morning, just as she was looking around and thinking that her work was nearly done, the antique man called her up and offered her fifty dollars for the chest of drawers, seventy-five for the highboy and twenty-five for the chair. Just like that! And she had been worrying about her money going so fast and no job in sight yet! The best agency had told her that morning as she stopped in on her way down, that there wasn't a chance of her getting more than ten a week till she could take dictation by shorthand, unless she wanted to go out to service, and then she could not say she was experienced, and that would be against her. She might not even make as much as ten a week.

With the receiver in her hand, she paused and looked

around the empty room, her eyes full of trouble, and just then in walked Nurse Bronson, having called to the colored woman at the back gate to let her in.

"What's the matter, child?" she asked at once, seeing the anxious brow and set lips, the tired look, on the little white face.

Romayne told her briefly.

"Don't you sell 'em! Not at that price, anyway. You tell him to wait a few days and you'll think about it."

"But he says somebody is there now who wants it. He may lose a sale if he waits."

"Fiddlesticks end! He'll only be the more anxious to buy 'em if you hesitate, and he'll give you more money, too. You tell him to wait and I'll see if I can't get somebody to pay more than that if you really want to sell."

"I don't," said Romayne; "they're all I've got that belonged to my mother, but I think I'll need the money."

"Well, wait till you do then. Don't sell those things cheap!"

Romayne told the man she would let him know that afternoon, that she did not really want to sell. He offered her another fifty dollars on the whole lot, but Nurse Bronson made terrible eyes at her and shook her head so vigorously that Romayne, after a moment's hesitation, said:

"I'll let you know at three."

Nurse Bronson seemed in a great hurry, although she had promised to take Romayne to see a man she had heard wanted a secretary. She said if she did not mind, she would try to come back later, or maybe not till the next day, and she hurried away again, leaving Romayne perplexed and troubled, wondering if she ought to sell her treasures, crying at the thought.

Nurse Bronson burst into the office where Evan Sherwood was sitting up a little while at his desk making out a report.

"Well, I've found the chance if you want to take it. Doesn't your Aunt Patty like antiques? Why don't you give her a chest of drawers and a highboy and a rocking-chair? They're really very nice."

"Just the thing! How much may I be allowed to pay?"

"The antique man has offered her seventy-five for the highboy, fifty for the chest, and twenty-five for the rock-

ing-chair. He added fifty when I made her tell him she'd
let him know at three."

"H'm! The highboy ought to be two hundred and fifty
at least, if it's anything of a highboy!"

"Don't make it too big or she'll suspect."

"How old is the chair? Could you get away with fifty on
that? And the chest of drawers could be anywhere from a
hundred and fifty to two hundred or more."

"Make it four hundred and seventy-five," said Nurse
Bronson grimly, "and make out yer check quick! There's
barely time before the bank closes to cash it."

Evan Sherwood wrote his check with great satisfaction.
It was almost as much as the one Romayne had insisted
on sending back to him. Nurse Bronson hurried away to
her bank, and at five minutes to three came puffing in
again.

"You haven't sold that furniture yet, I hope?"

"No," said Romayne, "I was just going to call him up. I
really think I ought to sell it. Two hundred dollars will
make a lot of difference to me just now."

"Well, I'm glad I got here in time. I was telling a friend
of mine who has an aunt up in New England that's just
crazy about antiques and she'll be glad to take 'em for
four hundred and seventy-five for the lot. I put 'em up
good and high, for there was plenty of money behind the
offer, and I knew they trusted my judgment. So now you
can take it or leave it, just as you like. They'll mebbe buy
'em later if you don't want to sell 'em now. And they're
people that might let you buy 'em back sometime if you
ever got prospered so you could."

"Oh! Why! Miss Bronson, you're just wonderful!" said
Romayne, brightening. "I never heard of anything like
that! Yes, I'll sell them at that price, of course. I must.
And you might tell the lady that if ever she wants to sell
them will she please give me the chance to buy them
back? I'll be willing to pay more than she paid me, if I
ever can."

"Sure! I'll fix that up," said Nurse Bronson, getting up
and bustling around to try and hide the satisfaction in her
eyes. "Well, here's the money. Nothing would do but I
should take it along with me, and I was to get a truck and
have 'em sent right up, so if you'll excuse me again I'll go
out and call a man I saw at the corner with a truck."

Romayne cried herself to sleep that night. She felt as if the last tie that bound her to father and mother and the dear old days was gone forever from her. She was very thankful, however, for the extra money, and the worried pucker between her eyes was not nearly so deep as it had been.

But the days went by and no job came to Romayne.

The old house was cleaned and vacated, and Romayne never walked that way any more when she went out on her fruitless trips to find something to do.

She wrote pathetic little advertisements and put them in the paper and was aghast at the price they cost. She began to wonder how many years one could live on four hundred dollars.

Twice on her journeys she had almost come face to face with Kearney Krupper, and had just succeeded in eluding him each time and slipping home by a circuitous route. Three times he had called at the house during her absence, three days in succession now, and she was afraid to go home every time she went out, and afraid to stay there lest he would come while she was there. She had told Nurse Bronson's sister that she did not wish to see Mr. Krupper, and that good woman had promised not to let him know when she would be at home; but Romayne had not any too much faith in the little woman's powers of evasion when she met the foxy ways of Kearney Krupper. She told her to tell the caller to write, but Kearney Krupper did not write. It was Romayne he wanted, not the answer to a message. It was her money perhaps more than all. For Kearney Krupper had ways of using money to an unlimited extent, and he was never satisfied with what he could lay his hands upon.

One night Romayne turned into Maple Street quite late. She had waited until the employment agency was closed, hoping that thus she might find some one in an emergency who wanted her.

The night was dark and warm, and she felt oppressed with the heat and murkiness of the atmosphere. Then suddenly, just ahead of her, she saw the man she disliked, swinging along on his rubber-heeled shoes and making scarcely any sound at all as he walked.

Her heart beat so wildly that she could hardly breathe and she almost reeled as she turned and slipped back into

the avenue, sick with the trifling adventure. It really was
ridiculous, she told herself afterwards, that just any man
should upset her so.

She walked down the lighted avenue for several blocks
before she stopped trembling and could control herself to
turn back, and when she got within a block of the house again
she turned into the dark little alley at the back and crept
around to the back gate. She had to climb the gate, for it
was locked, and there was only an ash-box to step upon,
but she made it, though she tore her dress and scratched
her arm, and when she finally made them hear her knock-
ing at the back door, they told her Kearney Krupper had
left a note for her.

There was no address and no signature.

"If you will call at my office in the Earnheim Building,
number 1166, at five o'clock to-morrow afternoon, I will
give you your brother's address and you can communicate
with him yourself. It is not safe for him if I send it through
the mail."

The Earnheim Building. That was away down town.
And that number would be on the eleventh floor! Five
o'clock! The building would be practically empty by that
time, and the elevators would have stopped running! To
meet Kearney Krupper in a place like that! Could she?
Dared she go alone? And yet, dared she not go, for
Lawrence's sake?

All that long night she lay tossing and troubling, and
when morning dawned she was no nearer a decision than
when she first read the note.

She could not eat anything, but drank a few swallows of
coffee.

She answered some advertisements in the daily paper,
went the rounds of the different agencies where she had
her name registered and had paid a fee, and about one
o'clock walked listlessly into a small park and dropped
down upon a seat, too tired and frightened to care how
she looked or who saw her. Very few of her friends were
in the city at this season anyway. She wished she dared
stretch out on the bench and go to sleep, but of course
that was impossible in a public park, secluded as the seat
she had chosen was, so she settled down with her arm
over the back and rested her head on her arm and closed
her eyes.

She was trying to concentrate her thoughts on the problem of the afternoon when a light hand touched her on the cheek.

She started up, frightened at once, thinking first in alarm of Kearney Krupper and ready to resent the familiarity; but there stood Frances Judson!

"Hullo!" laughed the other girl. "Ain't it queer I should find you here just when I was thinking about you. Say, your pa died, didn't he? So did mine! He had the delirium tremens. He never did stop drinking after that day. He just went from one fit to another and we hadta have him took to the hospital. Wilanna was awful sick when they took him and Ma couldn't leave her, but Wilanna got real better again. The doctor says she may walk. And now that there's no fear of her gettin' hit every little while, she's real happy and bright. She talks a lot about you. Why'n't you come around again? I s'pose you ben busy. I heard you'd moved? What's yer *add*ress? I'll come round and see ya sometime. I ben over to that agency acrost the park huntin' a new job. They don't charge no registry fees, and you don't haveta pay n'less they get you a place. I'm tryin' ta get inta the movies. They pay awful good, and I needta earn a lot, goodness knows, with Wilanna in bed yet, and Ma takin' in washin'. But Ma is awful set I should get a job tending children. I don't like it myself. Say, you had any word from——" and she lowered her voice to a sepulchral whisper, "Larry?" She seemed fairly to hiss the word out. "*I* did! I had two letters a'ready. One he told me he was lighting out and the other he asked me to do something for him. Well, I done it. He was a real good friend of mine and I didn't mind going out of my way to please him."

"I'm sorry that my brother is troubling you," said Romayne, a scarlet spot coming in either cheek. "He seems to be"—she searched about for a word—"all wrong somehow!" she ended desperately. The tears were in her eyes and she knew it, yet she had no power to stop their coming. How long was this girl going to torture her? And what should she say to her?

"Aw say now, don't take it ta heart so! He'll come out all right. Most men is that way, ain't they? I wonder sometimes why we like 'em so much, but we do. Say, I guess you didn't know Larry stayed at our house fer two days after he lit out on 'em, did you? He said he didn't want you to know he was in the city 'cause you would worry so. But I told him you wouldn't mind if you knew he was there 'cause we was friends, and you'd know he was safe."

Romayne turned a startled look on the other girl. Could it be true that Larry had fallen so low as to find refuge in a home like that? And they in trouble, too, poor things! She was aghast! And right there she told herself distinctly that Lawrence Ransom was a *sinner!* She suddenly realized that all along she had been trying to think that Lawrence had only been caught in a trap made by somebody else; that his own natural likes and instincts were for fine, high-minded things, and that he had descended to bad company only because he had been deceived and drawn into it little by little. But now, as she looked at the coarse little painted face beside her and realized that her brother had sought the company of such a girl, even in an extremity, the delusions seemed to fall away and she saw her brother as he really was. His life seemed to be built up of deceit and falsehood. And why should she, out of her sorrow and loneliness, make herself penniless to supply his needs, when he would have been in a good position to-day if he had done right?

Then it flashed across her that the real reason why she had been worried about money had been that she wanted to help Lawrence if he were really in straits. And now all at once she knew she must not. She knew that the only salvation for him was to come to want and to learn that he could not lean upon others. Oh, she had wanted to love and trust this brother whom she had adored from childhood, but he would not let her. Even now if he were sick and helpless she would give her life to save him, but it was not right to help him on in crime. He was being spoiled and she had helped to spoil him, too, she saw it now, by being so blind and always running to wait upon him and give him all she had.

These thoughts absorbed her so that she scarcely gave heed to Frances as she chattered on, till finally the younger girl suddenly arose.

"I must go," she said. "I promised Wilanna I'd get her one of the school-books off'n one o' the girls, and I must hurry or I'll be late to my appointment at the ten-cent

store. I guess I'll get the job if they pay enough. They told
me over to the agency it was real good pay and they
thought I'd suit. I got references off'n Rev. Stephens. He
give me an awful nice letter. You know he baptized
Wilanna when she was a baby and he ain't never forgot
us. Well, good-bye. Why'n't you come in and see us? Ma'd
love it. She likes your brother awful well, he's always so
p'lite to her, not like the other fellas, and she said she'd
like real well to know you better. Willanna'd just be
tickled to death to see you."

"Thank you," said Romayne, trying to smile. "I'll try
to, sometime. Good-bye."

She sat there half stunned for a few minutes, wondering
what she was going to do about it all, and whether she
really was going to meet Kearney Krupper and get that
address or not. There was a kind of sick apathy about her
that made her wish she could just lie down and give it all
up.

Her sad eyes wandered across the way unseeingly, till
suddenly she began to realize that she was reading the
words of a sign in great letters between the trees.

"QUALITY EMPLOYMENT AGENCY."

The words of Frances about an agency came back to
her and she wondered if it would be worth her while to go
over there and put down her name. She must get something, and even a job in a ten-cent store would be better
than nothing.

Listlessly she arose and made her way to the opposite
street, studying the front of the building. It seemed to be a
decent enough place, although it was a street that she
scarcely ever used. Frances had said you did not have to
pay anything unless you got a job, so why not try? There
were white starched curtains at the windows and the steps
were clean. She went in.

The trim, gray-haired woman at the desk looked her
over carefully. "Have you had experience?"

Romayne shook her head sadly.

"No, but I've got to get it sometime, I guess," she smiled
wistfully.

"H'm! Got any references I could get right away?"

"Doctor Stephens, the minister at the Presbyterian Church on Highland Avenue."

"That's all right."

The woman filliped the leaves of the telephone book over and called a number.

"I've got one place," she said speculatively, still taking an evident inventory of Romayne. "At least I guess it's still to be had. I just told 'em I didn't have anybody, but if this reference is all right you might suit. They want somebody terribly. It's a social secretary. Do you write a good hand? How soon could you be ready?"

Then the telephone answered and the woman gave her attention to that, while Romayne cast about in her mind what she should say. She had not come so near as this to a job at all, and "social secretary" sounded rather nice, although it was probably entirely above her abilities. What would she have to do?

Then she heard Doctor Stephens' pleasant voice.

"Oh, yes, I know Miss Ransom. She's a charming girl, belongs to a fine old Virginia family. A girl of great ability and good sense, I should say. Oh, certainly I could recommend her fully to do anything that she was willing to undertake. She is quite an unusual girl. I should say that any one who had her for a helper would be fortunate."

Romayne's face flushed with relief and pride. Even before this strange elderly woman it was good to have some one saying things like that about her.

"Well," said the woman, looking up to see if she had heard, "that sounds pretty good. You're lucky he was there, because I simply couldn't have sent you to this place without a recommend. They're very particular people. I've supplied them with cooks and governesses before sometimes, and they pay well and treat you well. Now, I'll have to call up and see if they've got anybody. They've been phoning everywhere for somebody. But you'll have to be ready to go right away. Hello! Hello! Yes, this is Quality Agency! Is this Miss Whitman? Well, have you got anybody yet? No? Well, I've found a girl. She has great references! What's that? Oh, how soon? Wait, I'll see An hour and a half! That's short notice."

The woman looked up.

"You'd have to go right away. You wouldn't have more than an hour and a half. Can you make it? They're leaving at five o'clock sharp, and they'll come right here for you. It's an out-of-town job, you know."

"But—who *are* they?" asked Romayne, her startled eyes full of anxiety.

"Oh, they're nice people," said the woman impatiently. "I don't have any others. The name is Whitman, and they have a lot of money and do things in style. You'll be well treated. It's good pay." And she named a sum that fairly took the worried girl's breath away.

"I'll go," said Romayne, catching her breath.

"Yes, Miss Whitman, she'll be ready. All right! I'll have her here at five o'clock sharp!" and the woman hung up the receiver.

"Well, you'd better step lively," said the woman. "Have you far to go? Here, sign your name and address before you leave. No, you needn't pay till you get back. I don't take money till I'm sure my people get together all right. Now, hurry! They can't wait if you're late! So it's up to you."

A moment more and Romayne was flying down the street toward the elevated station, trying to remember as she went whether there were enough things in her suitcase that she had packed for that house party to last her till she could get her trunk.

She did not see a high-power racing car that passed her as she was mounting the steps, nor notice that Kearney Krupper was driving it, and that he had marked the door she came from as she left the agency. She was intent only on getting the next east-bound elevated train and reaching Maple Street in the shortest possible time.

CHAPTER XXI

As THE elevated flew along Romayne began to count up the things she must remember to look after before she came back. She counted them out on her fingers. She must tell the people in the house and ask them to send word to Nurse

Bronson and Chris that she had a job and would write as soon as possible.

She must write a check to pay for her room, and another to pay her wash-woman, who would come with some clothes that day.

She must gather up the things on her bureau and in the drawers and closet and sweep them somehow into her trunk so that no one else would have much trouble in case she had to send for her trunk.

Her suit-case was just as it was when she came home from that house party. Each day she had thought she ought to take the things out and hang them up lest they be crushed beyond repair, but each day she had put it off, dreading to see the things that had been prepared with so much joy before her crushing sorrow came. But now it would be all right. She would just stuff one or two plain things in her hand-bag to supplement them for everyday work, and then she would surely be prepared for all emergencies. At least she would not be looked down upon for her wardrobe, and it was just as well to make a good impression even if she did not like the place well enough to remain. Anyhow it was all she could do at such short notice.

Then she would have to change her dress and fix her hair. It would never do to present herself as social secretary in a faded gingham. She could wear the little spring suit that had gone so blithely to the house party. She had not had it on since that day. She hoped it wasn't too rumpled, but then it had hung in the closet, and the wrinkles might have got out. Anyhow, it would have to do.

As she reached her station she glanced at her watch and found that twenty minutes of her precious hour and a half was gone. Forty minutes was all she really had, allowing for her return, and that would be a half-hour by the time she got to the house and told the people.

They helped her, those two good women with whom she was living. They sent the children out in the back yard to play and folded her garments for packing, they cleared out bureau drawers, using rare good sense in handing her little things they thought she ought to have with her.

They drew water for her bath and pressed out her suit, even rubbing out a spot they found on the front of the blouse. They wrote down her directions, and pinned her checks to them. They helped her fasten her collar. They telephoned for a taxi. They stuffed the last handkerchief from the wash in her hand-bag, locked her trunk, put the key in her purse, made a sandwich and cut it in tiny uncrummy mouthfuls and put it in a candy bag in the hand-bag for her to eat if she got hungry on the way, and they kissed her good-bye and stood on the step to wave her out of sight, without ever questioning her decision in the matter of going.

Romayne sat back in the taxi and tried to relax. She felt as if she had been catapulted through the universe at a terrible tension and she would never, never get her breath again. The top of her head was throbbing and her cheeks were blazing, but she was here, clothed in her pretty suit, her hair combed, her bag presumably packed with the necessary things and her suit-case at her feet just as it had been packed weeks ago. She almost laughed when she thought of it, a sick little hysterical laugh, all alone there in the taxi, rushing toward the agency, to think how different it all was from the time that the suit-case was prepared. Then she had been going off for a gay good time. Now she was going forth to meet utter strangers and go with them to an unknown destination, without ever having enquired anything about that agency or the people with whom she was going. Nurse Bronson would be horrified. She must write her at once as soon as she got somewhere and let her know it was all right.

But how did she know it was all right? She had only the word of the agency woman, and how did she know who she was? She had only the word of little painted Frances.

Well, she was a working woman now and working people had to take chances. She must take hers with the rest. She could not be guarded any more as her father and mother had guarded her. There was no one to guard her. Only Chris!

And then she giggled again, that sad little hysterical giggle that betokened she was tired to the soul and *needed* to be taken care of, worse than ever in her life before.

As the taxi lurched along she watched the metre and her watch alternately. There were only ten minutes left of the precious time, and suppose, after all, she should fail! Well, she had done her best. There was nothing she could have come without.

How thirsty she was, and how hot! She would give anything for a drink of water. The traffic was congested as they marked time at the main thoroughfare. Suppose she should not reach there in time! The thought recurred like a chorus at each crossing, till at last they reached the park and flew around the circle of it, bringing up before the door three minutes after a great high-power limousine drew up, just two minutes to five!

A young woman in a sport suit of the latest model, with a little close hat and bobbed hair, was standing in the open doorway of the agency with the proprietor, alternately glancing at her wrist-watch of platinum and diamonds, and looking up the street toward the elevated station.

"We can't wait a minute longer," the girl was saying. "My brother is very particular about keeping his appointments, and with traffic at this hour we couldn't possibly make it a minute later. She'll have to come on the train, I suppose, and that is so unsatisfactory. Besides, she might not come! They're always afraid of a strange place. I thought she *promised* to be here."

"She said she would. I think she meant it. There's another L train coming now from her direction."

"Well, if she doesn't come on that we'll have to go," sighed Miss Whitman with an impatient frown. "It's just two minutes of five. How tiresome! And I was so pleased to have accomplished what Mamma had tried and failed! Well, they all told me she wouldn't go on such short notice. I wish you had offered her more money."

But the gray-haired proprietor was watching the slim girl in the pretty suit who was paying the taxi driver. Was *that*——? It could not be! But she held herself the same way.

Miss Whitman was annoyed that the proprietor's attention should be turned away for a moment from the problem in hand. This woman was serving *her* and ought not to think of other customers now. She turned to see who had presumed to intrude at this inopportune moment, and took in the graceful girl from the crown of her becoming little hat to the tip of her pretty patent leather slippers, shiny suit-case, irreproachable hand-bag, wrist ruffled gloves and all. There really was no fault to be found with her, and she walked gracefully and carried herself with poise. Sophisticated as Miss Whitman was, she could not help giving a glance of approbation as she would have done to any stylish gown, or pretty face, that conformed to the passing mode. Then she turned back with a frown to Madame.

"There she is now," said Madame with relief in her voice.

She was thinking of the goodly fee the Whitmans always paid without a murmur when they were satisfied.

"What!" The Whitman girl looked up and down the street. "I don't see any one coming. No one came down the stairs after the train stopped."

"No, but *here*," sighed the woman as Romayne turned from the driver and preceded him, as he carried her suit-case up the steps. It was evident from his deference that he took her for a client of the place and not an applicant.

"*This!*" murmured the Whitman girl in amazement. "You don't mean—— How did you ever do it?"

And then Romayne lifted wistful blue eyes to her face in a brief glance, and addressed the elder woman.

"Am I in time? It's been rather a rush, and we got in traffic over on the Avenue."

"Just on time to the minute!" answered the proprietor with satisfaction. "Miss Whitman, this is Miss Ransom. I hope the arrangement will prove satisfactory."

Romayne gave the other girl a quick, shy glance of inspection.

"We haven't had much chance to think about it, have we?" she smiled naïvely. "I hope it's all right. I don't know that I understand exactly what my duties will be, but I'll do my best."

"I guess you'll do," said the other girl almost rudely after a second longer of prolonged inspection, her chin just the least bit haughty. This girl was just a shade too familiar. She must be put in her place. "You're here, that's the main thing. I suppose you can write a good clear hand, can't you?"

"Oh, yes," smiled Romayne with relief.

"Then come on! Here, I'll pay your fee. Don't bother, I've to settle my own account. Now, Madame, you'll be looking up that cook before we come home. You know, Mother said she didn't want the other one, she's too impudent. If you can just get Sarah everything will be all right. Now, Miss Ransom, if you'll just go right out to the car. James, take this baggage!"

They put Romayne in the front seat with the chauffeur. There was another girl and a young man in the back of the tonneau. Romayne was not introduced to them. It appeared she would have no part in the group at all. She was merely an outsider. It was her first experience in being among the working class. It rather amused her. She was glad on the whole that she had nothing to do, she was so mortally tired. Now at last she could relax a little and get rid of that terrible beating and trembling all over her weary body as if she had been clubbed. She was here, and she had a job. She might as well enjoy herself. She was going to have a ride at least, and she did not have to walk anywhere on her tired feet! Just be thankful, and wait for what came next.

Then they rounded the Park, and swung into the broad Parkway with the fountain purling in white feathered beauty ahead, and tall buildings looming at right and left as if reluctant to have the city give way to the beauties of Nature. And there, right before her on the left, loomed the Earnheim Building, with great letters on the side accusing her, as she was whirled away into a world of which she knew nothing.

And then, and not till then, did Romayne remember her appointment with Kearney Krupper.

She grasped the side of the car, caught her breath, and all but exclaimed, till she realized that nobody was paying the slightest attention to her, and that this was no time to mention forgotten dates. She must bear the consequences unless she wished to lose this obviously good job, the chance of a lifetime probably.

A second only it seemed, and the Earnheim Building was far in the distance behind her and a belated clock somewhere was tolling out five clear strokes, as if to mock her. She had left her brother and gone to seek her fortune! She had done just what he had done, and was living for herself and forgetting him!

Those were the first thoughts that the enemy found to fling at her weary young soul. And for a few dreadful minutes her conscience ran frantically around in her tired little being and kicked up a terrible time.

Then suddenly they rode smoothly out of the rush and traffic of the Parkway into the great cool Park itself, where rocks loomed and towered, covered with dripping moss and vines, and a deep stream flowed silently and unhurried, with trees arched overhead. It was almost twilight there, with a fresh green smell after the dust of the city.

Down upon her dropped a calm. Reason took the helm. She realized that she had not decided whether she was going to meet Krupper or not, and that it had been taken entirely out of her hands and made impossible for her to do. She could not very well make these people turn back to rectify something she had forgotten, when she knew they were in a hurry.

As she grew calmer she began to thank God in her heart that she had been saved from going to the eleventh floor in a lonely office to meet Kearney Krupper, alone. It seemed, at this perspective, quite an impossible thing to have done, and for a mile or two she sat and planned how she would write him a note and say that she was suddenly called out of town, making it impossible to keep the appointment, and that he might with perfect safety write the address in a sealed envelope and mail or leave it at Maple Street and she would get it on her return. She wondered why she had not thought of that before. But after a few more miles of beautiful roads even that dropped away and she was just thankful to be here. Whatever was at the end of the journey, this part of it was good, and she was glad for it.

They stopped a little after six at a suburban town and picked up Miss Whitman's brother, whom they addressed as Jack, and proceeded on their way out smooth highways into the country.

Romayne had had little opportunity for automobiling and she was enjoying every moment of the way. The sun went down like a fire opal behind the hills, leaving little flecks of coral and gold on the clear sea-blue and amber of the sky, and then darkness fell softly like a perfumed curtain about them and a single star looked out like an eye that watched and saw them all.

She did not care that they did not introduce her, that she was apart from their fun and noisy laughter in the back seat. She was glad, glad that she might just sit still and fly along this lovely road. It was good to feel the night about her, and not have any obligation to talk to any one. Her troubles and her burdens fell away like a garment, and left her soul there to revel in the silence all around, in the little sweet sounds of crickets, rusty-throated, along the edges of the road, the tree toads chirruping down in the valley, the distant lowing of a cow, a long sweet whistle from a boy coming home from his work, gay strains from a victrola in a little house up on the hillside as they passed, the laughter of children at bedtime, male voices droning a quartette on a dusky front porch at some friendly gathering. They were all like beautiful fragments of a world that was not hers any more, but which rested her just to know it was there again as it used to be before she had suffered so. She wondered why it was that God wanted her to stay here all alone this way and keep on living with this behind her, and nothing ahead but pain.

And then she remembered that that sweet Aunt Patty had said that the God who could forgive would also comfort and go with her and guide her, and she put up a little inaudible prayer that she might be remembered.

She began to feel the pangs of hunger by and by when the shadows at the side of the road grew velvet black and deep, and she wondered if she dared try a bite of that delectable sandwich that Grandma Bronson had put in her bag, but decided against it on account of the hawk-eyed James, who drove like an automaton, and who all too evidently missed nothing that went on. She wished to fade out of the picture as much as possible and not draw attention to herself; so she sat motionless and watched the wonderful night go by and forgot to be hungry.

They got out a flask in the back of the car and grew merry. With sudden friendly impulse they passed it to her and all unthinking, she turned to accept, for she was very thirsty, but she caught the fumes of liquor and drew back with almost a gasp. She had thought in her simpleness that it might be lemonade.

She managed to cover her awkwardness with a gentle "Thank you. No!" and turned back to her scenery again, thirstier than ever, and the Whitman girl drew back with a cold: "Oh, don't you care for it?" and a shrug of her shoulder. But long after the party in the back seat had forgotten the incident Romayne sat, with white face coming out of the darkness still and sad, and thought about it.

It was as if she had suddenly found her deadliest enemy riding in the seat beside her. The smell of that liquor carried her straight down into the cellar of her home, to the secret room, where she had gone with the officer that early morning, and seen the rows of bottles, and the machinery for rebottling, and smelled the whiffs of rank alcohol and read the labels and knew her shame to be real. Never again would she smell that odor of fermentation without being carried back to that cellar and the day of her first great sorrow. For now she could look back on her mother's death as a glad thing—rather than with sadness. She was glad that her mother had not lived to suffer all that she was suffering.

"And yet," she thought to herself as they glided into a

deep dark woods with the moon glinting palely out between branches overhead, "and yet, if Mother had lived, maybe it never would have happened. Mother was a sort of ballast for father—why wasn't *I?* Oh, if I had only understood the need! Oh, if I had been taught the evil that was possible all about for anybody to fall into!"

About midnight they stopped at an inn for supper. There was dancing and young Whitman asked Romayne if she would like to dance, but she thanked him and declined. She felt as if she were in a world that she could never be a part of, and she was beginning to be so weary and sleepy that she really did not care whether they liked it or not.

They hurried away after a little, and, revived by food and a cup of coffee, she was able to enjoy the ride once more.

Three hours later they turned into a rough mountain road, and for several miles had heavy going, among trees so tall that the sky seemed as far above as the tallest city buildings, and into a wood so dense that it seemed impenetrable. Here and there, like lovely wraiths, thin, white-footed birches stalked, picked out against the dark plumes of the pines; and spicy odors filled the air. The moon was only visible in glimpses now and then, and the way at the side looked like some great primeval forest. Romayne could hardly think that they were only a few hours away from the city.

Then suddenly they came out into a partial clearing and a great house loomed, built of logs in their bark, and rough stone, with verandas ranging all around like balconies, some of them lying against the hillside, and others looking down upon a sheer precipice, with a waterfall below. One could hear the distant sound of the water falling and echoing away into the aisles of the forest as the motor stopped.

A wide oak door was flung open and lights sprang out along the rustic balconies, where luxurious woven seats of grass and hammocks piled high with cushions invited one to rest.

Beyond the door she could see a fireplace almost big enough to walk into, with logs burning, for the night had grown cool, and Romayne was shivering in her coat that she had thought almost too heavy to bring with her at that time of the year.

Rustic balconies ran around the room above, and rooms opened in charming vistas beyond. Rich rugs and great skins of beasts were spread about the floor, and ancient carved oak chests and chairs that might have graced a throne room somewhere in strange lands were everywhere. Curious treasures from the Orient gleamed here and there like touches of great jewels on a lady's gown. It was a house that common mortals may dream about sometimes, or see in pictures in an architectural magazine occasionally, but seldom get an acquaintance with.

And into this mansion in the forest Romayne was led, and felt she had entered an enchanted palace. Up the wide oak stairs they took her and gave her a great room, all her own, with a white tiled bath that might have belonged to an old Roman house, and towels of such thickness and size, embroidered with W's, that she had to stop and examine them to see if they were just towels.

The Whitman girl unbent and visited her for a few brief moments, clad in a gauzy nightrobe of cobwebby embroidery with a wisp of rosy gossamer thrown over it, looking very young and almost sweet with her golden bobbed head and big blue eyes.

She explained to Romayne that the work was not hard— that her mother wanted some one to write a lot of notes, and keep up with the mail during her absence, and for the rest she would be needed to fill in when there were not enough girls at a picnic or party.

"There are more of us coming in a few days, of course," she ended, "and you're so good-looking I'm sure you can help out very well. Who's to know you are not one of my college friends? I'm quite delighted you're so sophisticated. I think we shall get along very well."

There was a bit of condescension in the tone, but Romayne told herself she must not mind that.

"Now sleep as late as you want to in the morning," said the girl on leaving her. "You must be tired after your hurry. Mother may not be here for two weeks or more, though she may drop in any time after to-morrow. There's no telling what she will do next. But until she comes your duties won't be very strenuous. Good night!"

Romayne felt better after she had gone. It was not going to be so bad, if they were all as nice as the girl. And the place certainly was wonderful. She hurried into the luxurious bed as fast as she could and was soon drifting off to sleep.

Did she or did she not hear some one calling across the hall—or was it all a dream——

"Say, Jack, when's Kearney coming?"

Kearney! Kearney? Who was that? Was she dreaming? In the morning she did not remember it at all.

CHAPTER XXII

"WELL, she's gone!" said Chris Hollister, bursting in on the Chief late that evening.

"Gone?"

"Yes, gone! Just like that!" Chris's face was blank with worry.

"Where?"

"That's the worst of it. I don't know. Nobody knows."

"But— what *do* you know?"

"Well, not much. Nurse Bronson wasn't at home, you know, and those two old noodles, not a brain between 'em, never asked her. That is, they say she got a job, but they don't know where. She didn't know herself. She was just going blind."

"But—how did she get it? Didn't they ask that?"

"Why, there seems to have been some kind of an agent, as near as I can make out and the people who wanted her were going out of town at once, but she wasn't told where. She didn't even leave the name of the folks. Said she would write and send for her trunk."

"Oh, she didn't take a trunk," said Evan with a relieved look. "Then she can't be going for long or else she'll send for it."

"Perhaps," said Chris gloomily. "Thing I can't figure out is why they didn't find out where she was to meet 'em. You can't tell what these rich guys are."

"You think it may be some of her former friends? Some of the gang?"

"Might. Or—Kearney Krupper. He's running loose, you know. He's a *fox!*"

Evan Sherwood sprang to his telephone.

"Get me the classified book and find the list of agencies," he said. Chris was alert at once.

"Why didn't I think of that? Still, she mighta met some one she knew and got the job. The old ladies did say she came back on the elevated and ran all the way from the second corner."

"That's something," said Sherwood. "Begin at the nearest."

But most of the agencies were closed at that hour and Evan Sherwood passed a sleepless night worrying about the girl who was "nothing more to him than the place in an African mission where his chance collection envelope went."

In the early morning he and Chris were at it again, and worked all day in relays in between the election business, which was getting more and more strenuous every day. For Sherwood had to write an editorial for the special paper they were publishing in the interest of a clean city, and Chris had to round up reports from the slum district, and there really were only so many hours in a day.

It was almost by chance and in desperation that at last they tried the Quality Employment Agency and were answered by the cool, crisp voice of Madame.

"Can you tell me if a young woman by the name of Romayne Ransom has registered at your office for a situation of any kind?"

Evan Sherwood had his question down to bare facts by this time.

There was a moment's consideration.

"Who is this?" asked Madame coldly.

"This is a friend of Miss Ransom's, who is anxious to locate her. She went away in a great hurry yesterday without leaving her address and her friends are worried lest something has happened to her."

Another pause.

"You couldn't give me your name?"

"Why, yes——" said Sherwood. It was the first time he had met with this request in his enquiries. "My name's Sherwood. Of the Citizens' League. Perhaps you've heard of me."

"Not Mr. Evan Sherwood," said Madame with a flutter in her voice. "Of course I have, Mr. Sherwood. Say, there's nothing wrong with that girl, is there? She had a reference from Doctor Stephens, and I've sent her to one of my very best customers. She seemed all right, but sometimes even a good reference isn't well founded. I always try to get good people. That's why I chose the name Quality for my agency."

"Nothing wrong at all with the girl," said Evan Sherwood heartily, "only that she's too fine for any job I know. We were just worried at her disappearance. You know there are foxes around looking for prey all the time, and she is somewhat alone in the world. Who did you say she was with? Whitman? Not the Gregory Whitmans? H'm! And she's gone away from the city. You don't know where? Oh, well, doubtless she will write soon. We just wanted to be sure she was with all right people. Thank you very much——"

He turned to Chris with an anxious face.

"Those Whitmans are all in the ring, aren't they? You don't suppose the gang has done it for some reason? You don't suppose they think they can find out something from her? Or get at those papers her brother has?"

"It might be, but they wouldn't have known to go after her through an agent, would they?"

"That's so, too. And yet——"

"Yes," said Chris. "And there's Kearney. But he's still in the city, or was to-night."

"Kearney won't leave now till after election. He has too much dirty work to do for his father, but watch him when it's over! Chris, have your detective find out where the summer homes of the Whitmans are, and, if possible, which they have gone to. The family may be scattered. They've likely run to cover. Find out where they *all* are. Then we shall have something to work from. We can't leave that kid out among the wolves!"

"I should say not!"

Chris hurried away, glad that something definite was going to be done. Now, if Romayne had only been willing to have married him! It was going to be tremendously hard work to take care of her this way. All that about God wanting her to be on her own sounded well enough, but when it came right down to brass tacks Chris meant to be on the job himself, unless he could go one better and get the Chief to do it.

Evan Sherwood went to his couch that night with satisfaction, feeling that he had done well to find out the starting of the girl, and the name of the people with whom she had gone. But he would not have slept so well if he had known that Kearney Krupper was several hours ahead of him in acquiring that knowledge, and that he was in a position to know where the Whitmans had gone without the trouble of resorting to a detective.

Now, Evan Sherwood believed in a God who guards and guides his own, just as his Aunt Patricia had written to Romayne, and he knew that his duty just now lay here in the city, at least until after that election. But he was not taking any chances so far as his own responsibility for Romayne was concerned. He knew that there were personal dangers for him in the election, and that he might be unable to do anything for her, even if she needed it, after election, because he might not be alive; so while he stayed at his post and worked with all his might, he was ferreting out information and writing down several directions for Chris to follow if anything happened to him. That African mission of his was surely becoming personal.

He called up Aunt Patty one evening on long distance in a chance moment of leisure in the hope that Aunt Martha was better and she might return and somehow get near to Romayne for him. But Aunt Patty talked in a whisper and said that Aunt Martha was lying at death's door, and might go at any moment, or she might linger yet for weeks. She had not had a moment to write as the nurse had been taken sick and had to leave. They had had difficulty in getting another, and Aunt Martha would not let her out of her sight.

So Evan turned away from the telephone realizing that he must not burden Aunt Patty with Romayne, and the days grew fuller and fuller of work, and nearer and nearer to election. The enemy was hot and heavy on the trail, and the number of abominable lies they had been able to rake out of the pit and bring to the light of day, and actually send masquerading in a cloak of righteousness, would be enough to amaze the angels. Evan Sherwood, sometimes, in his weariness, buried his face in his arms on his desk and wished he had never touched the dirty old wicked city. And then he would get up and go at it again.

He grew white and spent, and his friends urged him to rest. They sought to lure him to their homes to dinner and a ride in the cool evening. But he would not be lured. And nightly he called up Nurse Bronson, where she was on a case at the hospital, to ask if she had heard anything from Romayne. It was beginning to be an obsession with him, what had become of Romayne?

For strange to say, the detective had not been able to

discover where the Whitman family were gone. They were booked to sail for Europe, but there was no Ransom among their party. Some of them were announced in the society column as being in Bar Harbor, but an investigation through the proper authorities revealed no social secretary there except a Miss Jones, who had been with them for years, and was old with gray bobbed hair.

A son who had recently graduated from college through polo and football, with a smattering of engineering on the side, was supposed to be in the White Mountains, but had not as yet been located. It was rumored that a daughter was visiting college friends in the West, but that had not been verified nor the college friend located.

There were said to be a number of landholdings, with lodgings more or less spacious, in various parts of the United States where these favored people might flit at any moment, but no one seemed to know just where they had flitted this time nor for how long. The detective openly stated that he was up against it.

"It will depend on how the election goes, whether they come back soon or not," said Evan Sherwood with narrowed eyes on space.

The next day he went himself to inverview Madame and get all the facts.

"Why, I've just had a letter from Miss Gloria Whitman, about a cook," said Madame, delighted to have something to contribute to the great idol of the people. "It isn't dated and no address, so I expect she means me to write to the city number, but doesn't that postmark look like our state? I don't believe they're far away, for that postmark is dated yesterday. The rest is blurred."

Evan Sherwood went away with the precious envelope, and in some mysterious way, known only to detectives, they were able with the help of a microscope to discover the lodge in the wilderness whither Romayne had been spirited away so mysteriously. No one knows how the detectives work. It is as mysterious as the way a scientist can concoct a whole whale out of an innocent little tooth dropped eons ago, and develop a theory of evolution. But at least in this case it worked, and a lonely woodsman with a canny eye, travelling on foot—to all appearances—and having lost his way, was able to hover around and be fed, and linger with a sore foot until he had laid eyes on Romayne herself, had watched her playing tennis, on a perfect court in a lovely spot above the waterfall, with Jack Whitman; was even able to carry back with him a picture of her with her lovely hair in a long braid down her back and her slim body leaping for the ball with a graceful curve of her racket.

He carried with him somewhere concealed about his shabby garments a tiny camera of wondrous powers, and two days later Evan Sherwood sat him down alone at his desk and was able to see the great house in the forest, where Romayne was hidden, to watch her, as it were, sitting on the wide balcony framed in its fir trees and mountains, talking to this same Jack Whitman, or walking down a wooded path and looking back smiling, and behind her walked a man whose shoulders looked like Jack Whitman's.

There were a number of these views, all showing Romayne, with different people—some ladies and some more men. Most of them, it is true, showed her demurely keeping to herself. But there were enough with others, and it was this young Whitman that cut the deepest in the question, for Evan Sherwood had met him in the city and knew his face and figure well. He could not be deceived. And Evan Sherwood was not happy.

To all appearances the election was going well, and everything promised a glorious victory for the League, but still he was not happy, and he wished the election was over. He found he did not really care much now how it came out, that is, down in his tired heart he did not care, for he was worked to a thread—he just wished it was over. There was something he wanted to do. He did not know how he was going to work it out yet, because his pride was in the way. But he must do it.

Romayne was beginning to work into the new life beautifully. It was such a relief to be away from the things that had tried her soul, and from all the reminders of her shame and sorrow, that for the first few days she just relaxed and thought of nothing but the beauty of the place.

And because his special girl was not on hand, Jack Whitman did as he always did, took the first pretty girl that was handy. So Romayne was shown about the mountain, and the lake, and taken canoeing and tennising, and driving.

She could not get away from the fact that she was looked upon as a servitor on certain state occasions when guests were by, but for the most part there was an unbending toward her, and they found that she worked in well with the life. In school she had been a champion in tennis more than once, and found that her skill easily returned to her now. In the clear mountain air her color returned to her cheeks, and her eyes grew brighter.

"She's a stunning-looking girl," stated Jack to his sister when they were talking her over. "Where did you pick her up?"

"Now Jack, don't you go to spoiling her or Mamma will have it in for you when she comes. She must have a secretary this winter, and I want the honor of having provided her. It will make my life a lot more pleasant if she's of my picking. And you let this girl alone, and don't turn her head. She'll be falling in love with you next and then good-bye secretary, for Mamma won't stand for any of your nonsense with the servants."

"Might fall in love with worse," stated Jack languidly. "She's a peach, Glory, really she is. It's a shame to make her into a secretary. I'm half a mind to marry her!"

"You try it," flashed his sister, "and see what Papa will say! He doesn't intend you to marry that way. There's enough causes for excuses in the family now without marrying any more."

"There's worse I could hold up to him as an alternative if I wanted to that would make him beg me on his knees to marry her."

"If you're going to talk that way, Jack Whitman, I'll send her flying down the mountain this minute," threatened Gloria, "and I mean it!"

"Go to it if you like! I can follow, can't I? That never did work with me. If you keep this up I will take an interest in her."

Gloria studied him a minute with thoughtful gaze and knew that he was right.

"Oh, of course I know you're only kidding," she said politicly, with a smile. "I was just reminding you, for she is a striking girl and no mistake. I wonder where she got her clothes? She certainly has good taste. I'm going to let her come to the party next Saturday night if Harriet doesn't come, and you may dance with her if you'll promise not to make yourself conspicuous."

"She doesn't dance," said Jack glumly. "I asked her. She said her father and mother didn't approve of it."

"Fancy!" laughed Gloria derisively. "She's about a hundred years behind the times! Or is it more than that? Well, don't worry. I'll make her. I'll tell her it's a part of her duties as social secretary."

"Don't you bully her, Gloria, I won't have it!"

"No, I won't, Jackie," laughed his sister. "Trust me. I can work it."

But Gloria found to her surprise that she could not work it quite so easily. There were some things that Romayne, docile as she was in other ways, simply would not do. Romayne looked at her with her great eyes wide with unshed tears.

"Miss Whitman, I can't do it," she said. "My father has just died and I've been through a great deal of trouble, and even if I knew how or cared to dance I wouldn't feel like doing it. I did not know that a secretary's duties involved such things and if you feel that it does I would rather go back to the city and let you get some one else, for I do not feel I can do it. I would much rather not be downstairs at the party."

Gloria Whitman looked at her curiously, searching for a reason.

"You certainly are a queer girl!" she laughed. "Well, have it your own way."

Yet when Gloria came to think about it she was almost glad that Romayne's decision had been to keep out of the social affairs, for Romayne was too attractive for a mere secretary, and more than once Gloria had caught the glances of the young man who was supposed to be her own special property just then, stealing toward Romayne. Gloria Whitman liked her all the better that she did not try to be a rival.

The clear mountain days passed, and the sweet air and sunshine stole into Romayne's heart, healing the hurt and helping her to lay aside the fear and the burdens she had been bearing so many days.

She began to think about writing to her friends back in the city and letting them know how she fared. Not that she thought it mattered much to anybody except Chris. Poor Chris! She had forgotten him entirely, and he had been so faithful! She must let him know she was safe now and he need not worry over her any more.

There really was only one thing about her new position that troubled her, and that at times was very hard for her to endure. She found that it was almost unbearable to have so much drinking going on about her. It was not only because it was something she had been trained to feel was both common and wrong, but it kept constantly before her mind the shame through which she had been passing. These people were the kind who had helped her father to sin, and dragged her brother into what she could not help feeling was degradation. They drank partly to assert their right to do so, against the law of the land and the protest of a few fanatics—as they called them—who were trying to force everybody to do as they did.

They drank on all occasions. Highballs and cocktails were ever being passed. Flasks were the order of the day upon all rides and picnics. It was everywhere and apparently all their kind used it. They drank when they were hot and when they were cold, when they were gray and when they were sad. Sometimes their high, excited voices and flushed faces made Romayne turn sadly away and feel that she could not possibly spend her days among people who were so utterly different from what she wanted to be.

They laughed at her good-naturedly when she continued to decline it, called her "Miss Volstead," with a covert sneer in the end of the tone, but always pleasantly. It did not matter to them what their social secretary thought, of course. She was just queer, that was all. They let her go her way.

She usually went to her room after dinner, and avoided the evenings of merry-making, but sometimes even at dinner she felt uncomfortable at the intimate edge Jack Whitman gave to the tone of his conversation, and wished she were anywhere else as the tongues were loosed with the frequent glasses, and stories were told that went over the line of decency and good breeding as she had been taught to consider it. Always when this happened she drew aloof from everybody and slipped away as soon as she could.

Aside from these things her life was pleasant.

Mrs. Whitman had not yet appeared on the scene, though it was rumored she was coming the following week.

There was just enough work to keep her pleasantly busy without being strenuous. A large packet of mail to be attended to under the direction of Gloria, several big boxes of envelopes to be addressed and filled with the engraved invitations for certain social functions. Boxes and boxes stood in the little office where she worked.

"Mother wants to get all this out of the way so that your

time will be free in the fall when the rush will begin," explained Gloria. "Of course these won't be sent out until near the time for them. Mother is on a lot of boards and committees of clubs and things, of course, and she couldn't begin to keep up with them unless she got ahead in the summer. These are regular dates for every year, so there's no danger of their changing; the hospital reception, the Science and Art Exhibit, and those series of Friday night dinners and Thursday teas."

So Romayne worked happily away for the first two weeks, with pleasant intervals of walks and tennis and mountain roaming whenever she seemed really to be needed to make up a party, and the days passed so smoothly that sometimes for a little while she forgot the cloud under which she was living, and the anxiety over her only brother. Surely pretty soon she would hear from him. She had left her address for her mail to be forwarded. And why did not that nice Aunt Patty keep her promise about writing?

Then, one morning, it was announced quite casually at the breakfast-table, not at all as if it would interest her, however, that Alida Freeman, Judge Freeman's niece, who had been a close friend of Romayne's for a year or two at school, was to arrive at the mountain that evening.

The color sprang to Romayne's cheeks and a light to her eyes, and for an instant she felt a thrill of delight at the thought of meeting an old friend. Then, suddenly, there dropped down upon her a cloud of anxiety. Did Alida know about her father and brother? And what would Alida think to find her here in her present humble position?

All that day she carried a heavy, anxious heart as she went about her work. She did not tell any one that she knew Alida. She would wait and see.

CHAPTER XXIII

EARLY in the afternoon of the day of the Primary Election the Committee of the League of Taxpayers and Citizens were met in solemn conclave in Evan Sherwood's office.

"That snake Krupper is down in the Third Ward," said one of the members. "I've heard it from two or three sources already. He'll be getting in some of his funny business if we don't forestall him. Chris, you know how to handle him pretty well, why don't you take a couple of men and saunter down that way?"

"Kearney Krupper left a half an hour ago!" announced a member who had just come in. "Somebody brought him a message while I was there, and he looked scared and pulled out in a hurry! Got in that yellow racer of his and hit the trail for somewhere, hard. Going at seventy-five miles an hour, I should say, when he started."

Evan Sherwood and Chris looked at one another significantly and simultaneously.

"Kearney Krupper *left!*" said the Chief in a startled voice. "That means that they are afraid of something coming out. Which way did he go?"

"Out through the Park, I think," answered the newcomer. "Hey, Chief! What are you going to do now? You don't imagine you're going to catch him, do you, with that old Ford of yours? Why, man, he started half an hour or more ago, and he's got the fastest car around here!"

"I'm going to try!" said Evan Sherwood, seizing his hat and striding out the door.

"Oh, I say, Sherwood," shouted the others in chorus, bringing feet down from various resting-places and making for the hall, "don't you know you're a mark for a possible assassin to-day? For pity's sake stay in. Where do you think you're going anyway? The enemy will stop at nothing! We can't elect a dead Mayor! And after all this trouble, too!"

They shouted these things after him as he disappeared down the stairs, not even waiting for the elevator.

But Evan Sherwood and Chris Hollister were out of hearing before they finished, and the thought of the election had faded from their minds. They had more important matters now to look after.

The committee looked uncomfortably at one another, uncertain what they ought to do.

"That's the only trouble with him," stated a thin little nervous man fretfully. "He's always going off on some tangent where you can't follow him. If he would just stick to the matter in hand, and not worry about trifles."

"We can follow him!" said a tall alert man. "We must! It's our business to stop this foolhardiness. He doesn't belong to himself now, he belongs to the people who are voting for him. He's got to stop throwing himself open to attack this way. Johnson, isn't your car down there? We'll at least have to follow him and see that he comes to no harm."

They dashed down to Johnson's car and followed the shabby Ford ahead, just rounding a corner at breakneck speed in the midst of traffic.

"Now, just look at that!" said the tall man, pointing to the car they were pursuing. "That's the way he does! If anybody sees him they'll jack him up for not keeping the traffic laws!"

"This isn't the day to begin to criticize our Chief!" said Johnson grimly, putting his foot on the gas, and shooting around the corner on two wheels. "Our job is to protect him!"

The tall man gripped the side of the car. He had heard how easily a roadster was upset. Cautious, by nature, with an equally cautious wife, he did not drive a car himself.

They rounded another corner and shot into a straight road, Johnson hurling invectives at all the drivers he passed.

"Oh, drive that can off the road! Go out in a field and practice! Do you call that driving?"

The tall man wished he had never suggested following the Chief. A collision seemed imminent, yet, as by a miracle, they went on, threading their perilous way amid the traffic.

They were gaining on the shabby Ford, though it held its own in a rakish, persistent way. Three times Johnson attempted to get ahead that he might slow down and stop it, and three times was prevented by an oncoming car, or a great truck, sometimes two or three.

Then, suddenly, without warning, the Ford slowed down and drew up at the curb in front of a vacant lot. Johnson, coming like lightning behind, had just presence of mind to curve to the left and avoid smashing into it, and then to curve to the right—barely to escape an ice-cream truck that was bearing down upon him from the front. The tall man thought the end had come, but they righted themselves, slowed down and backed, coming to a stop in front of the pursued at last.

"Now, we must make him understand that he's *got* to go back," said Johnson in a low tone, and turned around to face a big fat colored man in overalls getting out of the shabby Ford with rheumatic deliberation, and leaning down to examine one of his wheels.

They went back to the office at graver speed, marvelling at their own stupidity, and when they reached the parking place they had left but a few moments before, there stood Sherwood's shabby Ford in its usual spot. But when they went into the the office Sherwood and Chris had not come back.

"Now, where the dickens have they gone? *How* have they gone?" inquired Johnson as he mopped his anxious brow.

"What in the world did he want to follow Kearney Krupper for? Does he know something that he is not telling us?" asked the suspicious member of the committee. "I can't understand why information is being withheld from us—if there is genuine information. I must confess I never liked these close-mouthed people."

"Well, aren't we going to do anything about it? I think we ought to do something more about it," said a little thin member anxiously. "We certainly can't run any more risks with our nominee."

"I think we ought to stay right where we are and run this election the best we know how. That's our job and that's what our Chief expected of us when he left. Sherwood's perfectly able to take care of himself and so is Chris; and besides, Chris is with him, and that's a whole battalion when it comes to danger." This from a man with a fine head and a strong jaw. "Harkinson, how about going down to that Third Ward? Will you and Spreicher go and see what's to be done? Mason, suppose you and I look in on the Sixth, and all of you phone over here to Johnson every little while with any information you have. Jones, and Smythe, you take the Fourth, and the rest of you circulate around, and keep the office informed. There may be a few more Kruppers let loose if we keep our eyes open."

"Well, I don't like the look of things at all," said the suspicious one, as he prepared to obey orders, and went grumbling down the street to the Fourth. Smythe always suspected everything he could, and when there was nothing else to suspect he suspected himself. He was not quite sure at that moment whether he ought to have joined that League or, not, with such an erratic chief.

*   *   *   *   *   *

The day had opened unpleasantly for Romayne.

She had come down to breakfast, as usual, a trifle early, and stepped out on the balcony for a breath of the crisp autumn morning before going around to the end balcony, where breakfast was usually served. At the farther end of the balcony she could see Mrs. Whitman, who had arrived unexpectedly just after dinner the night before and had taken very little notice of her except to give her a sheaf of letters which she wanted answered that night. Romayne had gone at the work at once and had not seen her again until now. Neither had she yet met Alida Freeman. She knew by the sounds that came up from the great living-room that Alida had arrived somewhere near midnight and was received with noisy welcome.

Romayne was wondering as she stood watching the sunlight sifting through the feathery pines, a never-ending source of delight to her, whether this fair view from the balcony would seem as pleasant to her if she did not like her employer as it had during the weeks that were passed. While she stood so, with the sunlight glinting her hair, Jack Whitman stepped out and stood beside her talking for a moment in his usual friendly way. Then came Mrs. Whitman's voice, halfway down the balcony, calling:

"Jack, dear, will you run in and get me my blue scarf, lying on my bed?"

Jack went at once and Romayne, turning, saw that Mrs. Whitman was approaching slowly with Alida by her side, and that she was observing her secretary with a cold stare as if she had just become conscious of her.

But Romayne was thinking then of Alida, and in the most natural way in the world she went forward to greet her.

"Alida!" she said with a glad little smile. "It is nice to see some one I know."

But Alida had a strange look of embarrassment on her pretty face and did not offer to take the hand that Romayne put out spontaneously.

"Why, Romayne! *You* here?" she said quite casually, as if Romayne might have been a favorite maid she had employed.

There was something in the tone more than in the words, something in the alien stare more than either, that sent the color in waves over her cheek and chin and brow. She felt as if Alida had lifted her little pink manicured hand and slapped her full in the face. She had never felt more humiliated in her life. In her bewilderment she stood still, just looking at her former friend, the color receding and leaving a kind of deathly pallor.

In the midst of it Jack came eagerly forward with the gay scarf in his hand, smiling at the guest and demanding to know if it wasn't a glorious morning. Then came Mrs. Whitman's cold voice:

"Miss Ransom, you may go and bring me those letters you wrote for me last night. I wish to get them off the first thing this morning."

Romayne went, hastily, feeling herself dismissed from the light of day, the ready tears beginning to sting their way into her eyes in spite of her best efforts. She was glad to retreat into the room just off the balcony, where she had been working the night before and left the letters. She gathered them up hastily, and waited a moment to wipe away the tears and get control of herself before she went out with them. While she stood there by the open window the cold voice of Mrs. Whitman came quite clearly:

"You knew my new secretary before, then, Alida?"

"Oh, yes, we went to the same school together for a time." Alida's tone gave the impression that the time was far back in youth, and that she merely knew Romayne by sight.

"Do tell me about her then," said the hostess eagerly. "We got her, you know, from an agency, and we don't know the least thing about her. We were desperate and Gloria had to take the first applicant that presented herself. I don't think she even had a reference."

"Well, Mrs. Whitman, we used to think she was a right nice little thing, but you know"—drawled Alida loftily—"she turned out to be the daughter of a common bootlegger! Imagine it! It was quite a scandal. If he hadn't been cunning enough to die in the nick of time, he would have had to serve a long term in prison. I don't know much about it myself, but I heard Daddy and Uncle Jud talking about him. Uncle Jud hasn't any use for any of them, of course. He had put up the money for the man to go into business and of course he never dreamed he would do anything like that! He pretended to be in the oil business. The son was a thief, I believe. That is, he stole an automobile, and there was a murder. I'm not sure about it, but I think he forged a check——"

"Oh, I say, Alida," put in Jack excitedly. "Don't put it over so strong. What difference does it make what her father and her brother did? She's an awfully nice girl. I don't believe——"

"Now Jackie dear," said his mother fondly, "don't get excited. Jack always does take up for people that are in trouble, no matter how bad they are——"

"But Mother, I know her! She's a peach. You won't think so when you get to understand her!"

"Oh, Jack, Jack! Your enthusiasm over a new face is amusing. I do wish you would grow up enough to have a little discernment. I shall have to write to Madame about this. I thought she understood not to send me anybody without the very best recommendations. I shall have to send this girl back at once if that's what she is. I can't have people like that around the house!"

"But Mother, she had great recommendations! Some minister at home, I forget who. Ask Gloria, she knows!"

"Oh, yes, Mrs. Whitman," put in Alida pacifically. "We all thought her quite nice. I'm sure you will find her a good worker. She was awfully conscientious in school and all that, and I wouldn't like you to dismiss her just for what I said. I really don't know much about it and I used to like her well enough myself. I've only told you what I've heard."

"You were quite right, dear," began Mrs. Whitman.

"But it's not fair, Mother," declared Jack hotly. "She's a peach of a girl. Wait till you know her."

Mrs. Whitman laughed indulgently.

"If you feel that way about her, I certainly shall send her flying, Jack. You always do lose your head over every new girl. Now take Alida down to breakfast. I've got to sign my letters before I can come."

Romayne, with her face as white as the little morning frock she was wearing, and her head held high, came out of the writing-room with the letters and handed them to her employer.

"Here are your letters, Mrs. Whitman," she said, trying to keep her voice steady. "And it will not be necessary for you to send me away. I should quite prefer to go if I am not wanted. Indeed, I could not think of remaining after what I could not help overhearing just now. But I want you to know that I have a good reference from Doctor Stephens, who has known me well, and that I am not without friends who can tell you what I am, if you care to inquire."

Romayne was trembling by the time she had finished this speech, but the older woman only looked at her coldly, appraisingly, as she took the letters, and she ran them over in her hand, looking at each address before she replied.

"I have not decided what I shall do about it yet," she answered, as if that ended the matter for the time. "These letters are very nicely done."

"But I have decided," said Romayne firmly. "I could not think of staying after what has been said——"

Mrs. Whitman's glances were like icicles. They made one shiver.

"You engaged to come to me for the season, did you not? Then you are bound to stay as long as I want you. I haven't decided yet what I shall do, but you will continue your service until I give you further notice. I will be in the writing-room at eleven to dictate some more letters. Be on time, please. I don't like to be delayed. And as for anything that may happen here, kindly remember that this is not a social engagement for you!"

She walked away then, leaving Romayne stranded, crimson with insult, angry and helpless.

As soon as she could get control of her muscles she turned and fled up to her room and locked the door. She walked to the window and looked out across the mountains with the morning sun touching their tops and the glint of the lake in the distance. It was all wonderful and glorious a few minutes before when she left her room to go down to breakfast. Now it was a blank of mingled colors blended by her tears. Her heart was giving great jerks of pain as if it were trying to come out and get away, and she felt weak and sick. She dropped into a chair and put her head upon the window sill, and her soul cried out to God in her loneliness and anguish.

A servant came to the door with a breakfast-tray, but Romayne sent her away. She did not want any breakfast.

Gloria came after a while with a message from Jack. He wanted her to come down and go for a horseback ride. He had had some horses sent over.

Romayne, white and dry-eyed because she seemed not to have the strength to cry about the terrible blow she had received, finally opened the door to Gloria, her head held up, her face haggard in its anguish. Gloria, bribed by Jack to carry his message, was touched on her own account and quite unbent to the little secretary.

"Don't be a fool," she said pleasantly. "Take all the good times you can get. Jack is crazy to take you riding and you'll feel saner when you get back and things won't look half so gloomy. I'm sorry they said things about you, but I don't think anybody meant to be mean. Alida was just telling me that you were an awfully nice little thing in school and very smart. I'm sure she didn't mean a thing. So don't mind her. She isn't going to be here long anyway, only a week. I don't care for her much myself, but Papa has business relations with her uncle, and she had to come. But don't mind her. Do eat your breakfast and go to ride."

"Oh, I couldn't possibly," said Romayne with tightly compressed lips. "And I'm sure your mother would not wish it. Please thank your brother and tell him I cannot go."

When Gloria went away and left her to herself again she tried to set her tempestuous thoughts in array and know what to do, but somehow the hurt in her heart was so great that she could not think consecutively. So that was what people were saying of her father! All the years of his honored citizenship, all the fatherhood of him, and the kindliness of him, all the respect that had been his forever until this happened, counted for nothing against that great sin of his! And the most astonishing thing about it was that the people who were condemning him had been his tempters and partners in it. But he had been caught in the act and they had not. That was the difference. No, there was one other difference: he was forgiven, and they were not. His sin was forever covered by the blood of the Saviour who died to take his place, and their sin was not even acknowledged by them.

Well, must she bear this? And must she stay in a house

where her brother was known to be involved in sin, and a fugitive from justice, where she herself was suspected of being a criminal also?

Was she really bound in any way to remain?

And yet if she went, where could she go? Who would take her if she was turned out of this place for a reason like this? Was there any one in the wide world who could help her with this taint upon her? Strangely, at that instant came a memory of the promise that Evan Sherwood had drawn from her, that she would call upon him for help if at any time she was in need, yet she put the idea from her as impossible and went on with her sad thoughts.

There was that nice Aunty Patty, but she, too, had failed— forgotten her. There was Chris. But she could not marry him. Even in her extremity she knew she never could.

Desperate thoughts flitted through her mind—of wishing she might fall over a precipice, or drown in the lake—but she knew they were unworthy, and put them aside. No, she had told Chris that God wanted her to be in this situation. He had put her on her own. Here she was and she must do what God had set her to do, yet how could she?

Then in the midst of her trouble a servant tapped on the door and told her that Mrs. Whitman wished to see her at once.

Mrs. Whitman was sitting at her telephone desk as if nothing had happened when Romayne entered. She looked up and signed to the girl to sit down.

"There is something I wish to say to you," she said crisply. "You knew all this about yourself when you came here, didn't you? You knew your father was a bootlegger and your brother was an escaped criminal, didn't you, before you heard Miss Freeman tell me so?"

She paused and looked Romayne through and through. Her words were like balls of lead that hit her in the heart. She seemed to have no power to resent them or deny. They were true, too true, but they were cruelly put.

"I want to ask you a question," went on the woman coolly, judicially. "Did you want to keep that from me? Were you intending to deceive me about it?"

"No," said Romayne, trying to speak steadily. "I did not think that had anything to do with my getting a position. I did not think you were hiring my father and my brother."

"Exactly," said Mrs. Whitman, "then why should it have anything to do with it now?"

Romayne hesitated for an answer.

"Because," she said, looking up with her sad clear eyes full on her employer, "you have insinuated that it had to do with my character also. And because, though some of what you have said about them was true, it was not all true, and not in the way that it was said. My father was a dear father to me, and I did not know what was going on until it was over. I know things about his life before this happened that make it impossible for me to stay where people will deliberately say such things to hurt me."

"Yet you acknowledge that the general facts are true, and you must know that people hold these opinions about them. You have got those facts to face. I don't see that you should be angry at people for thinking the natural thing about them. It is what you probably would do if you were in their place. And it would be very foolish for you to give up a good position just because your feelings were hurt. People in business are not supposed to have feelings. If you expect to be a business woman, you must be blind to personal hurts. You do not come here as a person, but to render a service for which you are paid. Outside of service hours your life is your own. We are not purchasing that, but while you are working you are not supposed to see or feel slights of any sort. You are not here for social and personal reasons. Do you understand me?"

"Yes," said Romayne, "I see what you mean, but you could not buy the best work that I can do in such a way. It would be work without any soul. I could not stay where I was not trusted."

"I did not say I do not trust you! I have just been talking with Doctor Stephens. I understand that you are thoroughly trustworthy, and I understand that your people were thoroughly respectable. It seems so until recently. Now, if you please, we will begin our work."

When Romayne finished that hour's work she was more worn out than she remembered ever to have been before. She gathered up her papers as she was about to leave the room.

"Mrs. Whitman," she said gently, yet with a certain reserve about her voice that demanded respect, "I shall have to think it over before I decide whether I can stay with you any longer or not, but there is one thing I must ask. I would like to eat my meals with the servants, please, or in my room. If I am an outcast I surely do not have to be put where I shall be constantly reminded of it."

Mrs. Whitman eyed her thoughtfully for a moment.

"There will be guests here to-night for dinner and you are needed to fill out the couples, Gloria tells me. You will have to be at the dinner-table to-night; it is a part of your duties. Take it as a duty and not as a social function if you please. You are being paid for it. You can do as you like about lunch."

What Romayne pleased to do was to go without lunch.

She went to her room, and after finishing the letters she had taken down, she went to sleep. She did not wake up until barely time for dinner, and her eyes were sad with dark circles underneath as she dressed hastily for the hateful dinner.

"I will go down to-night," she said to herself, "but I will not go again. There must be something else that I can do, somewhere. There will be drinking, and how can I ever get through it! I shall see the scorn in Alida's eyes every time I look up!"

But at the last minute she went downstairs, dressed in her pretty black evening dress and looking slender and lovely and most attractive. Just as she was being introduced to a stranger who was to take her in to dinner, in walked Kearney Krupper in evening clothes, and very much at home. He had arrived but a few minutes before, and they all greeted him jovially. "Hello, Kearney! Come at last!"

CHAPTER XXIV

KEARNEY KRUPPER was placed across the table from Romayne at dinner, and he did nothing but stare unpleasantly at her from the time that they were seated. Whenever she lifted her eyes in his direction his eyes were upon her, and their expression was not good to see. It was as if he were trying to disconcert her. There was something baleful, menacing, in his look that frightened her.

In vain she tried to put aside the feeling, to tell herself she was merely nervous about him. The feeling grew upon her until it seemed that she would have to scream and run from the table.

Everybody about her was drinking. The wine flowed freely. The young man by her side was a simple-minded creature who attempted to show Romayne that wine was good and she should learn to like it. His mentality was a light thing, like froth, and it was difficult to keep up a semblance of conversation with him; yet the eye of her employer was upon her, and for very pride's sake Romayne did not wish to appear noticeable. She was sure that Mrs. Whitman was beginning to notice Kearney Krupper's intent sneer at her, and she felt the eyes of her old friend Alida upon her from farther down the table. Her position became more and more unbearable. As the meal slowly neared its close, the talk drifted more merrily to general conversation. In this moment of release from her partner's babblings, she found herself praying softly.

"Oh, God! Help me hold out. Help me hold out till I can get away!"

At last the awful ordeal was over, and as Romayne arose she resolved in her heart that never again would she be placed in such a position in that household. When the morning dawned she would take her suit-case in her hand and go down that mountain on foot. She was done with being a social secretary. She would get a good, honest job and be her own mistress or she would starve. But she would get out of this awful place, come what might.

She watched her chance to slip away as the company broke into little groups, but when she looked up Kearney Krupper was just ahead of her, looking into her eyes with a leer.

In a panic she turned abruptly round and fled by way of the back balcony which overlooked the precipice. She had always avoided that at night. It looked so dark and terrible and made her shudder to look down, but now its black depths seemed almost friendly as she flew along and groped for the servants' staircase in the darkened hall. She could hear footsteps behind her and knew that they were Kearney Krupper's.

Dizzy with fear, she mounted the stairs, groped again, for the servants' hall was in darkness, and found her way at last to the door that she knew opened into the hall close to the door of her own room.

The steps were coming on uncertainly behind her, but she slid through the door and closed it softly, and quickly got inside her own door and locked it before the hall door opened again. If it were Kearney, and she knew it was, he would not know which door she had entered.

She did not switch on the light nor stir from her first position by the door. There should be no sound to guide him.

She could hear him now in the hall, and he was coming on toward her door, walking more certainly now in the lighted hall.

She held her breath, every nerve tense, and waited what seemed like centuries while he stood before her door and listened. Then he seemed to go on to the other doors on that same corridor, and listen once more. She thought she heard a knob turn, then another. He was trying the doors. Some of them opened and he paused to investigate, then went on. Finally his steps came back again toward her door and she felt the knob turn slowly in her door. By an almost superhuman effort she held herself rigid against the wall, not daring even to breathe.

Then she heard his voice.

"Romayne!" he said in a tone with all the disguises gone. "Romayne! I know you are there. It is no use to hide! I'll get you yet, my baby! You might as well come out!"

She closed her eyes, and it seemed to her that he could hear even that movement. How hateful it was to hear her name on his lips in that familiar way! Oh, if she might just die right here and now!

Oh, wouldn't God help her? Wouldn't He? She felt as if she dared not lift her heart in prayer lest that, too, might be heard.

There were footsteps at the far end of the hall. Some one must have come upstairs.

In a moment more she heard her enemy walk away from the door and call out a pleasant word to some one and a girl's voice answer. Was it Alida? She listened till it seemed to hurt her head to listen any more. There was silence. He must have gone down, and yet, she hardly dared stir. She did not dare turn on her light.

After a long time she moved a step at a time across the room and sat down by her bureau, very softly. If he should come back he must not know she was there.

She began to think about getting away in the morning. She wished she dared go to-night, but he would somehow find it out and follow her. He was a human serpent weaving a spell about her, and presently he would strike. She knew it now—perhaps she had been afraid of that all the time. She should have gone to some one and asked for protection. But who would have thought he would have come up here in the wilderness!

The memory of her dream the first night came back, some one calling across the hall, "When is Kearney coming?" She should have taken warning then and fled.

She sat a long time by the window, it seemed hours. The music was rioting downstairs. The voices grew louder in waves and then receded. Now and then some people would go out on the balcony and laughter and wild singing would float up like stench from a stagnant pool. It seemed that she was watching the effect of what her father had done. These people were scarcely sane. They had all been drinking until they were wild with mirth. They were not caring about life in any true sense. They were killing the true things in their souls, and trying to live on froth and forget that there were any grave things in the world, any responsibilities, any punishments.

And this was the kind of thing her father had been ministering to in the illegal business he had undertaken for her sake—that she, too, might shine in the unreal world of which they all were a part.

Well, if there was anything in life for her, it suddenly came to her that she must devote her whole existence to trying to undo what her father had helped to do. The thing became a vow to her and entered into her soul.

She did not think of going to bed. It seemed to her she must just sit perfectly still. She was calmer now, and she felt that somehow God was going to help her. When morning came she knew now that she must go. It would be better to starve or to work at very menial tasks than to stay in an unwholesome atmosphere like this. She thought it over carefully, whether she should try to steal away alone at dawn, or go openly, and decided on the latter. Probably they would give her protection and transportation to some railway station. She would tell them that she would try to send them some one else in her place. Thinking this out and making her decision gave her more assurance and calmed the wild beating of her heart and the trembling of her lips. She rested her head against the window frame, looking out into the cool, quiet darkness, wishing she dared climb out there and wander off alone. It would be easy to do it. The roof was a long, low sweep down over the lower balcony. A trellis below, where a great trumpet-vine flared, gave easy access to the ground. But out there she would have no protection at all if Kearney Krupper should discover her flight. So she sat with her head resting against the window frame, sadly watching a single great star that burned in the patch of sky she could see between the pines.

She must have fallen asleep for a few moments, for she was awakened suddenly by the sound of her key rattling in the lock, and then falling to the floor. There was some one outside in the hall working at her lock! It was Kearney Krupper, of course, and he must have another key. She could hear it slipping in the lock, as if it fitted smoothly. It was turning! She was trapped!

Without a second's hesitation, she sprang to the window sill and clambered out, a sudden strength coming to her aid, and stepped fearlessly out in the dark upon the balcony roof. It was slippery, but she did not hesitate and plunged down to the edge, where the trumpet-vine curled up and ran along the eaves.

Back in the room the door had been flung open, and some one had switched on the light. She could see Kearney Krupper's outline as he stood in the light looking for her. Then she took hold of the trellis and swung over, gripping her shaking hands to the light framework and wondering what it would be like if she fell. He was coming to the window now. She caught one glimpse of him looking out as she reached her foot for a holding below. He had seen her. What would he do? Would he follow and grasp her hands before she could let go? Would it do any good to scream? Would any one hear her above the jazzy din?

Then she took another step down, put down her foot for another, and missed it, and fell, down, down. It was farther than she had thought, but the branches made no noise at all as she crashed past them. She lay on the ground stunned and dizzy, and wondered dazedly what she ought to do next.

Then she heard steps come out on the balcony, swift steps, and she was stung back to fear again. She struggled to her feet and fled, off into the darkness of the forest, not knowing which direction she was taking, unable to think, only to flee,

* * * * * *

Chris Hollister had a queer-looking upstart of a car that was little more than a skeleton which he had rigged up himself, out of an old racing body and an engine that he had made as perfect as an engine could be. He was of a mechanical turn of mind and this car had been his toy, which he worked over in every spare moment and loved as some men love their horse or dog. It was as perfect a piece of speed as one could find anywhere and the little boys in the street where Hollister lived called it admiringly "the Humdinger."

For several days before election, whenever Chris had a moment of leisure, he had spent it working over this car, oiling it and putting it in absolutely perfect order.

There was little more to the Humdinger than four wheels, an engine, and a couple of bucket seats. Everything that could possibly be dispensed with in a car was gone. There was nothing to commend it to the eye, no luxury to allure one to ride therein, but it could beat anything on the road, Chris claimed, and no one had ever disputed the fact.

It was this car that Chris had chosen to ride in the morning of the Primary Election, instead of his little old roadster in which he usually went about town.

He had parked it in the area back of the office buildings, quite near to the janitor's entrance, out of sight, and he had come down early before any of the committee had arrived, before even Sherwood was in the office.

When Sherwood started out of his office with the declared intention of following Kearney Krupper, Chris was only a step behind him all the way down the three flights of stairs, and at the bottom of the third he touched Sherwood on the shoulder.

"This way Chief, I've got my racer here."

They sped out the back way and the Humdinger caught its breath with a silken sound and flew out on its way almost silently and out of sight before the committee-men on the fourth floor had begun to realize they must go after the two.

No one knew the wisest way to worm one's self out of traffic and into the open highway better and quicker than Chris. By the time Johnson was in his car and chasing after a shabby Ford, Chris and Sherwood were well on their way toward the Park.

Out along the smooth ribbon of highway they shot like a rocket going on its way. Travellers saw them approach like a speck in the sunshine, and lo, they were gone! People stopped on the wayside to stare and wonder, but found they were staring at space. Cars slowed up and swayed to the curb to let them pass, and children scurried out of the road.

Before three hours had passed, they got trace of their quarry at a roadside inn, where he had stopped for water in his car. There could be no mistake. Kearney's yellow sporting roadster was too noticeable. There were not two cars like that.

In five hours they saw a speck ahead which they were sure was Krupper, and then suddenly they lost sight of him and could not puzzle it out.

Chris had a crude map which the detective who took the photographs at the Whitman forest lodge had made for him. He got it out and they studied over it for some time, going back twice to make sure they had not missed the way, for it was lonely wilderness and there was no one to ask the way, and their difficulties were increased by the coming of darkness utter and deep and the fact that the moon would not rise until late that night. The forest was all about them and shadows lay thick like black velvet all along the road.

"Well, it's somewhere along this two miles and on the right-hand side," said Chris at last, turning the flashlight away from the paper in his hand and jabbing it into the inky blackness of the woods. "You stay here a minute, Chief, this road's gotta be hand-picked."

Chris walked away into the darkness. Sherwood could see the flashlight splashing into the night like a sprite, dancing here and there. The lights of the car were turned off and the engine was stopped. It was very still in the forest, and a single star burned above the Chief's head. He looked at it and wondered if this had been a fool's errand. Were they going to be balked by a mere trifle like getting lost in the dark? Then he saw the light pause, and flicker and blink out. For a long moment it was all darkness. He began to wonder if something had happened to Chris and whether he ought not to start the car and go after him. Then the light appeared again with a single wink, at intervals, and soon Chris loomed out of the shadows.

"All right, Chief! Found her!"

He climbed into the bucket at the wheel, and started the car softly.

"What's your idea?" asked Sherwood. "Some one about?"

"Might be. We're not far off. Heard music, I thought. Mighta been the wind in the branches."

They came to the road, a mere trail into the woods, and no sign but a "PRIVATE PROPERTY, No Trespassing."

As they bumped more slowly along the ruts, Chris spoke. They had come thus far from the city almost in silence.

"Chief, what you figuring to do when you get there?"

"I'm not figuring. I'm expecting to be led."

"Oh!" Chris looked at him furtively with the kind of awe he always felt when the Chief spoke that way. It reminded him of what Romayne had said about God wanting her to be in that situation.

"Well, I brought the warrant we had made out the other day for his arrest, anyhow. I just thought I'd let you know."

"I was depending on you for that, Chris."

Chris was silent a moment. Then he was supposed to be working out God's plans, without even being aware of it! Things were queer.

"You know it's just this side the border line of the state; it'll be legal all right," he added, embarrassed. "I looked that up. There's just a half a mile leeway."

"That's good," said Sherwood. "We might have had to kidnap him and carry him into the state to use it."

"How you figuring to carry him home after you've got him?" queried Chris after another mile.

"There's his car," suggested Sherwood.

"I see," said Chris. "How'll we handle it? Will we take him in this car or his own?"

"Better use his own, Chris, then we shan't be accused of stealing a car," laughed Sherwood, grimly.

"Then you'll have to drive this car, Chief. For I don't see letting you handle a prisoner with that lame shoulder of yours."

"We'll see how it comes out, kid!" said Sherwood with his arm thrown lovingly around Chris's shoulder.

"Yep! We'll see!" said Chris significantly. "*I'll* see!"

They were silent then till they lurched in sight of the great house in the distance and began to hear the jazzy hum of the music and the strange jangle of voices, with now and then a clear sentence startling whole out of the darkness as voices will sometimes carry in clear distance in the still open air.

They parked the car about a mile down the mountain, ran it into the woods behind a thicket and left it standing, and on foot the two crept stealthily up toward the house.

"We'll have to locate that car first," rumbled Chris, softly.

Sherwood assented silently. They said no more.

When they came in sight of the house they stood in the woods and took a long look. It was easy to see from the sounds that proceeded that a revel was in progress. The servants would likely be busy and there would be little interference with them. There seemed to be no dogs about. Chris laid a loving hand on a little weapon in his belt.

They made a circuit about the house, getting the lay of the land and cautiously approaching the wide-spread and deserted garage to which the roadway led. Yes, there was the yellow car, standing out boldly among the others, even in the darkness. They reconnoitred and found the servants were all in the house, eating and drinking on what the masters had left. They were evidently not expecting intruders in that remote place and at that time of night.

Chris went carefully over the car with a skilled hand. The key was in it and he found a neat little revolver of the best type. He put both key and weapon in his pocket.

"Better get this outta here, now," he whispered.

Sherwood nodded, and they went to work.

Fortunately the car was so placed as to be easy to remove. It had not been run into the garage at all, but left standing as it had been driven up, in the driveway, and they found little difficulty in pushing it out and down a road that evidently was used for trucks when they brought up supplies. They pushed and dragged, and lifted, and pried, until they got to the down grade and Chris could get into the car and guide it. Sherwood walked near to search out the way with a flashlight, for they dared not turn on the lights of the car so near to the house. But at last they had it down in the road quite near to the other car, and turned, satisfied, to creep back and await developments.

"We'll wait and see if we can locate him first," said Sherwood, softly. "They'll stop this party sometime before

morning and we may be able to separate him from the rest.
If we can't, we'll have to march boldly in and make our
arrest, but I'd like to avoid publicity if possible. It makes
such a mess, and might involve Miss Ransom."

"Sure!" said Chris.

So they took up grim watch among the trees, two stalwart
sentinels, weary but determined.

If only Romayne had known they stood there guarding her
how her faith and courage would have blazed forth.

But the clatter went on and on, and the two men in the
quiet wood were beginning to grow sleepy and impatient.
Almost they were on the verge of walking up to the house and
ending the suspense. Then suddenly they heard a noise in a
part of the house that had been dark and still. A movement
at the window, a curtain tearing and some one clambering
out. A white face, and a strange movement of shadows on
the roof of the veranda. Then a light at the window and
Kearney Krupper's face looking out. Something fell with a
soft thud to the ground.

The two men in the forest stood alert and tense, every
faculty working. The face at the window disappeared, and in
a moment more Kearney Krupper came flying out the lower
door and down the steps into the drive.

Some one sprang up from the ground and flashed away
into the darkness of the trees, a girl with a white face and
dark dress. They could see the gleam of white arms, one
hand held to the throat as she ran. The man was running
after her.

Simultaneously, like two panthers crouching for their prey,
Sherwood and Chris stole over toward the two. They could
hear the girl gasp as the man caught her, and fall with a
scream that was instantly smothered. Then they sprang.

The moon, which had been coming up quietly veiled with a
cloud, took that moment to roll out from behind the cloud
and shed full radiance into the night, and a soft brilliance
penetrated the denseness of the pines where they were and
made visible what before had been but a moving blackness
against more black. They could see that the man had the girl
down and was holding her by the throat. They could hear his
voice like the hiss of a serpent:

"I've got you now, Romayne Ransom," with an oath. "I'll
teach you to sneer at me and think you're too good for me,
and run away! I'll teach you to lie to me that you haven't any

money! I'll make you cringe and beg on your knees! I'll ruin you for life! I'll——"

But a great blow on the jaw brought an end to the awful threat, and a heavy hand grasped the man by the collar and lifted him bodily from the ground. Kearney Krupper had revealed himself with all his evil soul exposed there in the darkness when he thought no one was by but the girl, who was at last utterly in his power. And Chris lifted him as he would have lifted a snake, and flung him against a tree, where he lay limp and stunned, not knowing what had happened. Then Chris took handcuffs out of his pocket and shackled him hand and foot, and put a gag in his mouth. Silently and swiftly he worked, while Sherwood lifted the frightened girl and held her in his arms.

"Romayne, is it you?" he asked tenderly, not knowing he had called her so. "Are you hurt—dear?" and he put his face close to hers that he might be sure she had not fainted.

"Oh, is it *you?*" cried Romayne faintly. "Oh, I am so glad you have come. Please take me away from this awful place!" and she began to cry weakly and hid her face against his shoulder.

Evan Sherwood's arms were about her now in earnest and his lips against her forehead softly.

"My poor little darling!" he was saying. "My little darling!" over and over again, and holding her close, and she clinging to him.

Something wonderful had come to them both. They did not understand it; they had never looked for anything like this. It was as if a benediction had fallen upon them welding them into one, as if they had known and loved one another all their days.

Chris, surrounded by the darkness, saw, nevertheless, how it was with them and rejoiced. There were sudden tears in his good, kind eyes, but he was glad. Since he could not have her for himself, he was glad his Chief had found out the right way. And he fumbled about his prisoner and wondered how long he ought to let things go on. They ought to be getting away before any one in the house was roused.

They came to themselves in a moment more, and drew apart, half embarrassed, and then Sherwood deliberately drew Romayne into his arms and kissed her very gently on the forehead as if he were sealing something in a holy way that had just been ratified in heaven.

"Now, tell me, quickly," he said as she drew away shyly, though leaving her hand in his in a close grasp, and she told him briefly what had happened.

"Is there any one else here who will trouble you if you were to stay in your room until morning?" he asked anxiously.

"No, oh, no. They have all been quite decent—that is until to-day. Alida Freeman is here and she has told them about me. They look down upon me. I must go away."

"I see. Of course. But in any case, *now*, of course. Now we must work fast. It will not look well for you and Krupper to disappear together."

"Oh! No! Of course not," said Romayne with her hand clasped to her heart. "Is he going to disappear?"

"Yes. We're arresting him. We have a warrant. Would it be possible for you to get back to your room till morning and then let me come for you? Do they any of them know what has happened?"

"I do not think so," faltered Romayne. "I suppose you are right. I must go back to my room, and wait till morning. But how am I to get up there without any one seeing me? I have not been downstairs since dinner. They think I have gone to bed."

"You came down that roof," he said, pointing toward the house. "Could you go back that way if I put you up?"

"I think so."

"Wait a minute."

He motioned Chris.

"Prisoner all right, kid?"

"Yep. Not come to yet, but he'll be O.K."

"Manage him alone?"

"Oh, sure!"

"I'll stay then and come up for the girl in the morning."

"H'm!" said Chris, puckering his lips. "You can't take her in that car and ride into town. Make talk here even if you come after her in that."

"So it will, Chris, but I guess it can't be helped. She ought not to stay here any longer. She's been under a terrible nervous strain and they are very disagreeable to her."

"Well, you tell her to buck up. I'll telegraph when I get to a station and have 'em send two men and a limousine out, and they can drive the other car back. Let's see, what time is it now? About two? They oughtta be able to make it to that inn back there by nine o'clock. These folks won't come to after this bout till eleven in the morning at least. Tell her you'll probably be here after her between ten and eleven. That'll give you a chance to make a respectable getaway before the folks. Tell 'em her folks back home need her or something."

"Kid, you're great," said Sherwood with deep feeling in his voice. "I'll never forget what you've done this night."

"Aw, quit yer kidding," responded Chris quickly and sounding as if he were going to cry. "I gotta beat it back! Sure you're all right, Cap?"

"Sure. Only I oughtn't to let you go alone with that snake!"

"Aw, he's nothing! Knock the tar outta him easy as pie. Don't you worry about us. Got his clippers on him nice and tight and a bone to suck. Won't hear a peep outta him till I get him where I want him. Got a couppla guns, too, if I need 'em. So long, Cap! Better get a little sleep on these pine needles while you wait. You gotta good long stretch before you yet, and we gotta get around and see how that 'lection came out, yet, too."

Chris stooped and picked up his inert burden as if Kearney had been a child and stepped off down the mountain.

Sherwood stepped back to Romayne with his arm about her and together they watched until Chris was out of sight among the weird moonlit shadows of the wood. Then Sherwood drew her to him once more and whispered softly:

"Romayne, I love you. Will you let me take care of you the rest of your life?"

And Romayne hid her tired face against his shoulder and whispered yes.

That was a wonderful moment for both of them. They would have liked to wander out into the forest and tell their hearts to one another, and wonder over the miracle that had come to each in that moment of rescue, but Sherwood was mindful of the tongues that would need only a tiny start to make ugliness out of joy, and he called a halt in the beauty that was surging into their lives.

"We've got to put you right back into your room, darling," he whispered. "Any minute some one might come out and see us, and there would be no way of explaining it all that would not be embarrassing to you. We hope we'll have a whole lifetime of joy together, so we can bear to wait a few hours now for your sake. But when you get back into the room, have you any way of locking your door so that you cannot be disturbed till morning? I do not trust people who are drinking——"

"Yes, I'll put something through the key so that it can't be turned," said Romayne.

"Well, and you might draw a trunk or something across the door."

"I never did send for my trunk," said Romayne, "but there's a desk, and some heavy chairs. I'll fix it. But I'm not afraid *now*," and she looked up at him with a look that went to his heart even in the darkness. "And, besides, that awful man is gone."

"Yes, he's gone. You need not be afraid of him any more. And with his going a lot of other troubles are going to vanish also. You don't know what he's been to this liquor business—and other things. But I'll tell you later. Come!"

He folded her in his arms for just one more quick embrace and then softly they stole through the shadows close to the house, and he lifted her on his shoulders, and braced her until she was safe upon the roof. Then softly, slowly, she crept up, scrubbing her pretty little black evening dress most terribly, but what did that matter now! And when she was safely inside her window she waved him a kiss and slipped out of sight and Evan Sherwood disappeared into the shadows of the wood.

But he did not go far. He watched the house from a safe distance until the music at last stopped, the excited voices died away one after another, the lights appeared upstairs one at a time and blinked out again after a few minutes, and at last even the servants' quarters were dark, and every one seemed asleep.

Then and not till then did Evan Sherwood lie down on the pine needles and relax.

But not even then did he sleep. He did not intend to sleep. He was keeping watch over his beloved until the morning light should break. She was his beloved! He let that thought sink deeply, joyously, into his soul. She did not dislike his presence any more. She wanted him to take care of her. She had asked him to take her away, even before she knew that he loved her. He was watching over her now with her permission. He did not any longer have to do it through other people and by subterfuges. She was his, and he lay looking up at the pines in the moonlight and seeing a long vista of beautiful future ahead, until the moonlight paled and blushed into rosy light of the dawn. Then he got up, and after a brief reconnoitre to be sure all was well at the house, he went down to Chris's car and climbed in, and the Humdinger went down the mountain at a great pace till it came to the inn on the highway. There Evan Sherwood got a room, and shaved and made himself as fine as could be under the circumstances, and waited for his chariot to appear.

Shortly before ten o'clock there came a long-distance call for him and Chris was on the wire.

"Well, I got my little wild cat caged at last," he said nonchalantly. "Machine got there yet? They will be in a few minutes now. I told 'em they had to make it by ten. Anything you want done back here? Who? Bronson? Oh, yep. I'll have her on tap when you get here. Need me to meet you or anything? Well, so long. Take it easy on the way back!" and Chris hung up.

The limousine appeared almost on time, and Sherwood, fortified by breakfast, handed over the Humdinger to the two officers, who grinned an approving welcome with a somewhat overdone deference, he thought, said they were mighty glad he had turned up all safe after the scare, and then without further explanation stepped on the gas and shot away. But Evan Sherwood did not notice that they had not spoken of the result of the election. It had not once entered his mind since he started on his quest. He was only impatient now to be off and rescue the princess from the castle.

Alida Freeman was standing on the balcony when he drove into sight in the great beautiful car that Chris had somewhere dug up for the occasion, a car that Evan Sherwood's modest income could in nowise have provided for years to come. She was surrounded by three or four other young people, with Mrs. Whitman and Jack in the offing. Romayne was nowhere in sight. The young people were just straggling down to breakfast. It was after eleven o'clock.

"Oh, who is that stunning-looking man, Gloria?" called out Alida. "It looks like—why—I believe it is, that Sherwood fellow that's head of that ridiculous League. They say he's going to be the next Mayor. I suppose he just went into all this notoriety for the sake of getting elected, don't you, and when he gets the position he'll be worth knowing. I'm just crazy about him, and Uncle Jud has promised me an introduction if he really gets the nomination. How did he come to be here? Do you know him?"

Her words were so loud that the rest of the group on the balcony turned to look as he drew up in front of the door and stopped his engine. Mrs. Whitman and Jack hastened forward to greet so interesting a visitor, wondering whom of their guests he had come to see.

As Evan Sherwood stepped out of the car and came deliberately up the steps, looking about him coolly in search of some one, he knew he made a tremendous impression on the little jazzy-jaded assembly of pleasure-hunters, who were waiting for a new thrill each day.

"I am looking for Miss Ranson," he said in a clear voice, purposely raised so that Romayne might hear him if she were in the vicinity.

"Oh," said Mrs. Whitman speculatively. "She——You——"

"Yes," said Evan Sherwood as if she had asked him a definite question. "She is my fiancée. I have come to take her home this morning."

And then, while the astonishment was still upon the group, Romayne appeared with her suit-case and her little hand-bag.

"Mrs. Whitman, this is Mr. Sherwood," she said gravely. "I am sorry to have to leave you without any one, but it is impossible for me to remain any longer. I will try to send you some one if you care to have me do so."

"Oh!" said Mrs. Whitman in a small voice. "You didn't tell me."

"No," said Romayne, smiling pleasantly, "what difference would it have made?"

Then Evan Sherwood gathered his fiancée and her belongings into the big limousine and whirled her away through the forest into the glorious day.

"And that," said Mrs. Whitman, turning thoughtfully away from the last look down the winding trail, "is probably our future Mayor's wife, and we shall have to invite her to everything—or move away!"

"Well, Mamma, she's really quite attractive, you must own," said Gloria.

"I told you she was a peach!" said Jack glumly.

Said Alida:

"I always loved her dearly, and felt so sorry for her when she went through her trouble. But isn't it queer! I'm just crazy about him!"

They rode away into the day, and neither of them knew how long the miles had been for the glory of the way.

It was not until they rode quite into the city that they began to take account of the time and place. A noisy hurdy-gurdy was playing an old tune in wild time, and the madness of it went to their hearts.

"If a body meet a body,
  Coming through the rye,"

sang the hurdy-gurdy, and Evan turned laughing to Romayne and hummed in a clear tenor voice:

"If a body kiss a body,
  Need a body cry?"

and right there, passing in the street, he stooped and kissed her quickly.

"I guess we've come through the rye at last, dear," he said, and, as if to give him glad assent, a newsboy came flinging round the street corner crying:

"All about Evan Sherwood Nominated for Mayor by Large Majority!"

They stopped and bought a paper and read it on the way, and Evan turned to his smiling bride and said, "Yes, we seem to have come through, so far. Now, how soon can we be married? I want to take you to see my Aunt Patty."

"Why, I have an Aunt Patty, too," said Romayne happily; "at least she said I might call her that."

Evan Sherwood looked at the sweet face and began to speak, then closed his lips again. Why not keep that for a sweet surprise? So when he spoke he only said, "Have you?" and reached his hand to gather hers in a quick little grasp, before he stopped the car at Grandma Bronson's house.

BRING ROMANCE INTO YOUR LIFE

With these bestsellers from your favorite Bantam authors

Barbara Cartland

☐	11372	LOVE AND THE LOATHSOME LEOPARD	$1.50
☐	10712	LOVE LOCKED IN	$1.50
☐	11270	THE LOVE PIRATE	$1.50
☐	11271	THE TEMPTATION OF TORILLA	$1.50

Catherine Cookson

☐	13279	THE DWELLING PLACE	$1.95
☐	10358	THE GLASS VIRGIN	$1.50
☐	10516	THE TIDE OF LIFE	$1.75

Georgette Heyer

☐	13239	THE BLACK MOTH	$1.95
☐	10322	BLACK SHEEP	$1.50
☐	02210	FARO'S DAUGHTER	$1.50

Emilie Loring

☐	12946	FOLLOW YOUR HEART	$1.75
☐	12947	WHERE BEAUTY DWELLS	$1.75
☐	12948	RAINBOW AT DUSK	$1.75
☐	12949	WHEN HEARTS ARE LIGHT AGAIN	$1.75
☐	12945	ACROSS THE YEARS	$1.75

Eugenia Price

☐	12712	BELOVED INVADER	$1.95
☐	12717	LIGHTHOUSE	$1.95
☐	12835	NEW MOON RISING	$1.95

Buy them at your local bookstore or use this handy coupon for ordering:

Bantam Books, Inc., Dept. RO, 414 East Golf Road, Des Plaines, Ill. 60016

Please send me the books I have checked above. I am enclosing $_____ (please add 75¢ to cover postage and handling). Send check or money order —no cash or C.O.D.'s please.

Mr/Mrs/Miss_____

Address_____

City_____ State/Zip_____

RO—8/79

Please allow four weeks for delivery. This offer expires 2/80.

Novels of Enduring Romance and Inspiration by

GRACE LIVINGSTON HILL

Barbara Cartland

The world's bestselling author of romantic fiction. Her stories are always captivating tales of intrigue, adventure and love.

☐	11372	LOVE AND THE LOATHSOME LEOPARD	$1.50
☐	11410	THE NAKED BATTLE	$1.50
☐	11512	THE HELL-CAT AND THE KING	$1.50
☐	11537	NO ESCAPE FROM LOVE	$1.50
☐	11580	THE CASTLE MADE FOR LOVE	$1.50
☐	11579	THE SIGN OF LOVE	$1.50
☐	11595	THE SAINT AND THE SINNER	$1.50
☐	11649	A FUGITIVE FROM LOVE	$1.50
☐	11797	THE TWISTS AND TURNS OF LOVE	$1.50
☐	11801	THE PROBLEMS OF LOVE	$1.50
☐	11751	LOVE LEAVES AT MIDNIGHT	$1.50
☐	11882	MAGIC OR MIRAGE	$1.50
☐	10712	LOVE LOCKED IN	$1.50
☐	11959	LORD RAVENSCAR'S REVENGE	$1.50
☐	11488	THE WILD, UNWILLING WIFE	$1.50
☐	11555	LOVE, LORDS, AND LADY-BIRDS	$1.50

Buy them at your local bookstore or use this handy coupon:

Bantam Books, Inc., Dept. BC2, 414 East Golf Road, Des Plaines, Ill. 60016

Please send me the books I have checked above. I am enclosing $_____ (please add 75¢ to cover postage and handling). Send check or money order—no cash or C.O.D.'s please.

Mr/Mrs/Miss _____

Address _____

City _____ State/Zip _____

BC2—6/79

Please allow four weeks for delivery. This offer expires 12/79.
